Failing Adult

Failing ADULT

BEING A RESPONSIBLE ADULT
ISN'T FOR EVERYONE

ROBYN KERR

First paperback edition 2023

Book design by PublishingPush

978-1-80541-184-0 (Paperback)
978-1-80541-185-7 (eBook)

Dedicated to Alec

Chapter 1

I blame Julia Roberts and Drew Barrymore. It's because of them that I, and every other single, non-twenty-year-old, have unrealistic romantic standards. I've believed for years that some perfect-looking, slightly emotionally-damaged rich man would casually walk into my life, fall hopelessly in love with me and fix everything by helping me discover my hidden, big-money-making talent. This, however, has not been the case in my life. I appear to not have any talent, and men seem to not love me or even like me.

I'm sure everyone thinks life is out to get them, and maybe even most of them have fair points to support it, but I seriously think 'life' cannot stand me. I try to make the right choices, well, most of the time, but 'life' still keeps slapping me in the face. I admit I sometimes don't make things easy for myself and could definitely be better at this whole 'adult' thing. I can't cook, I don't have a pension plan, and I still watch cartoons while eating crisps and chocolate.

My therapist asked me once, 'When do you feel life began to cause you stress and anxiety?'

I said, 'The fourth of September, nineteen ninety-six. The day I was born.'

He then asked about the main trigger events in my life. I rattled off all the ones I could remember from my childhood and teen years, each one more pathetic and embarrassing than the last.

Paul, my therapist, then said a lot of fancy words that basically meant I was annoying him. My tales of my with-holding mother and awkward childhood weren't interesting enough for him. I decided that would be my first and only therapy session. I was already fragile, hence the need for a therapist.

Though sitting here now, in a police station at one o'clock in the morning, in my wine-soaked dress with a hint of something else, possibly blood (!), this new event in my life is definitely something I want to talk to a therapist about. This is me suffering peak, horrifying embarrassment and distress. I didn't know a wedding could cause so much screaming, anger and destruction. What can I say? My family know how to throw a party.

Well, I'm humiliated, above and beyond a level I thought possible (slightly my own fault). This time, I've managed to fuck up my life even worse than the last time I was here (definitely my fault). I've ruined any hope of a successful, healthy romantic relationship, and everyone I know thinks

I'm a parasite (actually, not my fault, I don't think). Yep, Dotty Peters, you are winning at life.

Nine days earlier

This is not my life. I am not getting fired. From a minimum wage job. Again.

'I'm sorry. When you say, "Letting me go," what do you mean?' I ask, confused and a little hungry; I shouldn't have skipped breakfast.

I mean, I know what she means, but maybe if I play dumb, she'll pity me because my bills are due. I'm trying to make good eye contact. I once read that good eye contact makes people respect you. It hasn't been proven in my day-to-day life so far, but that's got to change at some point.

'Fired. You are fired. You no longer work here.'

That's pretty clear, and she clearly does not pity me. Why does she have to be such a bitch, so early in the morning, though? Just once, I would love a nice, cool boss who gives me compliments and extra money when I need it. Well, since apparently I no longer have a job, maybe the next one will be.

'The thing is...' She places her hands on her desk and looks me dead in the eye. 'You don't fit in here.'

She waves her hands in my face, which I do not care for.

'This doesn't work, does it?'

I don't know how to take this.

She smirks, tilting her head. 'It's a personality thing.'

So I have a shit personality, got it.

Monday morning meetings are never good. She's pouting her lips now; she has perfect full lips. The kind of lips you pay for if you have money. I have a big bottom lip and a stupid thin thing on top; she has full ones on both. She has full lips, a perfect figure and gorgeous long black hair. It's completely unfair. Here I am, being told I'm basically unlikable by a girl at least five years younger than me while she paints her nails, seriously! She just pulled out nail polish from I don't know where and is now painting her nails. This is a new low. They say to take the lows with the highs, but what do you do when there are no highs? I mean, like no highs whatsoever.

'I mean, do you feel a part of the team?' she asks, not even looking at me. Too busy stroking her claws with a new bright colour.

How can I feel a part of the team when the team don't include me in anything? They all went to laser tag last week for Katie's birthday and didn't invite me. They asked me for a tenner for the collection and didn't invite me. Bastards. So no, I do not feel like part of the team as it goes. I hate this stupid office; I can't imagine a worse place to be fired from. This dull, beige, dirty office, with heavy seventy vibes. Who still has wallpaper in this day in age? This office is clearly why she's a bitch. She has to sit in here for hours. I totally would have redecorated.

This wouldn't be the best start to anybody's week, fired by a girl who doesn't even know who Shania Twain is. Shania Twain!

'We only want good vibes here. People who all have the same attitude to life.'

I feel like Emma, here, could have just fired me without all this extra stuff. I'm not appreciating young big-lipped Emma and her vibes right now.

She has always hated me and been the bitch in this working relationship. She once told me I couldn't wear buns in my hair 'cause it made me look homeless. She also said I couldn't not wear makeup because I looked dead without it. It's not my fault I'm deathly pale. I'm pretty sure telling someone to wear makeup is totally illegal.

'The team are in agreement that this is for the best.' She finishes off her paint job and starts blowing on her fingers.

What the fuck? She told the whole team that I was getting the boot before me. Is that allowed?

This is humiliating. The 'team' are the worst. They all silently agreed on day one that I was too old and sad to talk to. Stupid little Gen Z children. I didn't want to hang out with them anyway, making TikToks and creating memes; I'm a grown-up, technically. Did their videos look cool? Yes. Did they all look like they were having a great time at laser tag? Yes, but I didn't care, like at all. I was just as happy playing Guess Who with my roommate.

'You've been here eight months; you should be a better team player by now. Don't you agree?' she says a bit too condescendingly for my liking.

Am I meant to agree here? And it's only been seven months, actually. I should leave; this is bad for my self-esteem.

'You don't have a love for the job.' She sighs.

Oh, I'm sorry, Emma, is this hard for you? It's a shoe shop; it's a cheap shoe shop. Who wants to spend eight hours a day touching people's feet? Who would love that? Other than the obvious.

'I love shoes,' I say matter-of-factly.

'You gag when the customers aren't wearing socks. A love of shoes isn't enough; it's a no from us,' she says with a smirk on her stupid face.

Ok, I get this bitch doesn't like me, but why is she acting like such a 'see you next Tuesday?'

I'm twenty-seven. I need this job to pay my bills, not 'cause it was my ambition in life to talk to strangers about the dry skin on their feet. They show me and ask if it is normal. What the hell do I know about dry skin? I don't even know if my dry feet are normal. When I asked my roommate, she threw me a dirty look and walked away. How am I going to make money now? Oh god, I have like no money in my bank.

'Can I use you as a reference?' I ask, giving my nicest smile. I can't use the job before this one.

'No.' She isn't even looking at me. She's looking at her computer. If she starts playing Solitaire, I'll scream. We all know that's all she does in here when she's doing 'paperwork.'

'Can I buy one last pair of shoes with the discount?' I plead. There are these really cute pink flats.

'No.'

Bitch, it's for the best since I don't have any money. 'So, should I just...go?'

She turns to face me, completely serious. She's looking me dead in the eye again with her arms crossed.

I hope her nails smudge.

'It's embarrassing that you're still here,' she says, giving me a look of disgust.

If I could handle confrontation, I would totally call her out, but I can't.

So I get up, trip over her rug like a moron, and then leave. I wish it was more Julia Roberts in Pretty Woman than Mr Blobby, but these are the cards I've been dealt. The question now is, is it too early to start drinking? I need a drink, or at least cake.

I may be living in Glasgow, but not drinking before at least four in the afternoon isn't a standard I'm willing to lose – yet. So I find a quiet cafe and settle for a hot chocolate and two cakes. You should have seen the look on the barista's face – like we all haven't had two cakes before. I need to stay in town until Dani leaves the flat; I'm not ready for the humiliation of telling my roommate about my firing just yet.

I used to like people; I was a glass-half-full, people-are-mostly-good kind of gal. Then I became an adult, and that completely ruined me. I'm a complete cynic now. The glass is empty. Not half-empty, but empty-empty, dry as a bone. People are the absolute worse, and being an adult is the absolute worse. It's not all eating cookies and staying up late; it's dieting and going to bed early for work in the morning.

I mean, I always knew life was hard and all that, but does it have to be such a bitch?

It could be karma. I've made a few questionable decisions over the years, but I like to think I'm a good person, or I'm an ok person, at least. Well, I'm a person, and we're all God's creatures, right? Not that I believe in God; well, I'm on the fence. Actually, I *am* a good person, a good person who deserves a break. I grew up in a tiny village with no Primark. Haven't I suffered enough?

I had high hopes for today. I woke up with this sense of, what's the word I'm looking for? Not hope; I lost that a while ago. It'll come to me, but my point is, is it too much to ask for, that one aspect of my life goes well?

My family see me as the black sheep and have taken to pretending I don't exist. I only have one friend, a slightly unhinged friend, Dani, who has no moral compass or filter. She's also my roommate, so she has to be my friend. I have zero social life, and no man seems to want anything to do with me. Tinder might work for some, but it only attracts the three major negative groups for me, fuckboys, mummy's boys and overall loser boys.

What world are we living in when Boris Johnston has a beautiful wife, and I'm single? I might not be model good-looking, but I'm a solid seven. I have nice blue eyes, blonde hair (aren't men meant to love blondes?), and I'm relatively cute. What more are these men looking for? Admittedly, I have put on a little weight this year, and being five foot two, it shows. Particularly on my face, making it look very potato-like, and god knows what has been going on with my hair lately; it looks like broken straw. Maybe I'm a six, thinking about it.

I can handle the basic shit aspects of my life on a day-to-day basis: living in a box flat with Dani, who doesn't understand the concepts of clean-as-you-go, personal space, or that the toilet doesn't self-flush. That I can handle. I can even handle the fact that my bank balance is permanently in a minus, making a McDonald's a luxury. This, however, I can't handle. I'm faced with this whole new level of humiliation. Unemployment, and not just unemployed, but fired. I thought being a uni dropout was bad enough.

I knew getting called in at seven in the morning was a bad sign; the shop doesn't even open until nine o'clock. Stupid Dani got my stupid hopes up that it wasn't.

Now, here I am, sitting in this sad little eighties-themed cafe with the rest of the unemployables on a Monday morning, six in total, not counting the server who looks close to a nervous breakdown. His eyes are soulless; I think he could blow at any moment.

There is, however, an extremely attractive man in the corner, a beautiful Chris Evans lookalike, Captain America, not the ginger one. He's reading a paper like a proper grown-up; I bet he's drinking a proper drink too, like a black coffee, unlike me with my hot chocolate with cream and marshmallows, 'cause I'm a child. Four of the others are on computers acting like they're writing the next big blockbuster when we all know they ain't. This is Glasgow, after all, not New York City; they are totally playing online bingo or Candy Crush.

What kind of sociopath fires someone on a Monday? I spent all Sunday depressed 'cause I had to go back to work today; that was for nothing. Bitch could have said something on Friday; then again, that would have ruined my weekend.

I've never been fired before. I've quit jobs or not been taken on from temp status, but not fired. What do I do? Go home and cry? Sit here and cry? Phone Dani and cry? She would laugh. Either way, I need to cry. I could feel the urge building in the office when she said, 'It's just a no from us.'

Alright, Emma, so sorry my personality and overall self offended you so much. 'It's a no from us.' Who does she think she is? Simon Cowell hitting his red buzzer? I wish I had a red buzzer to smack across her stupid, pretty face. I mean, I know I wasn't the best shoe salesperson they ever had; I did make the odd mistake, but who doesn't? No one died; a guy just got a foot infection. It wasn't even a bad infection.

Chris Evans is staring at me, like, proper staring. Did he just smile? Is he flirting? Maybe today will actually be a good day after all. Oh my god, he's walking over, like, right towards me walking over. I quickly tighten my ponytail and wipe my face for any leftover cream. This is it; this is the start of my life turning around. He's going to ask me out, fall in love with me, and we'll get married and have gorgeous babies. I knew I was a seven.

'Excuse me,' he says with the sexiest Irish accent I've ever heard.

I'm blushing for the first time in so long; no one this good-looking ever talks to me. Well, that's a sad fact I just realised. 'Yes?' I say, which sounded sexier in my head and less breathy.

'I think a bird has shat on your head,' he says with an honest-to-god smirk.

'Oh.'

Yeah, I'm a six, maybe a five at this point. Kill me now.

'Thanks,' I say, resisting the urge to touch it.

'No problem. I told my girlfriend on the phone, and she said I should tell you to stop people staring and laughing.'

'Right.'

Girlfriend! Course he does. What does he mean, 'staring and laughing?' Who is laughing?

'Guess I'll get into heaven now,' he says, looking mighty pleased with himself.

'Guess you will,' I say, looking for the nearest toilet.

Why is he still standing here? Does he want a tip or something? After one more long stare, he turns and walks back to his table.

Well, I think that's enough social interaction for me today. Time to head home, cry and wash the literal shit out of my hair. If I knew this was what adult life would be like, I would have started drinking in my teens, along with everyone else.

Chapter 2

Home, my safe place, where I can block out the world.

I must say, lying on the couch eating crap all day while watching Friends for four hours straight has done wonders for my mental health. I wish I was Rachel Green. She's so put together and capable; that must be nice. Ross doesn't deserve her.

Our little living-slash-kitchen-slash-dining area might be small, but it's cosy. Dani's taste might be a tad on the colourful side with the blue walls, yellow couch and multi-coloured odds and ends, but it strangely works. I moved in two years ago after answering the ad for a roommate and cleaner. I thought the cleaner part was a joke – it wasn't – that bitch doesn't clean. But it's cheap, and it was here or my car.

Oh god, that was the front door slamming. Dani doesn't do quiet; I'm surprised we still have a door. Now I need to tell her what happened and relive the shame.

Dani walks in holding the mail, instantly fitting in with her very bright pink coat, purple hat and red boots. For the first month I lived here, I thought she was colour-blind.

'Friends night, is it?' she asks, throwing her coat and hat on the floor.

The table is right there; it's seconds away, and the worst part is they'll just sit there all night, until I pick them up. You should see her room, clothes everywhere. She has, like, five cupboards, which I guess must all be empty.

'I was feeling nostalgic,' I mutter.

'You look like shit,' she says, disgusted. Then screws up her face as she looks me up and down.

She jumps down next to me. Her long brown hair smacks me in the face as she lands. Which smells a lot like my shampoo, the thieving bitch.

Dani works as a waitress at a buffet restaurant. She calls it pain beyond my imagination, and she has seven tattoos, so I believe her. She hasn't been there long, a few months; she worked at a different place for over a year before that. That didn't end well; still a sore subject.

'Why was the mail on the floor?' she asks, turning her suspicious green eyes onto me.

She can be kinda intimidating when she looks at you like that, like she's reading your mind. She always seems to know when I'm freaking out or hiding something; maybe she can read minds. No, she would have had me committed by now if she could.

'What do you mean? The mail? I don't know.' Why can't I lie? It's such a normal, basic thing that people can do, except me, because I'm pathetic.

'You always lift the mail and put it on the table when you get home.'

She doesn't see the bin when it needs emptying, but this she notices.

'If you didn't lift it when you got home, then it came after you got home. How did you beat the mail?'

Jesus. 'I got fired,' I confess.

'You got fired from Clean Feet? I didn't think that was possible! That guy who licked the women's foot still works there.'

We lock eyes, disgusted at the memory.

I was working that day; it was a sad day. He touched my arm once by mistake, and I still feel dirty.

'She said I wasn't a people person, that I seemed to hate people,' I say, grabbing another Snickers from the table.

I was given a letter detailing my firing. Emma went on to list everything that was wrong with me; it was a lot. It seemed like overkill if you ask me, and also very hurtful.

'They said what? Who said that? Was it that cow, Emma? That's it; I'm going down there tomorrow.'

The thought of Emma having to deal with an angry Dani makes me feel a little better, actually. She looks so angry. She's biting the inside of her mouth, which means business.

'Thanks, but I'm ok.'

Yes, Netflix, I'm still watching. Stop making me have to find and lift the remote.

'It was a crap job anyway; I'm well out of it. Honestly, I'm fine.'

'No, you're clearly not; look at the state of you. I'll go in there tomorrow.'

Do I look that bad? I thought I looked cute in an I'm not bothering way.

'I don't need you making a scene and getting thrown out, like last week.'

It was at Tesco. It was bad, and I can't even talk about it. I have never been so embarrassed in my life, which is saying something. We got banned, banned from Tesco.

'Fine, but I'm sending bad juju her way,' she declares, putting her head on my shoulder. 'You got a nice letter.'

She gets up, grabs a letter from the table and hands me a gold-embellished envelope.

I have a bad feeling about opening this.

It's too nice.

I only know one person who uses paper this nice.

Oh god.

16

'Oh god.'

'What? What is it?' Dani asks, concerned.

Dani sits back down next to me and reads it for herself. That is definitely my shampoo.

'Why would she send me this?' I ask myself, confused.

'I don't know, babe, I would guess 'cause she's your sister... Inviting your sister to your wedding is like a thing people do.'

'Why?'

It's been two years; actually, it's been twenty months and fourteen days that I haven't heard from my sister or mother, no mail, no phone calls, nothing. I've only spoken to my dad and brother, but even that's been limited. My little sister is getting married, which stings on a whole other level. I mean, the older one should be first to be married; it's kinda rude, to be honest. My dad told me she was engaged, but I said I didn't want to know anything about it 'cause I was hurt and offended she hadn't told me herself. Next week! It's next week? I'm only finding out now, one week before? This day is just the worse.

'Are you going to go?' Dani asks.

'No. I don't know...Should I?'

We both look at each other, then back at the invite and shrug.

'Do you want to go?' she asks doubtfully.

Her look of disbelief as she asks this is understandable. I've literally been complaining about my family for almost two years straight. The thought of even thinking about going up there; I must be insane. They hate me, actually hate me. I'm not too keen on them either, after what happened.

'No, I do not want to go…but should I go?' Dani already says I'm too soft; this won't be helping.

'Shall we eat and drink? Then see what we think?' she rhymes off, smiling at her improv poem.

I need to eat and drink a lot; there's a lot to think about here, much to evaluate.

Two hours later and we're sitting at our little makeshift dining table having dinner. We started with snacks, then decided someone should make actual food. Dani thought she could make a proper table in our tiny kitchen, but she couldn't. Now we eat on a weird, kind of table-like thing with three legs. She painted it red, which doesn't help make it look like a table. It does make it look like a mailbox, a shit one.

The drink is good; Dani made us White Russians, which are delightful. The food, on the other hand, isn't so good.

'Should it be crunchy?' I ask, knowing it shouldn't be.

I've eaten a lot of pasta in my time, and it has never tasted like this. I feel like I'm eating bark.

'It's *al dente*. Don't be so uncultured,' she says, rolling her eyes.

'I guess the crunch gives it a little extra taste.'

'You decided if you'll go yet?' she asks, changing the subject away from her rubbish cooking.

'I don't think it's a good idea. Maybe if I had my life together, or if I had a life.'

'You have your life together,' she says through a mouthful of bark.

'Whose life are you talking about? I have no money, no career and no one loves me.' Well, now I'm depressed.

'I love you.' Dani pats my hand and then blows me a kiss. 'No adult has it all together, Dot. We're successful adults in our own way.'

We're sitting on garden furniture. We bought these garden chairs at B&M because we had no money for proper ones. We're eating our dinner on paper plates with plastic cutlery 'cause we don't own plates and can't be bothered to do the dishes. Our White Russians are in mugs as we have no glasses; this isn't what successful adulting looks like.

'Babe, I'm unemployed and poor.'

'You're doing alright,' she says through a mouthful of more bark. She can't be enjoying this.

'Alright doesn't cut it in my family.' They are overachievers.

'It doesn't matter what they think...it matters what *you* think...You're amazing...believe in yourself.'

She says it with such sincerity that I could believe her if it wasn't me she was talking about. So, I know she's full of shit.

'They will all be there...all of them,' I tell her, fear sending chills through me.

'You're not the same person you were when you left,' she says, taking my hand. 'You don't cry constantly every day, with snot all over your face anymore. Remember? You thinking he was going to come tell you he loves you, that he can't live without you. That was so sad and beyond pathetic.'

Good times.

'It did take you eight months, which was longer than it should have been, but you wised up.'

Aw, this isn't helping. 'Thanks, babe.' I'm sure she's aiming for supportive.

'You don't still love him, do you?' She gives me a look that says, if you do, I'll lose all respect for you.

'This isn't about him,' I tell her, although it's not *not* about him.

Adult life is complicated.

'I have an idea!' Dani announces, full of excitement. She leans over and raises an eyebrow. 'Shall we rage room?'

'Oh my god! Do you think they have space?' I ask, full of hope.

'Already sent Sarah a text. We're good to go.' She grins.

Fuck, yes! This is what I need. Me and Dani with blunt objects, violently smashing laptops and plates. Her friend Sarah working there has been my saving grace since moving here. Rage rooms are incredible, and my inner warrior needs a release. I never knew I had an inner warrior, but Dani assured me I did, and I do.

Chapter 3

I'm not going.
I'm one hundred percent not going.
I thought about it all night, and I'm not going.

The rage room helped me clear my head and make the decision. At first, when I took the baseball bat and smacked the fuck out of the laptop, I thought, *Family is important, and I should put aside my issues with them.* Then I took the golf club and smashed the ugly cat ornaments off the wall, which changed my mind. I stand by my issues.

It will be horrific, you know, for me. Maybe that makes me a terrible sister, but I won't go, and I don't feel bad about that.

It's a lovely day. I got rid of almost all my aggression last night, destroying statues to the sound of Fall Out Boy. I can hear the birds through the kitchen window. I've got pancakes; I'm not going.

'Do you think I should go?' I ask Dani as she plucks her chin hair at the kitchen table. I really wish she would do that in the bathroom; I eat here. I *am* eating here – right now.

'Babe, we went over this last night. No, I definitely don't think you should do that,' she says firmly, like I'm a two-year-old eating sand. 'You said it would make you feel like shit.'

'It's just...she did invite me,' I reason.

'She also called you a disgusting slut and said she didn't care where you went, as long as it was far away from her.'

She states this like she's reading the news.

'All true.' I nod reluctantly.

You see, the thing is, my sister, Jane, did say this. My baby sister, the girl I looked out for and taught how to do her makeup. Wait, no – she taught me. That's not the point. The point is that after the event, the situation.

It's a long, complicated story of lust and betrayal.

Alright, I slept with my boyfriend's brother a few times, alright, many times.

We've all been there.

If we lived in a city, it wouldn't have been such a scandal, but when you live in a small village with about one hundred people, it's like you've killed someone or voted Tory, both equal in their level of scandal. It was like living in Bridgerton times. I was ruined, and I thought that at least my sister wouldn't judge me, but she did. It didn't help that she was dating my boyfriend's best friend, meaning she had to pick a side, which took her about two seconds.

My mother was mortified, destroyed and shamed. You would have thought I had been arrested for murder; her whole reaction was a bit much. My dad was ok, just confused over why I did it. He doesn't think highly of either brother, but at least he didn't stop looking me in the eye. Then there was my big brother, poor thing. He didn't know what to say or do, so he pretended nothing had happened. All different reactions, with the end result being me shunned and blamed for everything.

Mum decided I was no longer a part of the family. She said I had embarrassed them all and made them look dirty and undignified. She said the respectful thing to do was for me to leave, so I did.

For some reason, I decided Glasgow was a good choice, so I went on Gumtree, found Dani, and I've been hiding out here with her ever since. I like Glasgow. You have more than two choices for a meal out, no animal poo smell everywhere, and no one looks at me with hatred in their eyes; that's always nice.

'Maybe this is her olive branch,' I suggest.

'Maybe she knows you won't go and is trying to act like the good guy,' Dani replies. 'Did I get them all?' she asks, pointing to her chin.

I inspect her chin. 'Yeah. So I shouldn't go?'

'Jesus Christ, do you really want to go to the place where everyone hates and judges you for being human?' she pleads.

'Well, it is nice this time of year.'

'It's October,' she says like I'm stupid. 'The Highlands in October, that doesn't sound nice; that sounds cold.' She gives me a look of distaste before turning away to stare at her chin again.

I don't actually want to go; I just want Dani to tell me not to go over and over again. Then I won't feel guilty for not going, not that I should feel guilty. I mean, she clearly doesn't want me involved, anyway, since it's only a week away. I'm not going, I'm not feeling guilty about not going, and I'm not changing my mind about not going.

Decision made. Time to move on with my day, my day of doing absolutely nothing, because I'm unemployed.

Does she want me there?

It's a couple of hours later, and I've moved to the couch. I'm still staring at this stupid invitation. Why invite me? I didn't even know she knew where I lived. Did Dad tell her? I don't want to go; I don't. I don't want to face them all, and I absolutely don't want to see or talk to James or his stupid coward-ass brother. On the other hand, it's my sister, my little Jane. She can have her bitch moments, but she is my sister, and it's her wedding.

We were close, once upon a time. Most sisters go through that hate-hate phase growing up, where they fight, don't talk and fight some more. We didn't, though, probably mainly due to the fact there's a four-year age difference but still, we never fought longer than twenty minutes. Now look at us: two years without a word.

My ten-year-old younger self would be so disappointed. I always said I would always be there for my brother and sister. In my defence, Jane turned on me. Ok, it was me that made the mistake, but isn't blood supposed to be thicker than water? Ain't it funny how life works out sometimes? I thought I would live in that village my whole life.

What is it with women anyway? As soon as they get a man, all other relationships basically go out the window. I'm not saying I won't do the same when I find someone to love me, but for now, I'll judge the others who do it.

When everything blew up with James, she completely turned on me, as if our relationship meant nothing compared to her relationship with Andy. Andy is the man who stole Jane's heart. James met him at football. They both joined the five-a-side team and bonded over a love of Call of Duty.

Andy only lived a couple of towns over, so he was a brand new face in our little village. Jane was gone, head over heels, before he even had one foot in the door; she was a bit desperate, actually. With the five-year age difference, Andy wasn't keen, him being twenty-five and her twenty, but my little sister was persistent and wore him down in five months flat. Shame James wasn't the love of my life; life would have been so much easier.

I did like James, but it wasn't real love. We got together when we were young and stupid; our village didn't have many choices. That sounds bad; I mean, he was cute and sweet. It was simple and uncomplicated. I did like a lot about him, and we were happy enough. Then his brother moved to the village for good; he had lived with their dad growing up. He would visit every now and again, the first time being the Christmas after James moved to the village.

I remember the first time I saw him, Billy. I was fifteen at the time; he was eighteen. I thought he was so cool, a grown-up teenager with his spiky, gelled hair and cool puffer jacket. He had blond hair and blue eyes, like a young Leo DiCaprio, which definitely made Christmas more interesting. Then he left to go back to his dad's, and that was that. Nothing ever happened until...

'What are you doing? Get up and get dressed!' Dani demands, walking into the living room.

'Why?' I ask, confused. I'm not moving. I have plans of lying on this couch in my jammies, doing absolutely nothing as I stare at this invite.

'What do you mean, why?' She's standing over me in a way where I'm starting to fear for my life. 'Have you forgotten?'

'No.' Shit. What have I forgotten?

'Jason's party,' she states, completely deadpan.

Oh god, her nephew's party, a kid's party. I don't want to go to any party, let alone a kid's one. I'll need to get dressed, do my hair and get up. No, no, I need to stay here.

'I don't want to,' I say, full of fear.

'Tough, I'm not going alone, and you can't sit around here staring at a bit of paper all day.' She rolls her eyes at my pathetic self.

'I only got fired yesterday; I need time to process everything,' I plead.

'Twenty-four hours is plenty; now move,' she demands.

She grabs my arm, and before I know it, I'm off the couch. She's pulling my T-shirt off me and pushing me towards the shower.

'Babe, I don't think I'm ready to be around people right now,' I reason, trying and failing to fight past her and get back to the couch.

'Babe, I really don't care.'

I can't even move her an inch; I'm so weak. 'Isn't it a small thing? I mean, just family, it is a Tuesday.'

'Tuesdays are cheaper. Now stop being a child. Get in the shower and then get ready,' she demands as she shoves me into the bathroom and blocks the doorway.

Suddenly working with people's feet doesn't seem so bad. I think of ways to run away, but she would only catch me in a matter of seconds.

'I don't have anything to wear.'

'It's at Adventure Planet; we ain't going dancing,' she replies, deadpan and with a slight serial killer glare.

'Do you really need me there?' I'm getting desperate now.

'You know I do. You have forty minutes,' she says with a slam of the bathroom door.

Looks like I'm going to a kid's party, a weekday party at a play area filled with mums and screaming children. Fun.

This isn't my week, and it's only Tuesday.

I'm sitting at our kitchen mailbox as Dani wraps a Spider-Man backpack badly. I don't even look good; my hair's still wet, my T-shirt needs ironing, and I couldn't be bothered putting makeup on, which I now regret. Dani, on the other hand, looks fantastic. She's wearing a cute green floral wrap dress, she's pinned her hair up, and her makeup is flawless. She looks ready for a tea party in the royal gardens, not a six-year-old's birthday party.

'Should I change?' I ask, hoping she lets me.

She turns around, looks me up and down and then looks away. 'You look fine.'

That bad, great.

I was going for a cool, casual look: black jeans and a pink Barbie top. It isn't working, though. My jeans are very washed out, and my T-shirt is too tight.

'Here,' Dani says as a T-shirt smacks me in the face. 'Put that on. You'll look more rock chick than middle-aged weirdo.'

Thank you very much. It is a cool T-shirt, a vintage, black Pink Floyd number.

'Is this clean?' I question her, pulling it over my head.

She avoids eye contact. Dani isn't dirty; she's just unbelievably lazy. She only does one wash a week. She doesn't even separate the colours, like an absolute savage.

'It's clean-ish.' She shrugs.

Fantastic.

'Right, it's wrapped. Let's go.' She pushes herself up and looks nervous.

'It'll be good, babe. We'll have fun.' I try to reassure her.

'It definitely won't be,' she states, rushing out of the living room.

Yeah, it won't be.

This is torture.

I thought Dani was being dramatic when she said this place was hell, but she most certainly was not. I've heard 'Let It Go' and 'You've Got a Friend in Me' about forty times each, five balls have smacked me in the face, two kids have kicked me, one literally pushed me over, and to top off my evening, I sat in yoghurt. So, I smell, I'm bruised, and now, I definitely don't want children.

This building is big, but you wouldn't think it since there are about a thousand children here and, like, no parents. I mean, this party is a kid drop-off, but only about ten of them belong to us. It smells too. I don't know what that café is serving, but it smells like sadness.

Dani isn't having the best night either. We're sitting next to April, Dani's stepsister. Jason, the birthday boy, is her stepsister's son. She loves Jason but can't stand April, a fact she doesn't try to hide. They are sitting across from each other. April is feeding her newborn baby girl, and Dani's arms are crossed; the vibe coming from them is absolute hatred. We didn't choose to sit here; Jason begged us to. The youth are so naïve.

'Where's your husband? Still cheating?' Dani asks April, staring at her with zero emotion on her face.

This might seem cold and extremely bitchy on Dani's part, but about one minute ago, April asked Dani when she was going to lose weight because being in her thirties and fat was pitiful and embarrassing.

'One of my friends was in that restaurant you used to work at the other day. You know, the one you were fired from,' April spits.

'I wasn't fired; I quit,' Dani fires back.

This is a sore subject, but long as she doesn't mention...

'You mean the chef dumped you, so you then quit.' April smirks at her. 'No, wait, he dumped you for that girl, your friend, right? The young one.'

Oh god, her age, she went for her age.

'It really upsets you that I look younger than you, doesn't it? With you being seven years younger.' Dani smiles sweetly at her.

'It's catching up with you, or can you not see that wrinkled forehead and those chin hairs?' April emphasises the point by stroking her own chin.

Shit, I must not have seen a couple! 'Aren't you scared this inner bitch of yours won't sweep into your daughter?' Did I just say that?

Even Dani looks shocked.

'Aw, little Gus Gus speaks,' April sarcastically says, turning her evil soul onto me.

Who the fuck is Gus Gus?

'Listen, you horse-faced cow,' Dani whispers with intense rage. 'Why don't you...'

'Auntie Dani, come play on the bouncy castle with me,' Jason pleads, breaking Dani's wrath on his mother.

'Course, sweet boy, let's do it.' Dani beams at him, jumping up off her seat to run over and join him.

This leaves me with walking poison. 'So, how's maternity going?' I ask.

I hate awkward silences.

'DOT! Come bounce!' Dani shouts from inside the kid's play tower of horrors.

I'm scared to stay where I am but terrified I'll break something going in there.

'You're definitely single, aren't you?' April says, giving me a look of utter disgust.

'COMING!'

Well, turns out I was right. I'm injured.

My wrist is killing me.

We're back at the table, but thankfully April is not.

'Would you stop stroking your arm? You're fine,' Dani moans at me through a mouthful of cake.

'It hurts,' I whimper.

'You didn't fall; you hardly even moved,' she scoffs, looking at me completely unimpressed.

Hardly moved! Is she insane? I was at the top of that death trap when some tiny Antichrist came charging towards me, knocking me over, and then I went arse first down a horror slide as a bunch of twelve-year-olds laughed at me.

I'm not enjoying any of this, especially the judgemental looks from the three mothers that are actually here. The colourful language I used as I rolled down that slide wasn't very child friendly.

The friction marks on my wrist are painful as fuck too.

'When can we leave?' I'm completely done with this.

'We can't leave; we've been here twenty minutes.' Dani reasons.

Twenty minutes! Feels like days.

'What the fuck?'

Oh great, April's back.

'Are you actually eating the cake?' April rages.

'Yeah, but don't worry, Jason had the first piece.' Dani smiles and gives a charming thumbs-up.

'You let him cut the cake?' April is fit to burst. She's standing over Dani, and if it wasn't for the baby in her arms, I think she would be choking her. 'I left for five minutes to change Sophie.'

'Two minutes is all we needed,' Dani tells her before turning back to her cake.

'You are such a bitch,' April spits.

'There's my two girls.'

I turn round to see Neil walking towards us, Dani's father. As if things couldn't get more tense.

'Hi, Daddy.' April beams at him and walks over to hug him.

Dani doesn't get up or stop eating her cake. 'Hi, Neil,' Dani calls over her shoulder.

'Dani,' Neil replies. He sits down across from Dani as April takes her seat next to him. 'Aw, did you cut the cake without me?'

'I wouldn't do that,' April sweetly tells him. 'She did.' April grasses on Dani.

'Dani!' Neil says in disappointment as he shakes his head. 'Why would you do that to your sister?'

'She's not my sister.' Dani states the fact.

'Don't start, Dani,' Neil warns. 'This isn't your day; it's not about you.'

'Let's go, babe,' Dani tells me.

Dani stands up so fast I suddenly feel under pressure to move quickly and stand up super fast, getting a tiny head rush.

'JASON!' Dani walks over to the tower of horrors to find her nephew. 'BABE, GRAB MY COAT, PLEASE.'

Ok, so I'll do that. I turn round and see April and Neil staring at me. I quickly grab our coats and bags.

'Thank you for inviting me,' I blurt out before running away.

I can see Dani walking towards me; she looks angry and upset. I can also see Jason in the background; he looks so upset.

'Let's get the hell out of here. I need a drink,' Dani declares.

God, so do I. I already needed a drink *before* dealing with her family.

They really do make me feel better about mine, though.

'More tequila!' Dani shouts so loud I think Mexico heard her.

We're pretty drunk by now, and I'm starting to get over my traumatic evening. Five cocktails, eight shots and a rum and coke will do that for anyone, or was it eight cocktails and five shots? Or was it six shots? No, five! I threw up the sixth one.

I like this place. We're in a cool Mexican restaurant; it's bright, lively and loud, not children loud, adults having fun loud. We're in a nice booth near the band, and I'm loving the music the guys are playing. We don't know any words to any songs, which means Dani can't sing, which is amazing cause she's shite. It's busy, so when I started crying, no one really noticed, or they just pretended they didn't; either way, I like it here.

'I need chips,' I declare to no one in particular.

'I love chips. You can't go wrong with chips; they know what they are and just accept what they are, you know,' Dani says in a serious tone as she sways away to the music.

I do get what she means; chips are a sound snack, decent. I also want ice cream – coconut. Coconut ice cream is so underrated. I haven't drunk this much in so long; it feels great. I totally understand why people do this every day; I don't get how they afford it, though. Glasgow is another world; I grew up with one pub, just one. Glasgow has many, so many, like, many red dots on a map, many.

'Oh, sweet Mary, check out the state of you two,' Matt announces.

Dani's friend Matt has arrived and is already insulting me. I say Dani's friend, but I think we're also at friend stage now. They met doing community service together. Matt got arrested for jumping on stage at a Take That concert. Apparently, he touched Gary Barlow's leg; it's his claim to fame. Dani was serving the court because she chained herself to a bar in the West End. They refused to make her an Old Fashioned, and she said it was because she was a woman. They actually didn't have the ingredients. Where she got the chain was anyone's guess, she can't even remember.

I like Matt. He does sometimes make me cry with his blunt sense of humour, but what he says is true, as Dani points out. He looks like Colin Farrell, so I was more than a little upset when I found out he was gay; I love Colin Farrell. But Matt's not charming or loveable like Colin Farrell. He's actually sulky and a pain in the arse at times.

'MATT!' Dani screams as she jumps into his un-waiting arms, landing on her arse.

'Babe, you alright?' I ask, not looking or getting up.

'I'm great!' she announces, getting right back up and into her seat. 'Sit down, Matt, get yourself a tequila. TEQUILA!'

'Well, it'll take some work to catch up with the two of you, but I'm up for the challenge,' he says, sitting next to Dani.

'Tell me something, Matt, do you think I should go to the wedding?' I ask.

'What wedding?' he asks, confused, as he downs two shots back-to-back.

Impressive.

'The wedding, the big one, the only one, you know, the wedding. The person's wedding that I didn't even know was having a wedding. I mean, when did they get this wedding? No one told me.' Am I making sense? Cause I am in my head.

'You're not making sense, Dotty.' Matt says, downing another shot. He's gonna make himself sick.

'You don't get it. Dani, he doesn't get it,' I wail.

'Matt, what you not getting?' Dani asks, dancing in her seat.

'The wedding!' I explain.

'The wedding Matt, Do you think Dotty should go?' Dani whispers.

'I need more alcohol,' Matt declares, making his way to the bar.

'He didn't answer, Dani. He didn't answer if I should go.'

'Wait, my job is shite.'

Did she just figure that out?

'We need to go to this wedding; I'll call in sick or quit, whatever. Let's go, let's go up north and go to this wedding.'

'You think we should? Would you really quit?' I ask, knowing the answer. She hates that job.

'Absolutely, we should go up there and, like, hike or something. We could shout at the people who were mean to you.'

She's making a lot of sense.

We don't have anything better to do.

'You have a point, babe,' I tell her.

'Yeah, we'll go and get those guys told, put them straight. They don't get to talk to you like that, do what they did, no. And we'll tell that friend, get that bitch told too, just like you told that cow April tonight. That was amazing,' she tells me proudly.

She's right; the girl is right. I mean, why am I scared? They should be scared of me. I've grown as a person; I'm a force to be reckoned with. I feel a tad sick.

'Alright, I got drinks and more drinks.' Matt is back with the drinks like a hero.

'MATT, WE'RE GOING TO THE NORTH; IT'S HAPPENING!' Dani shouts to the world.

'Cool,' Matt says, confused. 'When?'

'This week...like this end...this few days,' Dani tells him.

'This weekend?' Asks Matt.

'Friday,' Dani agrees.

'You will come? Like, come, though? Dani? Cause I need that,' I ask, suddenly feeling scared.

'Babe, of course I will. I got back your, 'cause I will be as...something, plus I want to see these brothers,' she slurs.

'The famous brothers. Can I come?' Matt asks hopefully.

Fuck it.

'Yeah, let's go back to that, yeah, to up there and put things back,' I say, channelling my inner warrior. 'We can walk places to the...place. Amazing.'

I'm feeling hella strong right now and pissed.

'Oh, I love it, I love it. The drama will be amazing,' Matt says.

Drama, there will definitely be, but I am a strong, confident woman. I can take on anything life throws at me.

Where are my chips?

Chapter 4

I want to die.

Every inch of me hurts.

Tequila is not my friend.

I'm currently lying on my back, in last night's clothes, on my bedroom floor, and the ceiling has many spider webs, urgh. After doing another five shots – why I thought five more was a good idea is anyone's guess – we went to the chippy, which was amazing. I got a sausage supper, and it was epic. We then headed to the squinty bridge to see if we could walk across it in a straight line. We couldn't, but we tried eight times, just to be sure.

Oh, I have a text.

Hey sexy, love your body, I want to come over and I'll show you how much.

God, as if I wasn't feeling sick enough already, how do people find their husbands on this thing?

Tinder always seems to know when I'm having a bad day. Why do I still have it?

He's named Barry, and looking at his pictures, he's clearly a fuckboy.

Blocked.

After the bridge, I think we walked home, but I think it took longer than usual 'cause my feet feel like they're not even there anymore, completely numb. I very slowly turn my head to my feet. Jesus, they are disgusting. I must have taken my shoes off last night; it's vile. It's a good thing I got fired 'cause the thought of going to work and smelling people's cheesy feet is enough to send me over the edge. I need water, but I can't move, but I need water. Life is so hard.

It's been three hours, and I haven't moved. I've just been sitting here, scrolling through my phone. Every time I attempt to sit up, my head gets heavy and I fall back down. I wish I had hoovered last week; the floor is covered in my hair. I feel so sorry for myself. I texted Dani asking for some water, but she still hasn't replied; hopefully, she's not dead.

Don't ask me how, but I have somehow managed to make it to the living room. It's the most impressive thing I think I've ever done, and I was even able to grab Coke and snacks from the kitchen on my way. I haven't managed to eat anything; it was a just-in-case, forward-thinking decision. Don't know why I'm holding the bottle of Coke like a baby; I think it's comforting me in some way. I have Golden Girls on, too. I love these old gals and their wacky adventures.

I was a little concerned about Dani until I heard a sort of wailing sound coming from her room, so she's fine. No matter how bad my hangover is, it hasn't made me stop thinking about this stupid wedding all day. It hurts. She didn't tell me when he proposed, send me pictures of her dress, or talk over all the little exciting stuff. We're sisters; I'm the only sister she has.

I can't go to this wedding; too much time has gone by. I've missed everything, and more importantly, she hasn't wanted me to be a part of anything. I did try when I first left. I tried to stay in touch, but they both never answered my phone calls or texts. You can only try so many times before it seems pointless.

'Dotty!' Dani cries as she literally crawls into the living room. 'I'm dying,' she dramatically announces as she lies on the floor.

She looks like a swamp creature. I can't even see her face through that bird's nest on her head. She's wearing granny knickers and an inside-out T-shirt; it's got yellow crap all over it, which I'm hoping is custard.

'Hi, beautiful,' I say sweetly.

'My hair smells like ash. Did we smoke last night?' she asks. She looks like death. Her poor skin is pale and blotchy, and her eyes look dead.

Oh god, I must look like that, too.

'My memory is patchy at best.' Did we smoke?

She slowly gets up and makes her way beside me. She smells so bad. So do I, but that's my dirt and smell.

'Is that custard on your top?' I ask nervously.

'Yeah, I made some last night,' she replies as she cuddles into me.

God, that smell is strong. I'm trying hard not to gag, but between the smoke smell and overall mank, it's hard.

'Why did you make custard?' I ask, confused.

'I wanted something yellow to eat, and we didn't have any bananas.' She yawns in reply.

'Yeah, that makes sense.' It does. I wanted something blue last night, but luckily I passed out before I could find anything.

It's insane how close you can get to someone in a short space of time. One month after moving in here and it was like I had known Dani for years. True, she can overshare at times, especially when it comes to her bathroom habits. I knew everything about her IBS three days into living here.

'I like Golden Girls. I'm Dorothy,' she says, holding out her hand for my Coke.

'Have you brushed your teeth?' I narrow my eyes at her.

There isn't a chance in hell she's drinking my Coke with manky custard breath.

'Yes,' she lies. 'Smell my breath and see.'

I have two choices here, smell her breath and possibly die, or give her my Coke. It's a tough call until I remember she paid for the chippy we ate last night and handover the Coke. I'm not doing double standards here; I brushed my teeth last night. No matter how drunk I get, I will never not brush my teeth. She downs practically the whole bottle and then holds it out for me to take; I decline, which was the bitch's plan all along.

'I've decided I'm not going to the wedding,' I say firmly.

'What?' She sits up straight and looks shocked.

'I'm not letting them control my actions,' I tell her.

'What happened to last night?' she demands.

Is she angry? She sounds angry, yet she's the one who said I shouldn't go.

'You were right; I shouldn't go. I shouldn't have to deal with them.'

'You're wrong; we're going to that wedding,' she states, taking one of my Snickers.

'I don't want to.' Why do I sound fifteen?

'Tough, it's happening,' she warns.

'Why do you suddenly care? You said my family all sound horrible and basic.'

'They do, but you were right,' she says, giving me a knowing look.

I don't know what I should know or what I'm right about. Dani thinks I'm always wrong, and she's always right. I'm actually right a lot. Dani once said that Tom Hanks was in Finding Nemo, and I said he wasn't. I was right that time. Wait, what is she talking about?

'What was I right about?' I ask, confused.

'You don't remember what you said last night?' she asks, shocked.

'I only remember the chippy and the bit from the bridge.'

'Oh, yeah, the bridge.' She smiles. 'Did we make it across straight?'

'No,' I say sadly.

'Aw...well, last night you said that you wouldn't miss your baby sister's wedding for the world...that no matter what has happened...you would be there for her, as a big sister should... you promised, and you made me promise, that I wouldn't let you back out...so I won't, we're going.' She's determined; her eyes are like steel.

Damn my drunken state. Drunk me has betrayed me once again.

Why did I say that?

It's true, I guess, but why did I say it?

'Besides, I think it's about time you finally had your say about what happened. Don't you?' She looks at me with puppy dog eyes.

No, I don't; I think I want to run away, far.

'I don't think I can do it,' I admit.

'You can; you're not going alone,' she says, taking my hand. 'Anyone tries to fuck with you; I'll hurt them.'

It would be a sweet moment if both our hands weren't sweaty. She quickly takes hers back. Fair.

'So we're leaving next Wednesday,' I say, terrified.

'Next Wednesday? What about the hen night, rehearsal dinner and all that other rubbish? No, Friday. We leave on Friday.'

'You want me to spend extra time with my family?' I ask, horrified.

'Yes, we can't just go up for one night,' she says, drinking the rest of my Coke.

'Why?' I ask with a pouting lip.

'You have a lot to say.'

I ain't saying shit.

'No, I don't. I don't want to say anything. I only want to make it out without having a breakdown.' I say, completely serious.

'As someone who did therapy more than once, there's things that need saying.'

'As someone from an emotionally stunted family, those things need to stay buried.' Deep, they need to be buried deep, like the deep end of the ocean deep. 'And I mean, saying these things out loud hasn't helped you with your family.'

'Those people aren't my family, except Jason,' she states matter-of-factly.

'Well, I'm not sure that I want my those people to be mine,' I retort back.

Did I study English, because surely I should be able to speak better than this?

'Fine, we'll just go up there, say nothing, do nothing and then leave,' she says with more than a hint of sarcasm.

'Perfect.'

'You need therapy,' she states.

'I did therapy,' I snap.

'You did *a* session,' she snaps back.

'It was expensive and pointless.'

I see my Disney+ subscription and chocolate as my therapy. I mean, I already know my faults; I don't need to pay someone to point them out.

'You know, Friday is in two days; that's not a lot of time to get wedding-ready,' I point out.

'Plenty of time to prepare,' she says confidently.

Dammit.

Wait.

This isn't a lot of time to prepare.

How do I lose two stone in a week? I'll never get an eyebrow appointment. This is already a disaster.

What will I wear?

Oh my god! What will I wear?

It's amazing what a shower can do. I feel like a new woman; I'm clean and fresh, and it feels fantastic. I even feel better about going back home, kind of. Not really; I'm fucking dreading it.

I'm sitting here watching some Superstore waiting on Dani finishing her shower. She's been in there an hour now. She says, who needs a boyfriend when she has a power shower? I didn't shower for two days after she said that.

I'm thinking about what I'll say when I get back home. Looking for inspiration from my favourite Cloud Nine employees, I wish I was more like Dina, direct and forceful; no one dares take her on.

I'm starting to picture my mum's face when I walk through the door; it won't be friendly. I wasn't that close to my mum before it all kicked off, but after, it was horrible. She said things; I said things; she screamed; I cried, and she screamed some more. I will always remember the last thing she said to me.

'You are not the daughter I raised; you're my greatest failure.'

Don't mothers say the sweetest stuff?

Appearances are extremely important to my mother, and I certainly didn't uphold the family name. I always felt like the one letting the side down. My sister and brother are picture-perfect: smart, attractive, talented, and loved by all. I love that my sister and brother do so well at life, I just wish they didn't do so well at life. I mean, Jane is a student dentist, for God's sake. She got all As in school, did ballet and made my dad cry with her performance. What the fuck is that?

Then there is David, the golden boy. He's a singer, but, like, a really good one, high level, but without the money. He also brought my dad to tears with his performance in the school show. I made my dad cry, too; I dropped a hammer on his foot. I was twenty-three. At least they haven't made my mum cry, but then again, I've never seen her cry in my life. I don't think she has tear ducts.

I didn't do well at school, I have no talent in any form, and I just got fired from being a shoe shop assistant. That's all kind of acceptable, but cheating on my lovely boyfriend, a well-loved policeman and also the son of the local bed-and-breakfast owner, with his brother, a not well-loved jobless loser (my mum's words), well, that definitely wasn't acceptable.

In my defence, yeah, I don't actually have a defence, but I didn't set out to hurt anyone. I thought people knew me well enough to know that and knew I wasn't a heartless tramp (also my mum's words); it turns out they didn't.

Now I'm heading back, jobless, single and two stone heavier. Talk about winning at life. I wonder if I could just fake my own death? We'll call that Plan B.

As for seeing *him* again, I have no idea how I feel about that. That's a lie; I feel petrified. I think that was what hurt the most. With everything going on at the time, I thought I at least would have him supporting me. He hung me out to dry. I get that he loves his brother and didn't want to lose him, but he started it. He asked me to leave James. Then he turned his back on me; he was a coward, pure and simple. I wasn't blameless; I know this. I'm not the victim, but I was the only one that lost everything: my family, friends, my whole life, banished. What happened to it takes two, and all that rubbish? It was so stereotypical, blame the woman, scarlet letter, a ruined woman. I hope that one day, I'll be able to move past all this ill-feeling.

'I feel fantastic, like a new person,' Dani announces, walking in all clean.

'I feel the same. I'm actually hungry. You hungry?' I ask in hope.

'I could eat,' she says, smiling, taking her usual seat beside me.

Thank god Dani is coming with me.

'Chinese?' I ask hopefully.

'Oh, yeah, what we watching? Father of the Bride? Wedding Crashers?' she asks, grinning.

'Funny!'

I wouldn't even think about going if it wasn't for Dani. She'll keep me calm, protect me, and stop me from doing something stupid. Actually, she definitely won't stop me. I do stupid things like ninety percent of the time, and she never stops me. Oh my god, what am I going to do? It's only one week away, one week!

I can handle one week. I'm giving up before it's even begun.

'You need to relax, babe. I can literally see your little brain moving ten to the dozen. Don't be scared; you know why?' she says, raising her eyebrow and giving me her best smile.

'Why?'

''cause they should be scared of you. I would be,' she lies.

Maybe she's right. I bet they've got on with life like nothing happened, all forgotten, the scarlet letter girl gone, then bang, I'm back. Oh god, they will be terrified. I'm kind of looking forward to this trip all of a sudden.

'Where are we going to stay?' Dani asks.

Crap.

I forgot about that part.

We have nowhere to stay.

Perfect.

I've been lying in bed now for two hours, trying to figure out where I could pitch a tent. There's one in Argos for forty pounds; not bad. We can't stay at the house because, well, we can't stay at the house. It wouldn't end well, probably in murder. The only other option would be the local bed-and-breakfast. I would rather die than go there, since it's James's mum's bed-and-breakfast.

Most mums are overprotective of their sons, but this crazy mother bear takes the biscuit *and* the cup of tea. She does everything for her baby boys, mainly James, her perfect little baby. She does his washing, makes his dinner, she even changes his sheets, and he doesn't even live at home! I truly believe that if it had been James I cheated with, it wouldn't have been such a thing. She told me I was a worthless, selfish whore who broke her family.

So it looks like it'll be a tent in a field: I'm sure Dani will understand. What is wrong with me? I thought I was the one that was being feared. I am a strong woman. I think I've grown a little. Well, I better at least act strong. I'm booking that bed-and-breakfast under Dani's name. She can check in, and I'll just sneak in at night. Yeah, that'll work.

Chapter 5

It's times like these that I wish I had lived in the 40s when it was all about natural beauty. In the last two hours, I've been plucked, waxed, dyed and painted. Don't get me wrong, I look incredible. I forgot how nice I can look with a bit of care. I would do it more often if it wasn't so goddam expensive. This has cost me two hundred and eighty-five pounds so far. I'm unemployed; I don't have eighty-five pence. Although my hair does look so good, I might just have to stop eating to get it done more often. I went for a more platinum blonde look that paired with my new eyelashes, and my eyes are seriously popping. I don't know why Dani insisted on me getting my toenails done, along with my fingernails. Who cares if they match?

Now that I am looking presentable, I feel it's time we leave the beauticians. What else could they possibly do to me? Haven't I been through enough pain? I've waited in this tidy little back room for twenty minutes now, ain't nobody got time for this. I still need to find an outfit.

'Sorry about your wait, Miss Peters.'

Oh good, the mistress of pain is back, hopefully, to set me free. Her actual name is Gail.

'We about done?' I plead.

'One last finishing touch,' she replies.

She smiles as she puts on her gloves and turns on some machine on the counter.

'If you could just lie down on the bed and open your legs.'

I'm sorry, what? Open my what?

'Open my legs?'

'Time for your Hollywood,' she sings, all cheery.

What the fuck does Hollywood mean?

I mean, it's called Hollywood, so it can't be that bad. Hollywood is a fun place, right? Dani booked everything and told me to trust her, so I guess I'll just lie back and open my legs.

Ok, this is happening.

'Little bit wider,' she tells me before opening them herself.

Alright then. Oh god, that's hot, oh that's hot, is she smearing it?

OH MY FUCKING GOD.

OH, MY SPECIAL PLACE, MY SPECIAL PLACE IS BURNING.

OH GOD, SHE'S STILL DOING IT.

'Could you just pull your skin here?'

She's guiding my hand to help her torture me. What a sadistic bitch.

FUCK FUCK FUCK.

'Ok,' she says happily.

At least someone is; I'm thanking god she's finished.

'If you could just now lie on your side.'

What?

No, seriously, what? Why?

'Could you lie on your side?' she says again, slightly losing patience.

Bitch, give me a minute to focus on what's happening. I slowly move onto my side; I think I might know what is about to happen.

Oh god, yeah. Yeah, she's doing it; she's waxing my ass.

FUCK.

Oh, oh! That actually feels nice. Feels clean, fresh. Good job, Gail.

'All finished. That wasn't so bad, was it?'

Calm down, darling. I may feel fresh, but you did still just wax my bum hair clean off.

'You could have warned me,' I pout.

Dani and I are currently leafing through rails and rails of nothing good, trying and failing to find knockout outfits. Why do women love this so much? I feel like I've been looking at the same stuff for hours, and everything I try on makes me look like a different-coloured potato. It doesn't help that this shop is rammed with good-looking, skinny women. Where are all the curvy girls?

'If I had, you wouldn't have done it,' she says, holding up a yellow satin number.

Absolutely not.

'I'm blonde. Blonde and yellow doesn't work,' I point out.

'Cameron Diaz makes it works,' she reasons.

'Cameron Diaz is stunning and a size zero,' I say, trying to think of a famous blonde wearing yellow and looking ugly.

'So what colour you hoping to find?' she asks, impatient and annoyed.

'I don't know…blue?'

I can rock a blue.

'Blue could work on you.'

What does she mean, "could" work on me? I look amazing in blue; well, I don't look horrendous.

'What about you?' I ask her.

I already know she wants green.

'Green.'

She loves a green.

'I feel sticky,' I whisper to her.

'Too much information, Dotty.'

She knows I mean from the wax. However, even if I wasn't talking about the wax, she once went into great detail about a disappointing sexual experience she had on a boat. And I mean *great* detail.

'We should go to that place on Bath Street with the prom dresses.'

'Prom dresses?' I say, trying on a hat.

I should wear hats more often.

'That hat looks stupid on you,' she says, taking it off me. 'It's not just prom dresses. They have lots of other, less over-the-top dresses.'

'Can we get food first?' I plead as my stomach rumbles.

'Fine, but only a quick one; we only have today to find these dresses.'

I feel like I'm shopping with Paris Geller. It's been hours, I hate shopping, but I especially hate shopping under pressure; I need food.

'How about the German place we love?' I ask excitedly.

'No, we'll bloat.'

Aw, for god's sake, I love that German place; been thinking about it all day. Everything makes me bloat anyway; I hate being a woman.

'Fine, where do you want to go?' I ask, sulkily like a teenager.

'Salad Land.'

I would rather starve.

'You want to go to Salad Land?' I ask in disbelief, giving a look of disgust.

She must be taking the piss; I'm not even sure she can name three vegetables.

'I like salad,' she says, holding up a short red dress.

When I say short, I mean short.

'I wasn't planning on pretending I'm a prostitute,' I tell her.

She holds it up in front of herself and narrows her eyes.

'You may have a point,' she says, putting the dress down.

'How about the Cuban place? They have salads too.' I reason with her.

'Fine, but if I feel fat trying on dresses after this, you're to blame,' she warns, before walking over to a peach dress.

'I can live with that.'

I feel so much better. I was getting hangry; my bitchy side was seconds from exploding out of me. It's amazing how skipping just one meal can turn you into a demonic cow. All is good now, though; I have my Porn Star Martini, chicken tacos and chips with guacamole. I'm happy. Dani has had four cocktails, so I'm guessing she's happy.

I remember the first time I came here. I had just moved to Glasgow and was feeling like a total loser. Dani said I was depressing her, so she brought me here. It's lovely; the food is great, the staff are lovely, and the cocktails are strong. What more could you ask for? The first time we came here, Dani told me her life story and demanded I tell her mine, which I did, 'cause I was drunk. She then told me to get a grip, which I didn't. We bonded over our failed relationships and dysfunctional families, and we've been close ever since. She was my saviour.

'Would you hurry up and eat that before I shove it down your throat myself?' she rages at me.

How can you not love her? She's delightful.

'Would you stop rushing me? I'm stressed, unemployed, I have no outfit, I need to deal with my family tomorrow, and I've been violated,' I declare as my eyes widen.

It really has been a week.

'Being waxed isn't a violation, you drama queen,' she says, downing her drink.

'She took my hair, Dani, all of it. I'm hairless down there; she left me with nothing.'

'That's what a Hollywood is. Would you rather have a wild jungle growing down there?'

'I'm from the back end of nowhere; we keep our hair from nowhere.'

That didn't sound right. Oh, who cares? I'm tired and hairless.

'Well, here in the city, we don't do hair. I basically had my whole body waxed; you don't see me complaining. Plus, what if you pull up there?'

'Well, that's definitely not happening, is it?'

She smirks as I finish the last of my chicken.

'Good, finally! Now drink up,' she demands.

She is like a dog with a bone.

'Can't we just wear something we already have?' I suggest, hopefully.

'I'm going to pretend you didn't just say that.'

I down my Porn Star as Dani waves for the bill.

I know we don't talk often, but please, God, let us find dresses, or at least let Dani find one before I kill her.

'This is it, this is the one; I'll blow them away with this.'

'Yeah, very good, Dani. I'm thrilled for you,' I say in a huff.

We're standing in front of a full-length mirror in the changing rooms of Monsoon. We only came in here as a joke. I mean, we're too young to shop in here, not to mention too poor. Dani is wearing a silk, floor-length, green dress; it's backless with a low neckline. She looks incredible.

'My ass does look a tad big, but my boobs look fantastic,' she says, adjusting her size Ds.

Bitch, I only have Bs. I'm wearing a pink satin thing; it has both glitter and sequins. I look horrendous.

'So, we good? Can we go home now?' I say, folding my arms.

'You're like a five-year-old; we're out here for you.'

'I hate shopping; I'm too fat for this mirror.'

I sit down on a nearby chair. Dani walks over and kneels down beside me.

'Dotty,' she's putting on her calm but annoyed voice.

'What?'

'You're gorgeous...you're funny...kinda smart and a decent person.' She puts her hands on my face. 'Anyone who doesn't see that is a moron...Now, are you a moron?' she asks, raising her eyebrow.

'No,' I mutter. 'But.'

'No, no buts,' she tells me, standing up. 'Get up. We'll try one more place and then head home. God knows you can't wear that thing.' She laughs, pointing at the pink mess on me.

I hate shopping.

One more shop turned into three more shops, and by the end, I just picked the last thing I saw. It's blue, that's the only good thing about it, to be honest. Dani wasn't too keen, but she could tell I was close to breaking, so she agreed on the dress, and we left. Now we are safely back home, away from the dresses and judgemental salespeople.

'That hair on my back is back,' Dani announces, walking into the living room and jumping down next to me on the couch, tweezers in hand. 'Get it,' she demands.

I love my friend, I do, but plucking her one weird white hair out of her back isn't my favourite thing to do in the world; I can't imagine why. She takes off her T-shirt and turns away from me.

'I can't see it,' I say, screwing up my face.

'Well, I felt it, so it's there.'

Great, I need to feel for it; I don't think we're this close.

'Oh, there it is, got it.'

'Thanks, babe.' She pulls her top back on and turns to sit back next to me again. 'Can't be having that when we're away. What if I pull?'

'Are you serious? Sorry, babe, but there ain't any talent up there.' I break the news to her.

She doesn't seem to realise where we're going. She can't pull when there's nothing to pull.

'You haven't been there in, like, two years. There could be an army of fit men up there by now. I need to remember to pack my no!no!'

'Why? You just waxed every speck of your body.'

'Babe, I'm like a fucking gorilla; my hair grows by the second. That reminds me, I need to get my nipple hair plucked; my waxer doesn't do nipples.'

I used to think I was the only one with nipple hair before I met Dani. It's not something women talk about, is it? Nipple hair. It was actually nice to hear; it meant I wasn't a weirdo. Turns out it's common. What a shit thing for God to do to women.

Prick.

'Can't believe we leave tomorrow,' I say as I feel the nerves pulsing through me.

'I'm actually excited; you've spoken so much about these people, it'll be nice to put faces to names.'

'Well, I'm glad you're excited; I'm absolutely fucking bricking it,' I admit.

'I think we'll have a great time. You just need to remember one simple motto.'

'What's that?' I ask.

She smiles. 'Fuck them.'

Chapter 6

Fuck them, fuck them, fuck them.

Nope, this motto ain't helping; I still want to run away. I'm sitting on the edge of my bed, counting to ten, which is also not working.

'We're grabbing a Starbucks on the way, right?' Dani says, bouncing into my room.

'What the hell have you done?' I exclaim.

Dani has just bounced in here with new bright ginger hair. Did she do that last night? It looks alright, actually.

'You like it? Thought I would mix it up a bit; new place, new do.'

She ain't half enthusiastic as she tosses her hair.

'It's bright. How did you get it so light?'

'Well, I dyed it red first, then stripped it.' She grins at me, pleased with her handiwork.

'Is that what that smell was in the bathroom? I thought you were removing more hair with that cream.'

'No, it was the dye and remover; they're strong ass chemicals,' she tells me with widened eyes.

She sits down next to me on the bed, giving me a concerned look, like I might make a run for it any minute.

'I do like your hair,' I tell her truthfully.

It actually looks natural on her.

'You ready?' she gingerly asks.

'I know I've said this a lot, but I can't go. I'm feeling very stressed.' I shake my head, trying not to cry.

'Your bags are packed, there's petrol in the car, we're going,' she tells me, determination in her eyes.

Something tells me she plans on getting me there no matter what it takes.

'They will say things, treat me like I'm...the devil. How do I handle that? I'm not one for confrontation, and what do I say to James?' I'm panicking; my voice is breaking.

'You do the best you can, then when you can't keep going... I'll push you the rest of the way,' she whispers, pulling me in for a hug. She pulls away and smiles at me with a look of love.

I can see it in her eyes, and it warms my heart to have that in my life from someone.

'Alright, bitches, we ready?' Matt shouts from the front door.

'Is that Matt?' I ask, shocked. Why is Matt here?

'Yeah, and he's late.' She jumps up and starts walking to the door.

'Matt is here,' I state, confused.

'Yeah,' she repeats, looking at me confused.

I don't know why she's looking at me like I'm the cause of confusion. Matt being here is the confusing part.

'Why?'

''cause he's coming. Did you forget you invited him?' she asks with a look of joy in her eyes; she loves a bit of drama.

'Yeah,' I whisper.

Of course I fucking forgot. This is perfect. I now have a bigger audience to my despair. I wonder if he would be very upset if I withdrew my invite; I don't actually remember inviting him. Who am I kidding? I could never disinvite anyone from anything.

She stands up and looks down the hall.

'Well, he has his bags with him and snacks, so…guess he's coming.' She shrugs.

'Are we getting this road trip on the fucking road or what?' Matt calls from the hall before appearing at my bedroom door. 'Oh my god, what have you done to your hair? You look like Kathy Burke in Gimme Gimme Gimme.'

'You cheeky bastard, I do not!' Dani gingerly touches her ginger locks. 'And you're one to talk; look at what you're wearing. This ain't fashion week at the Met.'

Matt has decided to dress for the occasion and is wearing navy trousers, a blush pink shirt and a navy waistcoat.

'It's called putting in the effort. You might want to try it sometime, you scruffy cow,' he replies to an angry Dani.

She then proceeds to shove and smack him out of the room.

Well, isn't this fantastic? Haven't seen the family in two years, and now I'm rocking up with two loud, convicted Glaswegians. Looks like I'm going to make Mummy even prouder.

We've been driving for three hours now, the three longest hours of my life. Having never been on a long road trip with either of them, I didn't realise that:

A. They know every word to every song.
B. They love every song.
C. They can't sing in tune to any song.

Three hours! For three hours, I've been trapped in this car. I can't even complain because it's not my car. This isn't helping with my anxiety, let me tell you. It also turns out that Matt has the bladder of an eighty-year-old. We've stopped like a billion times so he can pee. Each time he does, he buys a new drink, so we're in this endless cycle of stop and pee, stop and pee. To add insult to injury, I'm sitting in the back seat because Matt gets car sick; I call bullshit on that.

So I'm getting crushed by suitcases because Dani drives a Mini. Three people and their luggage mean no room to breathe for me. It's fitting: having the journey from hell to hell itself.

'I need to pee again,' Matt whines.

What the hell is wrong with him? I think he might have a problem; I would see a doctor for sure. Did he just put his seat back again? Prick.

'I'm driving like a hundred hours today, Matt, so could you chill it with the sparkling water? I'll stop one more time, then that's your lot, we clear?' Dani says, frustrated.

Thank god, I thought it was just me that was close to killing him, and it's six hours she's driving. What is with the sparkling water anyway, seriously? What is wrong with him? It's like drinking static.

'I have a weak bladder.' He looks guilty.

'Yeah, alright, Matt, but I have a weak attention span, so the longer I drive, the more likely I am to crash the car,' she says, turning up the radio.

She better be joking. Oh god, is that Britney? Britney makes her sing louder. Britney and the Spice Girls.

'Look, up there,' Matt starts pointing wildly at a petrol station. 'Pull over there.'

'Alright, I see it.' Dani hits his hand away from her face. She shakes her head, driving the car over to the exit.

I could use a snack; I need extra comfort food on this trip.

We pull into the petrol station in the middle of The Highlands. It's very pretty here, actually; shame I can't appreciate it because of my horrendous situation.

'Right, go pee,' Dani demands.

Matt hurries out of the car, a man on a mission.

'I could really do with stretching my legs,' I plead.

'Fine,' she barks. 'But this is a five-minute stop, tops.'

Dani jumps out of the car, coming around to the other side to release me from my cage.

Aw, fresh air, it's beautiful. We lean on the car; in my head, we look sexy and edgy. In reality, we look like unkempt, sad women close to breaking down. I should have worn a better outfit; I need to stop dressing for comfort over stylish. Instead of wearing a cute skinny jeans and jumper combo, I'm wearing old pink joggers and a non-matching blue jumper. Dani doesn't even look much better. She also goes for comfort and is wearing a bobbly grey lounge jumpsuit thing.

'He should see a doctor about his bladder,' I tell her. This isn't natural.

'I thought we would have passed a town by now.'

'Maybe he has a urine infection,' I suggest.

'Actually, we should definitely have passed a town by now. I checked the route, and we should have passed like three towns.'

She knows.

'Why haven't we passed a town?'

'Maybe, he drank a lot last night,' I say, pretending I can't hear her.

She turns her big accusing eyes to me.

'Have you given me the wrong address?' she asks sternly.

'Not, exactly. I have taken us the long way around. The scenic route,' I confess. This is actually only half the truth. 'You said you had never seen The Highlands before.'

'I did say that. I didn't, however, say I wanted more time in the car with the two of you.' She's upset.

I don't understand why I'm in the same league as Matt. I'm a delight to travel with. Speak of the devil; Matt is back.

'I'm good to go,' he gleams. 'What have I missed?'

Clearly, he's picking up on the tension.

'I need food before I leave Dot on the side of the road,' Dani tells us.

'Ok,' Matt replies, confused.

'There's a service station not far,' I tell her.

'You can't be trusted,' Dani rages as she climbs into the car.

'What have you done?' Matt whispers.

'Let's just get a McDonalds into her, quick.'

I'll buy her two meals; that'll put things right.

Right, so it was a little further than I thought, by like forty minutes. I didn't realise the next possible stop for food was this far, but we are here, in line and soon will be eating greasy fast food.

'You two better know what you're having 'cause I want no extra time added.' Dani warns us.

'Why you being a bitch to me? I didn't do anything,' Matt asks, annoyed.

'It's her fault,' Dani snaps.

'I've said sorry like twenty times,' I say, pleading my case.

She'll be fine once we eat. I hope.

'Did anyone else think Inverness was bigger? How is this a city?' Matt asks, clearly puzzled.

Inverness is tiny, especially compared to Glasgow. However, we are not in Inverness. Finally, it's our turn.

'Hello, what can I get you?' The disheartened girl behind the voice machine asks.

'Hi, can I please have a McSandwich meal with a Coke, large?' Dani starts.

'That's McDonald's,' the unimpressed girl tells Dani.

'Oh, sorry, em. I'll have a Chicken Royale then, with a Coke and large,' Dani says, confused.

Matt lets out a snort, clearly enjoying himself.

'That's Burger King,' the girl replies, as deadpan as before.

'Dot! Where the fuck are we?' Dani snaps at me. Because clearly this is my fault.

I can see why she's confused, what with the huge KFC signs literally everywhere, including one right in front of our faces.

'You're at KFC,' the girl answers her, again deadpan. Maybe this happens a lot, although I don't see how.

'KFC?' Dani ponders. She's not really a KFC girl.

Matt reaches over her. 'Can I have a Twister, please, with a Coke Zero?'

'Do you want Southern Sweet Chilli, Original Kentucky Mayo, the Twister Wrap of the Day or the Twister Box Meal?' the worker asks.

'Fuck! KFC has upped their game. I haven't been at one of these since, like, two thousand and six, so just whatever you think,' he says, leaning back into his seat and shaking his head in disbelief.

'Can I just get a burger?' Dani asks her. 'That can't be too complicated,' she tells us.

'The Zinger Burger Box, the Fillet Box meal, the Zinger Stacker meal, the Zinger Burger meal, the Zinger Tower meal, the Fillet Burger meal, the Fillet Tower Burger meal or the Trilogy Box meal?' she rattles off.

Right! I get that we are clearly annoying this girl, but we are also clearly a bit thick. Well, they are.

'We'll have the Twister Box Meal with Original Kentucky Mayo and a side of coleslaw with a Coke Zero. We will have the Boneless Banquet Box meal with a Coke, barbecue dip and a side of corn. We'll also have the Trilogy Box meal with a Coke, gravy dip and mash,' I call over Dani's shoulder. I eat out a lot.

'We don't do Coke. Is Pepsi ok?'

'It's perfect,' Dani replies in a hurry.

'Pay at the next window,' she tells us, clearly thrilled to be done with this order.

'Thank you,' Dani says before pulling away to the next window.

'You couldn't have done that earlier?' Matt snaps at me.

'Sorry, I thought we had all ordered at a drive-thru before. My mistake,' I fire back at him.

'I'm healthy; I don't live off fast food,' he states proudly. 'How was that, Dani? Did we order fast enough for you?'

'Piss off,' Dani warns.

'McChicken, McRoyal, McLovin,' he sings.

'I swear, Matthew...' she warns him.

I can't help laughing.

'Don't you start,' she says, trying not to laugh by biting the inside of her mouth.

'That's twenty-seven thirty-eight,' an equally unimpressed KFC worker says.

'Dot,' Matt and Dani say in unison.

I hand over my card reluctantly. You know you're getting old when you remember prices being half the cost of what they are now.

We are fed and back on the road. It's been a nice, quiet thirty minutes in the car, if a bit boring. The silence is broken by Matt.

'Let's play a game,' Matt huffs, rolling his eyes.

'How about I Spy?' I suggest.

They both look disgusted at the idea, giving me a look of disappointment.

Whatever.

Ten minutes later, with no better suggestions, we're playing I Spy.

'I spy with my little eye…something beginning with…K,' Dani says proudly.

K. What starts with K? Kent? No, that's a place in England. Kangaroo? Kiwi? Kettle? Why isn't my brain working? There isn't a kettle here. K. What starts with K? There are no Ks. What the hell is she talking about?

'Keyboard? Matt answers.

Keyboard? Where is there a keyboard?

'Yes.' Dani sulks.

'What? Where is there a keyboard? You're both cheating,' I accuse.

'It's on my iPad, babe,' she says, looking at me through the rearview mirror. She looks at me like I'm her huffy child. Narrowing her eyes.

'I spy with my little eye...something beginning with...G,' Matt says, with absolutely zero interest.

If he's not interested, then why is he answering with the correct words?

G, what starts with G? Golf, Guns. Is there a gun in here?

'Grass?' Dani answers.

'Yeah,' Matt sighs.

Son of a bitch.

'Let's play Stop the Bus,' I announce.

'Don't be a sore loser.' Dani says as I pout in the back.

'How much longer? No offence, but I'm struggling to put up with the two of you,' Matt says as he opens a packet of cheese and onion crisps.

Great, a lovely cheesy smell to go with the KFC smell. My window doesn't even work; this could be the worse day of my life.

We've now been driving for seven hours in total. It's safe to say we all now hate each other and will probably never speak again. Turns out we can't all be alone together for longer than three hours in a confined space. I Spy got out of hand, and Dani's singing got us beyond rattled, so that had to stop. Me and Matt then got into a very heated argument about Cobra Kai and who was the best fighter, which lasted nearly an hour.

We now haven't spoken in fifty-four minutes, and it's been amazing. I haven't had to listen to Matt's whining, Dani shouting at Matt for whining or both of their singing.

'It says we're almost there,' Dani says, breaking the peace and quiet. 'But that doesn't make sense,' she continues. 'This isn't a village; it's a town…a small town…but a town.'

Time for me to be honest; she might kill me.

'Yeah…so the thing is…I need another night…before I face my family,' I confess. 'So I booked us into a cute little bed-and-breakfast…and then we'll go tomorrow.'

Matt turns round to face me and gives me a look of, well, I guess I would call it confusion, horror, maybe even murderous? Dani is just staring ahead. I think she's actually pretending she's somewhere else or counting to ten.

'But the wedding is tomorrow…we can't just rock up on the day,' Matt says hysterically, waving his arms around like he's a mime. 'Dani, tell her this is stupid.'

'She knows she's stupid…but the wedding isn't tomorrow; it's next Thursday,' Dani says deadpan and raging.

'WHAT?' Matt screams. 'She's kidding...right...? Someone tell me this is a joke.' He looks from me to Dani to me, his head spinning faster than a roulette table.

'I can't...it is next Thursday,' I stutter. 'You didn't know that?' I ask pathetically.

'Why are we here a week early? None of these people even like you; they didn't even invite you until a couple of days ago. Why wasn't I told this?'

Well, that was so much harsher than it needed to be. He has a point, though. Neither of us did say anything, but I forgot he was coming. So Dani is to blame if you think about it.

'That's why we're here a week early...to have it out,' Dani says, punching the air.

'No...that isn't why...We're here for the hen party, reception...and other crap,' I correct her.

'Why?' Matt asks, exasperated.

I actually don't know; I don't have an answer to that question. Why are we here so early?

'Dani!...It's her fault,' I say in protest.

'Eh, alright, Dotty, lay it on my door, why don't you? It wasn't my idea for this stupid detour. Where are we?'

'The bed-and-breakfast,' I tell them. 'That's it there.' I point to a rather crap-looking building as we pull up outside. It looked better in the photos.

'I only took off this weekend,' Matt announces.

'You own your own business, Matt,' Dani says as we pull into the car park.

'That's not the point,' he snaps.

'Is this free parking? You know I ain't paying for parking,' she announces, like we didn't already know that.

We once parked twenty-seven minutes away from a restaurant because the parking fee was two pounds.

'It's free.' I checked online.

'Do we have our own room?' Matt enquires.

Matt is in for a fun surprise. Since I forgot he was coming, I only booked one double bedroom. He's going to moan like such a little bitch.

If I still spoke to my therapist, I feel like they would agree that today has been a testing day. I'm lying here in a small double bed, in a human sandwich. It's so small that I'm pretty sure it should be classed as a single, and I'm with two people who want to kill me and each other.

'I swear to god, Matt, you touch me one more time with that foot, I will cut it off,' Dani states with pure hatred in her eyes. It's dark, but I can see it.

She pulls the covers off him, to which he immediately pulls them off her. Being in the middle is so much fun. It was agreed by them when we walked in that I was in the middle, since everything was all my fault. So now I'm sandwiched between them, Dani on my left, facing me, Matt on my right, facing the window.

It's only ten o'clock, but they were so pissed at me that they said they were going to bed as soon as we checked in. I think the room had a lot to do with it; it's not great. I've seen worse rooms. Ok, the shower pressure isn't the best, the sheets don't have the nicest smell, and the window doesn't close, meaning it's freezing, but it could be worse.

'MATT, stop taking my covers!' Dani snaps.

'It's not fair that your giant ass needs half the covers,' Matt hisses back.

One point Matt.

'Jealous? 'cause your skinny non-ass only needs a napkin?'

Oh, there's venom in her voice.

Not her best, though. She's funnier than that; she must be tired.

'Guys! It's been a long day...let's not fight,' I reason.

'Fuck off,' they say in unison.

Maybe they'll reunite in their hate for me?

'I've never been this cold in my life,' Matt announces dramatically.

Since I'm from up north, I'm used to this temperature, but the Glaswegians can't cope, it would seem.

'We've only been in bed for about ten minutes. Once the body heat kicks in, we'll be warm and toasty,' I say, patting them with a hand each.

'Didn't we tell you to fuck off?'

God, Matt.

'I wouldn't be so cold if I had had a decent shower…not been spat on by like four drips of water,' Dani tells us. 'I still have shampoo in my hair.'

They start breathing a little heavier. I think they're counting to ten to stop themselves from killing me. We count to ten too much to be considered sane.

I'm so uncomfortable; I'll never sleep in this position, especially with Matt's feet on top of me. They might be hitting Dani every now and then, but they are actually on me, freezing hairy feet, on me.

I don't like this silence.

'Guys…this is a weird request, but can I get a hug?' I ask 'cause I'm having a bad day, week, month and year.

I try not to be emotional in front of Dani; she doesn't know how to deal with too much sadness or distress. She's a let-it-build-up-and-then-explore-it kind of gal.

'Are you serious?' Matt asks, bewildered, turning back around to face us. 'Are you this scared of your family? 'cause if so, I don't think I want to meet them.'

'It's just been...an...' Fantastic; I'm crying. I must have been holding it in. 'Emotional week.'

'Oh, babe.' Dani grabs me, pulling me in for a bear hug.

'Why did we...come so early?' I sniff.

'I don't actually know; it seemed like a good idea.' She narrows her eyes and shrugs. 'But it wasn't.' She lets me go. 'You're good now, right?'

'Should we just go home tomorrow?' I ask.

'Yes,' Matt retorts.

'Shut up, Matt,' Dani says, dismissing him. 'It's going to be fine. At the very least, we'll all have a few nice days in the country. Matt, you did say we should take a trip away.'

'Yeah, to like Paris or Berlin, not the arse end of nowhere,' Matt says, sitting up. He turns on the lamp, blinding us all.

Dani sits herself up. I feel left out, so I sit up too. Paris sounds so much nicer than this right now, although this isn't hard to beat.

'We could go home and then come back just for the wedding,' I suggest, with absolutely no intention of coming back.

'I'm not driving all the way home to drive all the way back up here in four days.'

'I can't spend a week here. There's nothing here; it's like a ghost town,' Matt rages.

This isn't even the village.

'Yeah, I don't want to lie. There really isn't anything up here; we will be very bored,' I tell them. Hopefully, Matt makes Dani takes us home.

Matt turns away with a face like I just slapped him.

'We're going. If we hate it after twenty-four hours, we leave…agreed?' Dani says, holding out her hand for us to shake.

'Agreed,' I say, shaking her hand.

We both turn and look at Matt. He rolls his eyes, turns off the lamp and shuffles to lie back down on the bed.

'Agreed,' he huffs.

'I mean, you must be curious about what they are all up to,' Dani says.

'Couldn't care less.' I'm clearly talking utter shite.

'Course you don't, babe,' she says before shuffling back down.

'You think he's single?' Matt interjects.

'Which one?' Dani replies.

'I don't know. Which one do you want to be single?'

What a question, Matt. I shuffle back down the bed.

'Let's just sleep,' I tell them.

Tomorrow will be fine; it'll be good. Please, god, let it be good.

Chapter 7

I've never been a fan of breakfast; nothing against it, but I prefer lunch and dinner. I think it's 'cause I'm so tired in the morning, so all I'm thinking about is how I could still be in bed. If it's a case of breakfast or sleeping, I will always choose sleep. I may not know much about breakfast, as someone who doesn't usually attend, but even I know that this is shit.

I don't understand why these people opened a bed-and-breakfast. Their rooms are horrible, the building is falling apart (there are slates from the roof in the garden), they clearly can't stand people, judging by how they greeted us at the door last night, and this breakfast is the most disgusting thing that has ever existed.

The 'continental' buffet consists of prunes, black bananas, raisins, crackers (really! crackers), beans and cheese, but not slices of different cheeses, a block of cheese, with no knife. The cooked breakfast has two choices, scrambled eggs or porridge. It doesn't even say scrambled eggs and toast, just scrambled eggs. There isn't a full Scottish breakfast. Who are these inhumane people?

The breakfast room is another horror show. I didn't see it last night 'cause we went straight to our room, but it's horrifyingly ugly. The main issues are that it is the size of a cupboard, it has black walls (seriously), around sixty pictures of frogs, a pink carpet (no, honestly, it's bubble gum pink), yellow chairs and orange tables. They're clearly serial killers or emotionally disturbed. Why do these people own a bed-and-breakfast? Of course, my darling companions are being supportive and understanding as we sit here, in it together, knowing in their hearts that I didn't know this place was complete shit when I booked it.

'I wish I was dead and didn't have to look at you two,' Matt says, throwing his napkin on the table.

'You just put your napkin in your beans,' I tell him.

'Napkin? Dotty, that's a bit of blue roll,' Dani says, screwing up her face at the offensive napkin/blue roll.

When we came down to this Kermit shrine room, I did suggest we go to Starbucks, but this was included in the price. Dani loves a bargain. She must feel pretty stupid right now.

Oh god, Katie Hopkins' less-friendly sister just walked back into the room. Now, there's no one in this world that I have a lower opinion of than Katie Hopkins, just to illustrate how horrendous this women's customer service is. She's carrying our breakfast. We're the only ones here, so it has to be ours, although looking at it, I wish it wasn't.

'Porridge?' she spits, literally.

'That's me,' I answer as she drops it in front of me from five feet in the fucking air.

As the plate smacks the table, about a third of the bowl spits back out at me.

'Thank you.' Yeah, thanks for the third-degree burns.

'Eggs?'

Ew, she spat again.

'Here,' Dani says as she pushes away from the table to avoid the third-degree burns I just got.

No burns, but there is now egg in her hair, runny egg. Why are they so runny? I'm no chef, but isn't that salmonella on a plate?

'Thank you.'

No matter what happens, Dani can't not be polite to service staff; it's like a waitress code.

'You don't want anything else, right?'

She isn't asking; she's telling us.

'No, thank you, that's perfect,' I reply. I, too, now have the waitress code due to Dani drumming it into me.

As she storms off, slamming the door as she exits, I look around the table at the four angry eyes on me.

'It is just scrambled eggs, undercooked scrambled eggs,' Dani rages.

I take a bite of my porridge for something to do. Oh, shocker, it's vile.

'It's horrible, isn't it? I can see it on your face,' Matt says.

I can't be sure, but I think they've made it with water, like actual savages. Isn't that how they make it in prison? Milk isn't even expensive; that bitch is evil.

'It's lovely.' I can't say it's liking eating paste, can I? They don't need any more reason to turn on me.

I'll move it around the bowl and pretend I'm eating it.

'We need to go to Tesco,' Matt announces. He hasn't uncrossed his arms since we sat down; he's a five-year-old child.

Of course we're going to Tesco; otherwise, we would starve. I don't think they fully understand how remote my home is. This is going to be the worse week of my life. It's one thing to have to deal with all those people, but these two moaning will send me insane.

'Do you want more juice?' I ask with a please-stop-blaming-me smile.

'Juice? It's lime cordial,' Dani says before she bursts out laughing.

'It's seriously not funny, Dani,' Matt says as he pours himself another lime cordial. Oh, god, he just spilt it onto the bubble pink carpet.

That's it; now I'm laughing. Matt pouring the cordial on that manky carpet has pushed me over the edge for some reason. They do say you either have to laugh or cry.

'What's with the frogs?' Dani says through tears of laughter.

'The frogs? What about these chairs? I feel like I'm sitting on a banana,' Matt says before he bursts out laughing.

'COULD YOU ALL KEEP IT DOWN?' Bitch face shouts from the kitchen.

'OH, GO SUCK ANOTHER LEMON!' Matt screams back.

Now we're in fits of laughter, the kind where you can't stop and you don't know why. Oh god, Dani just fell off her chair! She can't even get back up for laughing. Matt picks up a banana and holds it out for her to grab, which only makes us laugh more. Dani sits back up, and we slightly simmer down.

'We need to go before lemon face comes out and kills us,' Dani states.

The three of us slowly stand up and make our way to the door. The door to the kitchen opens as we do, and me and Dani rush out the door as Matt falls down, running.

'Wait,' Matt pleads.

I go to help him.

'Leave him! Every man for himself!' Dani says, making a run for it.

I'm a follower, so I hesitate, then run after her. I don't need to worry; he's back up in no time, overtaking me and running for the car.

We're about five minutes from my mum and dad's house, and I'm terrified. I've been scared for the past three days, but now, driving closer and closer, I'm shaking. Dani won't stop singing, and Matt is in the back sleeping, his car sickness a thing of the past. I think he's pretending to sleep because no one could sleep through her singing.

'It says we're five minutes away,' Dani says.

'Yep, yep, yep…we are…we are five minutes away,' I say, slapping my legs over and over again.

'You alright there, babe?' Dani asks, I think, slightly worried about my state of mind.

'Course…I'm excited. That's what I am…buzzing.' I can't stop shaking.

'Everything will be good. If you stop shaking.' She pats my leg.

'I'm trying.' I really am.

'Ok, why don't you do that breathing trick, like you're in labour?' Dani suggests.

'Thanks, babe, but the only thing that's going to calm me down, is driving in the opposite direction.'

We drive the next three minutes in silence, then before I know it, or I'm prepared for it, we're here, outside my childhood home.

'What the fuck is this?' Matt says, sitting up in between us.

Matt and Dani are sitting up straight, staring out the front window, shell-shocked. Matt's mouth is literally hanging open, and Dani has a look on her face like she's trying to divide five hundred and seventy-four by forty-two. I should have told them, but they would have said stuff and teased me. My family kind of have money.

'Why are we sitting outside a mansion?' Matt asks, pointing to my house.

It's just big; it's not overly grand inside or anything. We have the usual basic rooms, living room, kitchen, bathroom, five bedrooms, the office, mud room, gym...Alright, it's a mansion. We weren't spoiled, though. Well, my brother was, to be fair.

'Are you rich?' Matt asks. 'Dani, stop making that face; you look stupid.'

'I'm not rich...my mum and dad are comfortable.'

'That's what rich people say. Dani, did you know she was rich? I wouldn't have slagged you off so much if I had known you were minted.'

'Babe, we're outside a mansion.' Dani is out of her shock-induced coma.

'Can we move on from this?' I beg them.

'Move on? It's been a hot minute.' She tells me.

'I'm really looking forward to this wedding now…it's going to be so nice and fancy,' Matt says, full of excitement. He's actually smiling.

'We're really underdressed,' Dani states.

I begged her to change before we left the room, begged, but she said it was her most comfortable outfit. The most comfortable outfit Dani owns is purple joggers and an orange T-shirt. At breakfast, in that room, she fitted in perfectly. Matt is wearing skinny black jeans and a Spice Girls T-shirt, which looks good in Glasgow but not in the country. I'm wearing grey leggings with a pink jumper; Matt called me a basic bitch. We look like poor art students on a budget.

'Right, we doing this or what?' Matt says, getting annoyed.

'In a minute…I just need a minute,' I say, not making eye contact.

It's been ten minutes.

Now it's been fifteen minutes; this is getting pathetic.

'For the love of god, Dotty, get out of this mother fucking car!' Dani says with her head on the wheel.

'Are you trying to kill me? She is,' Matt says to himself. He's sitting back with his eyes closed.

Sorry if my personal trauma is boring you, Matthew. I will get out of the car; I just need a little time.

'Maybe we should just take a drive first,' I suggest.

'A drive? Babe, my ass is numb 'cause I've been driving for days,' Dani says, lifting her head to stare into my eyes with her irritated ones.

It hasn't been days; it's been two half-days.

'Fine...fine...I'm getting out of the car...Ok...? I am getting out of the car...now...right now...right now.'

'GET OUT OF THE CAR!' Matt interrupts, screaming.

'Babe...get out of the car...or I will drag you out.'

Alright.

One.

Two.

Three.

Three and one quarter.

'Remember, they should fear you; you're Dotty Peters,' Dani says, taking hold of my hand, which she squeezes a little too hard.

'If we could take a little drive around the village first, I would really appreciate it,' I say to Dani.

She looks at me with sympathetic eyes, nods her head then takes a deep breath.

'No,' she says firmly.

'It's just; they don't know we're coming.' I confess.

'Excuse me?' Matt says, concerned. 'They don't know?'

'You said you told your dad!' Dani shrieks.

'I was going to, but then I didn't.'

She looks so mad.

'Have you told us anything we need to know? Or kept all the important information to yourself?' Dani demands to know.

'I honestly don't know,' I tell her truthfully. I can't even remember what I've told them.

'Out,' she demands.

'Babe, this is all a bit much…and I'm sure they're watching us right now…which means they already know I'm here, so… job done.'

She doesn't look convinced.

They share a look. This can't be good.

'Last chance, babe, or I'll need to take matters into my own hands,' Dani warns me.

Whatever she's thinking, I think it's what needs to happen because I seriously can't move my legs.

'Do what you need to do,' I tell her.

It is what it is.

Chapter 8

How did I get here?

I mean, I know how I got here physically, but how did I get to be in this situation? Standing outside my childhood home, scared to knock on the door after being physically pushed out of a car. Matt opened my door as Dani pushed me out onto the ground; it was mortifying. The three of us are now at the front door, staring at the bell.

'For the love of god,' Matt mutters as he pushes past me to ring the bell.

'Thanks, Matt; I'm starting to lose the will to live,' Dani whispers.

Hopefully, my mum doesn't answer, or my sister. Yeah, it'll definitely be one of them.

The door is opening...the door is opening...the door is...

My mum. My mum is standing right in front of me, holding a candle stick. Dotty Peters was killed on the entranceway stairs by her mother with the candle stick.

My mum, or Anna as her friends call her, is still an attractive older woman. She wears her age well and looks more in her early forties than late fifties. Slim build, blue eyes, she still dyes her hair and has kept her brown bob the same shade for the last twenty years. She looks absolutely livid.

'Dorothy...what on earth are you doing here?' my mum asks, with such disdain that it takes my breath away for a second.

She's the only person that calls me Dorothy; it's my actual name, but I hate it.

'Hi, Mum.' I wave. Why did I wave? I'm such a freak. 'This is Dani.' I point to Dani like she can't see the five-foot-four ginger behind me. 'And Matt.' I need to stop pointing. 'They are my friends from Glasgow.' I point to the car like it's somehow Glasgow.

'Ok...could you now explain why you have brought strangers to my home?' she asks, looking at my partners in crime with disgust.

Sorry guys.

'We're here for the wedding,' I offer.

My mum looks confused and horrified in equal measure. 'I was worried you would come here and cause trouble.'

She takes a very long, deep breath. I have no idea what to do.

'We were invited. Well, Dotty was, at least,' Dani says.

'Speak when spoken to, my dear,' my mother says as she turns to look Dani up and down.

'Oh my,' Dani says in return, looking at her shoes.

'Time for you three to head back home...I won't have my daughter's wedding ruined.' And with that statement, she slams the door in my face.

'Fuck me...she is horrible; I get you shaking now,' Matt says, startled. 'We're leaving now, right?'

'Fuck, no,' Dani says, pushing past me again and banging hard on the door. 'Sorry, she took me aback for a minute there, but I got this.'

'Babe, let's just go. I knew this wasn't a good idea.'

The door swings open once again.

'You all need to leave.'

Mum is raging.

'Look, I get it; Dotty shamed you or whatever.' Dani starts ranting. 'The little minx that she was. But I just drove like a week to get here. We have been through it; you should have seen where we stayed last night, Jesus.'

'Babe, I don't think...' I plead to Dani.

'And I nearly crashed like five times on those shit one-way country roads, so we're staying,' Dani tells my mother matter-of-factly. 'It's her sister's wedding; she was invited, so get used to the idea.'

Happy with her statement, Dani stands back; actually, she hides behind me. Matt is very quiet as he looks at the clouds with intense interest.

'I can assure you, young lady, none of you were invited.'

Great, Mum just called Dani "young;" she'll be talking about this for months.

'Mum, I *was* invited. Why do you think I came?' I ask.

'To cause destruction; that is what you do best, isn't it?' Mum says, putting a hand on her forehead like some damsel in distress.

Come on, Mum, grow up.

You cheat on one person one time, and suddenly, you're branded for life.

'Destruction?' Matt sniggers. 'Come on; it was an affair, not murder. She didn't serve time.'

My thoughts exactly.

'MUM, WHOSE CAR IS OUTSIDE?' I hear my brother shout from upstairs.

We all kind of just stare at each other; it's weird.

'Guess you all better come in then,' Mum says, walking inside.

'Can I not do that?' Matt begs us.

'Yeah, that doesn't sound like a great time,' Dani agrees.

'Either of you leave, I'll scream,' I warn, following my mum into the pits of hell. Here we go.

We all walk into the sitting area, yes, a seating area. Mum always said calling it a living room was common; she has issues. Matt and Dani stand in the corner, completely still; no eye contact, nothing.

'I'll go get your brother, I suppose,' Mum says, leaving us alone.

'Oh my god, look at that!' Matt rushes over to the fireplace, picking up my mum's gold elephant statue.

That thing costs more than Dani's car; my heart is in my mouth.

'Please put it down...gently,' I beg.

'Why? How much is it worth?' Matt asks, passing it from one hand to the other.

I will murder him, I swear.

'A lot,' I warn.

He puts it back, causing my heart rate to relax.

'This place is immaculate,' Dani says, running her hand down the wall.

'Do people even live here?' Matt asks, looking around the room. 'Hospitals aren't this clean.'

'Yeah, but they're rich; bet they have like six cleaners.' Dani says, bouncing down on the couch, a ten grand couch.

'True.' Matt agrees, bouncing down next to her.

Oh god, Mum loves that couch more than any of her kids.

'We do not have six cleaners,' I say, sitting down gently across from them. We only have one cleaner.

Footsteps. I stand up in preparation.

Within seconds my big brother is standing ten feet away from me. It might only have been two years, but he looks so different. His hair has gone from shaggy to shaven, clean-cut. He has lost weight, at least a stone, he wasn't fat, but now he looks great, healthy.

'DOT!' he screams, running over to pick me up in a big bear hug.

At least he's happy to see me; I'll take that.

I've missed my brother, but I didn't realise how much until this very moment. He still smells the same, coconut and mint from his shower gel with a hint of smoke, a habit that Mum still doesn't know about. His hugs are always so comforting and safe.

'Alright, David, she doesn't have much time, so...' Mum says, ruining the moment.

'What do you mean?' David asks, putting me down and pulling away to face our mother. 'You're not staying?' He turns back to me, his eyes showing concern.

'Well, we...' I start.

'No, they aren't.' Mum interrupts.

'You aren't?' my confused brother asks. 'Jane is getting married; you need to stay.'

'We are.' Dani announces.

I actually forgot they were over there for a minute. I look over to see that Dani has found her feet and is walking towards us. Matt is just sitting there, staring at my brother; he's *really* staring at my brother.

'You are?' David asks me, completely hopeful.

I turn round to see my brother smiling at me, full of enthusiasm and hope. My sister invited me, and my brother clearly wants me here, so.

'Course I am; I wouldn't miss it.'

Yesterday's car journey was the worst, last night was the worst, and now, this lunch is the absolute worst. It doesn't say much about how the rest of the week will go.

It started off ok, once my mum got over her small stroke at the revelation that we were staying. We all agreed to have a small bite; after that breakfast, we were all starving. Dani's face lit up like a Christmas tree when Mum brought out the scones. Matt ran to grab the seat night to David; I'll need to break it to him soon that my brother is straight. It's me, David and Matt on one side, Dani and Mum on the other.

Once the food was demolished, we tried the whole small talk thing. Dani swore about eighty times in ten minutes, and Matt told a slightly explicit story while staring at my brother the entire time. So, it's safe to say my mum isn't impressed by my friends. Technically Matt is Dani's friend, so I take no responsibility for him. Then an extremely awkward silence appeared, and it hasn't gone away yet; it's been twenty-five minutes.

'So, Mrs Peters….this is a big house.'

Aw, Dani is trying to engage my mother in conversation.

'The garden must be huge.' Dani smiles, looking like she wants the ground to open up and swallow her.

Well, she tried.

'This house is beautiful, by the way. Huge as well,' Matt nervously remarks. 'What is it you do?'

'My husband owns his own company,' Mum flippantly replies.

'Nice. Me too,' Matt tells her proudly.

'Really?' my mother asks, completely uninterested.

'It's a vape shop.'

Mum looks at me with disappointed eyes. I don't even vape.

Was that the door? Judging by my mum's now worried, twisty face, it was the door.

'DAVID, WHOSE CAR IS OUTSIDE?' Jane shouts.

My sister is home.

We have never had many guests here. Mum doesn't like strangers touching her things, or family members, or friends. A new car in the drive is out of the norm for us.

'In here, sweetheart.' Mum calls.

I doubt she heard her, but Mum never shouts. Wait, sweetheart? She has never said sweetheart to me. Whatever.

'David, you in here?' Jane asks as she turns into the dining room.

There she is, my baby sister. All five-foot-seven of her, she got the tall gene. You have never seen a girl look so much like both her parents, except maybe, Maya Hawk. She has Dad's brown eyes, Mum's nose, Mum's mouth and both their natural brown hair colour. She's a perfect combo of both beautiful and elegant.

She doesn't look beautiful right now, though; she looks bewildered and slightly pissed off. It's the look she had when they cancelled her school talent show in primary five. Her face is confusing since she invited me here.

'Dot?' she asks like she's the only person who can see me.

'She came home for your wedding.' David says. 'Is that not amazing?'

Clearly not.

'You're here for the wedding?' she asks, confused. 'My wedding?'

Oh shit. She didn't invite me.

'You invited me,' I say, 'cause I don't know what else to say.

'No, I didn't...Why would I invite you here? It's the biggest day of my life.'

'Isn't that why you would invite her?' Dani asks.

'Who are you?' Jane asks her, narrowing her eyes in distrust.

'Dani...I'm the friend...this is Matt...he's my friend,' she stutters, clearly struggling to understand what is happening. 'Matt, say something.'

'I like your jacket,' he says, pointing to Jane's jacket as if she would have forgotten she was wearing one.

'What is happening?' Jane asks no one in particular.

'I knew you were lying,' Mum says, pointing at me with venom. 'You couldn't let your sister have her day?'

'I was invited; I got it the other day...How else would I know it was even happening?'

'It's called Facebook, Dot,' Jane retorts, sitting down across from me.

'You blocked me on Facebook,' I retort back.

She did, the bitch. Blocked me on all social media; they all did, and David doesn't have any. Whatever, I'm over it.

'Did you invite her?' Jane accuses David.

'No...I don't even know what the invites look like,' David says in his defence.

'Well, now that it has been established that Dorothy was not invited...it's about time you all left.' Mum says.

Jesus, Mother, most parents would be happy to see their child after two years.

'They can't,' argues David.

'David.' Mum snaps at my innocent brother.

'Mum,' he snaps back. 'Jane is getting married…Dot should be here…Jane.'

Well, this is awkward.

We all just sit in silence. Matt and Dani are staring at Mum in astonishment, as they should be. Mum is staring at Jane, David is staring at Jane, Jane is staring at me, and I'm staring at the last scone.

'Fine…she can stay.'

Well, thank you, little sister, you're too kind. Mum looks like she's about to faint, and Dani has the biggest grin on her face.

'But they can't stay here.'

'Jane,' David pleads.

'No, David…James will be over here with Andy all week…I'm not having him feel uncomfortable.' Jane states.

I heard of a family once that had a choice of staying together and dying, or separating with a chance of surviving; they chose to stay together. They loved each other so much that they couldn't live without each other, a loving, amazing family. It's enough to make you sick, isn't it?

'Where are they supposed to stay?' David asks.

We all look at each other, knowing full well there is only one choice.

'We'll figure it out.' I reply.

I could really do with a nice virus right about now, just bad enough to keep me bed bound. I keep asking myself the same question: why the hell did we come this early? Or why at all?

'Jane, aren't you going to invite them to your thing tomorrow?' David asks a livid Jane.

The room suddenly got really tense, well, more tense than it already was, and it was tense as hell before.

'It's short notice,' Jane states.

'They can make it. You can make it...right?' David demands, sitting up straighter in his chair.

'Well, we have no plans...because we don't live here.... but what are we making exactly?' Dani asks with her little eyebrow kink.

'The girls are going to a spa for the bridal shower,' my mum says, finding her voice again. 'It's a private event.'

Well, that was subtle. Why didn't she just say, you're not welcome like she has done about us being here?

'Like a hen?' Dani's excited now; she basically just jumped out of her chair.

'No, it's a shower; the hen is on Tuesday,' Jane answers, and I can see the instant regret on her face.

The room has a lovely silence now. David is itching to say something, Dani is loving the drama, and Matt hasn't stopped looking at David. I don't even think he knows what's happening right now. I mean, I don't care if we miss it, but if she invites us, then we need to say yes.

'Jane! A word,' my brother demands.

David gets out of his seat and goes round to Jane. She stands up as he practically pushes her out of the door. Mother doesn't look happy. I don't know if it's being left out of that conversation, or the possibility of having to be in another one with us.

Nice, silence again.

Thank god; they are back. They both take their previous seats.

Oh god, Jane looks guilty. She's going to ask us.

'You should come to the hen...both of you.'

'We would love to.' Dani answers for us.

'Thanks,' I tell her. We lock eyes for a split second, and I actually see my sister, my sweet little sister. Then it's gone, replaced by disdain.

'What about this spa? Cause I could really do with a rub down,' Dani tells the room.

Oh, there's that lovely silence again.

'Yeah...course. Come to that, too...if you want.' Jane says.

'Perfect,' Dani says, excited.

'Yeah...perfect,' I say in utter disbelief.

Who should I ask about the price of all this? I am jobless, after all.

Chapter 9

After another fun-filled thirty minutes of weird small talk (to be fair, Dani did most of the talking), we made our excuses and left. I did want to see my dad, but his sixth sense must have kicked in, warning him of danger.

So here we are again, in the car, sitting outside the place we need to go into, with me refusing to move. Me and Dani are in the front. Dani is staring out the window, losing the will to live as Matt sits with his head in his hands.

'Dotty, it has been a day…made only bearable with the inclusion of your hot brother…Can we please go in here, get drunk and forget this day ever happened?' Matt begs, lifting his head.

'My brother is straight,' I say.

'Of course he is,' Matt replies with a wink.

'Look…as much as I was scared to face my mother,' I say, ignoring him.

'With good reason,' Dani interrupts.

'This is different…this woman despises me.'

'You're not your mother's favourite person either,' Dani interrupts again.

She's not wrong, but my mother won't do me any physical harm; I wouldn't like to think.

'This woman wouldn't spit on me if I was on fire.' I'm not even exaggerating.

'Your mum would think twice about it too,' Dani interrupts again.

'Yeah, alright, Dani, I get it. My mum thinks I'm a piece of shit...but you think she was bad...Just wait until you see how this bitch reacts. She's every Disney villain, all rolled into one,' I stress.

'I mean, after the last twenty-four hours...does it matter if one more person treats you like a whore?' Matt suggests.

He has a point. What is one more person hating on me going to do?

'What if she refuses to give us a room?' Dani asks, suddenly concerned.

This is a strong possibility.

'I don't know,' I reply.

The closest town with any sort of accommodation is an hour and a half away. Which isn't ideal, but I think I would prefer it.

'Dani...if she doesn't get out this car in the next minute...I'm going to take a bitch fit,' he says, rubbing his temples in exasperation.

'Dotty...please get out of the car...I can't handle your emotional breakdown and his whining at the same time. Plus, I need to pee.'

Ok. I can handle this; I'm ready.

'Ok, I'm ready...you can push me out of the car again. Whenever you're ready,' I tell them.

'You heard the woman, Matt. Get the door, and I'll shove.'

It's the only way I'll move these days.

It looks the same, like a scene straight out of the eighties. Smells the same, like floral perfume. Kim loves a floral scented candle. The last time I was standing in this hall, the crazy bitch was throwing eggs at me. Seriously, eggs! The house is lovely; once upon a time, it used to be a farmhouse. She converted it into a bed-and-breakfast years ago when she moved up here. It's a very impressive story, actually: single mother, abandoned by her husband, uproots and starts over in a small village. It's basically every Hallmark movie plotline. I mean, she was left like ninety grand in her dad's will, so she had help.

The whole single mother thing is the reason she's so over-protective. James told me when he was younger, this boy in his class pushed him over; it was over a game of football they played or something. Then the next day, Kim pushed the boy's mother over, right there in the playground at pick-up time. That woman got pushed over; I got egged. I thought she would hit me, to be honest. I think I got off easy, considering I hurt her precious boy. James was always such a mummy's boy; I think he felt guilty for his brother choosing Daddy, even though he was the one who stayed with her.

'Dotty, this is getting boring; ring the fucking bell,' Matt demands.

We're standing at the reception desk; the bell is right in front of me, but alas, I cannot press it. We are surrounded by weird dead butterflies and tiny creatures in frames. I don't understand taxidermy. It's dead; why frame that? I bet she wants to kill and stuff me. Oh god, we should leave.

'Give me strength,' Matt says dramatically. He pushes past me and rings the bell. 'You're welcome,' he snaps.

He stands back behind me and Dani. Probably for cover, and he hasn't even met her yet.

I can hear her footsteps coming from the kitchen. Great, now I'm sweating. She opens the swing door separating us and stops dead in her tracks. If looks could kill, I would be stabbed, shot and maimed.

'Dotty.' Kim says my name with so much disdain and disgust that my soul freezes in fear. 'Heard you were back,' she states, looking me up and down with a smirk. 'Not looking your best, are you?'

I've felt small in my time, but right this second, I feel like a traffic warden, hated and despised. She walks slowly towards us, like a lion approaching its prey. Of course she already knew I was back; Jane would have told Andy, Andy would have told James, and James would have called his mummy.

'Kim,' I stutter. Nice, Dotty; real strong and confident.

'Guessing you and your little Glasgow gang here want a couple of rooms?' She asks.

'Gang?' Matt asks Dani.

She just shrugs, looking confused. 'We do...please,' Dani says to Kim.

'She your bodyguard?' Kim asks me, not taking her eyes off me. 'You all have some nerve showing up here, to my home, wanting a room.'

'I said please,' Dani says in confusion. 'And you are a B&B, right?'

Dani looks to Matt, who has lost all interest, I think.

Please, God, kill me now.

'I know this is...weird,' I start, not really knowing where I'm going with this.

'Weird?' Kim laughs.

'Ok, it's inappropriate then,' I offer.

'I'm sorry, I know this is an awkward moment...she broke your son...and did whatever to the other one,' Matt says, as I stare at him in shock.

Not Dani; she's grinning.

'But...I need to sleep tonight...Last night I had to listen to that one.' He points to Dani. 'Snoring all night... Imagine listening to a thousand pigs being slaughtered...the sound is worse than that.'

He's not wrong.

'And that one...'

Oh good, my turn.

'Her feet are like ice blocks...and she hits...I'm talking slaps, punches and kicks...so please...please...give me a room...I don't care about them...just please give me a room.'

Selfish bastard.

After a very tense few minutes...

'Must be your lucky day...' Kim says. 'I have had a cancellation, so you can have one triple room between you all...as long as all three of you stay away from me...at all times.' She gives each one of us a stern stare. 'And know that I am doing this for your sister.'

Understood. Oh god, we're sharing. I know that room, too, it's not the best. It's not even used unless absolutely essential.

'Oh god, we're sharing!' Matt cries.

Rude! He's the worse one to share with. I'm a delight. I do get where Kim is coming from. If I could insist Matt stay away from me for the next three days, I would too.

'As for my sons, I hope you know to stay very clear away from them,' Kim says with a murderous look. 'Both of them.'

'But will they stay away from her?' Dani replies.

There she goes, all unfiltered and making me want to kill her.

'Sorry...Please still give us the room,' Dani pleads.

'Do you have a room in a shed?' Matt asks. ''cause I would take a shed room.'

I need a drink. This week is turning me into an alcoholic, and I don't even care.

I feel much better; I feel happy and calm.

I love alcohol.

After we got to our room and dumped our bags, we lasted about two seconds before we all agreed that getting drunk was the only thing to do.

That was three hours, six gins, two ciders and a shot of a weird green thing ago; now we're all having a much better time.

We came to The Blackburn, the only pub the village has; it's old and smells of beer and cigarettes. Basically, it's like walking back into the nineties. It's only a forty-minute walk away from the bed-and-breakfast, which wasn't met with the most positive response from the city people. They ain't walkers, but they wanted alcohol. I wanted to drive over to another village, away from everyone, but no one was willing to drive and surrender the alcohol. At first, the staring in the pub annoyed me and made me want to cry, but now I'm drunk and couldn't care less.

That's not true; I still care, but considerably less.

It's packed in here; it always is, 'cause I mean, what else is there to do in this time capsule of a village? You've got the Quinns at the bar, an older couple who stopped talking to each other about twenty years ago but still come here every night for their pint and vodka with soda. There's Ieuan sitting by the bathrooms; he's a Welsh guy who moved up years ago to get away from people and the world. I understand him more and more as the years go by. You also have the Semple family, all eight of them; they have six children. Why anyone would have six children baffles me. They're actually alright; they have never given me a dirty look and say hi when they see me. Then there are the usual farmers and their helping hands.

It's strange; I grew up here with these people, but I feel like a complete outsider, and not just 'cause no one talks to me. I think being away, in the 'big' city, has changed me.

'I feel like I'm in The Wicker Man,' Matt states, downing his pint. 'I bet they are all discussing how to kill us slowly, make the pain last.'

'Would you shut the fuck up? You're going to give me nightmares,' Dani says, looking around the room with suspicion.

'You're both stupid,' I state, taking a gulp of my drink.

'Can't believe we're here for a week…I might go insane, you know,' Matt says dramatically.

'I swear, you two better stop the whining. No one forced either of you to come,' I say a tad too loud.

The Semple's all just turned and stared at me, all sixteen eyes of them.

I definitely get braver the more I drink; I should get really drunk at the wedding. No, that's a bad idea, or is it?

'Forced?' Dani asks. 'Babe, if I hadn't said I would go, you wouldn't have come,' Dani says, sitting back in her chair proudly, like she just did math in her head, which she can't do.

'Then we wouldn't all be here, would we?' I retort. 'And Matt wouldn't be sulking.'

'He ain't sulking 'cause he's here…he's sulking 'cause he got dumped.' Dani says each word with a point in Matt's direction.

'Thanks, Dani, real supportive,' Matt says, rolling his eyes and pouting. 'And I didn't get dumped…it was mutual.'

'He said he was moving out 'cause he met someone else… how is that mutual?'

Jesus, Dani, tell it how it is, why don't you? We should work on her sympathetic tone.

'Because we agreed that...it was alright...would,' he snaps at her.

'Was it also mutual that you leave for a few days while he moves his stuff out?' Dani asks with all the empathy of a goldfish.

'Is that the reason you came?' I ask, suddenly offended. There's me thinking he was being supportive.

Wait, no, I didn't; I thought he came for the drama. Oh, I'm drunker than I thought.

'Yes,' Matt replies.

'It's not that I don't feel for you, babe, but these things happen...and you were only together three months,' Dani says, widening her eyes at me.

'Four, actually,' Matt retorts. 'Who wants another drink?' He gets up and moves over to the bar before either of us gives an answer.

'Well, that was harsh,' I say, softening towards Matt. He does look all heartbroken.

'Tough love, babe.'

'Please don't give me tough love,' I beg.

'The way this week is going...I won't...though I'm seriously starting to think that I might have to check you into some sort of facility when we get home. There has to be somewhere to send people like you,' Dani says, completely serious.

She has a point, to be fair. I was thinking the same.

Is that...? It can't be; he can't be here. I can't deal with him on top of everything else.

It is him. Of course it's him. I'm tired, emotionally drained and drunk—perfect timing for him to show up.

As if my week wasn't already a disaster. Billy has just walked through the door. What is he even doing here?

Great, he's seen me. We lock eyes for a split second before I look away. It hasn't been enough years; I need more time. Of fucking course, James just walked in behind him. Who I also lock eyes with for a split second. That's it; I'm just going to look at Dani.

'Why are you staring at me like that? You look consti-pated.' She narrows her eyes at me.

'They're here!' I whisper as low as I can.

'What?' she basically screams.

'They...are...here,' I hiss.

'What the fuck are you saying?' she shouts.

'Who just walked in, looked at you and left?' Matt asks, appearing out of nowhere with a fresh beer and a round of shots. Tequila rose, absolutely not.

Wait! They left? Thank god.

As he sits back down, Dani turns her head around to look.

'Who's that walking over?' Dani asks.

What? I whip my head around to see what humiliating situation I have to deal with now. James!

Shit, he's too close to run, so I do the other grown-up thing to do: I hide under the table.

'What is happening?' I hear Matt ask from above my head.

Ew, it's very sticky under here.

'Babe, this isn't a great look. You know, coward,' Dani advises me in a whisper above my head.

Like I don't know this already.

'Seriously, Dot, is this how you want to deal with me?' James asks me in a charming superior tone.

I would rather not deal with him at all.

'Don't know who you are, but there's no one under the table.' Dani tells him.

I can always count on Dani to have my back.

'Her ass is in plain sight,' James argues.

'I think you're drunk; there isn't anyone under there. You should just carry on with your night elsewhere.'

Dani will never admit defeat. If you show her undeniable proof that she is wrong, she will still say she's right. Like now, I'm clearly under this table, but Dani will stand by me and her lie that I definitely am not.

I can hear the familiar sound of James sighing.

'Dorothy Peters, can you please get up?'

He won't leave, even though I would clearly rather be a thousand feet under the sea, swimming with sharks, than be here. Stubborn git.

I reluctantly climb out and sit back on my chair. To then be met with a smug-looking James looking down on me. Literally.

'Babe! When did you get here?' Dani asks in a very over-the-top way.

'I see Glasgow doesn't agree with you,' James arrogantly tells me.

'So your mum already told me,' I fire back.

'She said she had seen you. Didn't think you would have the nerve to come back, let alone ask my mum for a room. You really don't have any sense of decency,' he angrily says, folding his arms. Clearly, time hasn't been a great healer.

Before I can respond, I'm beaten to the punch.

'You didn't think she would have the nerve to come to her sister's wedding?' Dani says, matching his fiery tone. 'Or you didn't think she had the nerve to come back to her home town, where her family live?' Dani asks him, shaking her head in confusion.

'Clearly, she hasn't told you the full story,' James patronises.

'We know it,' Matt interjects. He's been sitting inspecting James through this exchange. 'She cheated on you, probably because of your shit personality, then decided she wanted a change of scenery. Now we're all here for a wedding. Do you have a problem with that? I couldn't give a shit if you do; I'm just wondering why you would. It's been two years.' Matt calmly says. He takes a drink of his beer, sitting back in his chair like a fucking boss.

I might have forgotten I invited him, but I'm absolutely delighted that I did. James is stumped. I can see his little wheels turning, trying to think of a smart comeback.

'I couldn't care less that you're all here. I only care that my mum's put out.'

'Your mum owns a business, and last time I checked, we had paid her,' Dani points out to him. 'And after meeting your mother, she doesn't need you defending her.'

'Side note, was that your brother, by any chance, that ran away like a little bitch when he saw her?'

Holy shit, Matt!

'Don't talk shit about my family,' James warns.

'Don't walk over here or anywhere and try to act disrespectfully to my friends,' Matt warns.

'Like I said, you should leave and carry on your night elsewhere,' Dani advises James.

James unfolds his arms and turns to face me.

'You always did need someone else to fight your battles,' he tells me, his voice filled with venom.

'Why are we battling? It's done; it's in the past,' I calmly and patiently tell him.

He smiles, shakes his head in disbelief and leaves, shooting one last look of disdain at Matt, who simply grins back at him.

'Yeah, I would have cheated too,' Dani announces.

'Agreed,' Matt replies.

Guess that's one down, one more to go.

It's two hours later, and Matt has retired back to the bed and breakfast. He said he was tired, but he just wanted the bed closest to the heating. The room is so tiny, it doesn't matter which bed we have; with three of us in there, the place will be like a sauna. With the strong wind up here, though, I don't think he's taking any chances.

Me and Dani have moved to the bar stools. I was trying to show my giving side by giving our table to Dawn and Geoff. They are the sweetest people in the village; they raise money for charity, bake amazing cakes for everyone's birthday, volunteer at every local event, they just help people.

Dawn is a teacher and tutors the slow kids at weekends (I was one of them). Geoff is a gardener; he looks after all the old people's gardens for free in his spare time. I mean, they are actual saints. They thanked us with a smile and bought us a drink. Saints.

The pub is now packed; every Tom, Dick and Harry is here. There are a lot of judgemental eyes staring back at us now. Dani being a loud, sweary Glaswegian isn't helping, but what are you going to do?

'When the fuck is the karaoke starting?' Dani asks, looking around the bar.

Oh yeah, Karaoke Saturday; I forgot she'd seen that poster. That's why she was so keen to stay; I only wanted more alcohol. If these people didn't hate me before, they will for sure once she starts singing; even Dawn and Geoff will turn on me.

'Soon, babe.' God help us all.

We have been to many karaoke nights, and Dani has sung at many karaoke nights. I have never, nor will I ever, sing karaoke or sing anywhere publicly again, much to Dani's disapproval. She gasps and points to the back of the bar, where Alice is setting up the karaoke machine. Alice runs the pub with her mum, Ellen. I have no idea how they do it without killing each other. Working with my mother would be literal hell for me.

Dani has sat up so straight in her excitement that she looks like a meerkat. She jumps out of her seat and rushes over to Alice. She nearly runs right into her, making Alice jump out of her skin. I look around the pub at all these familiar faces; it's the same but not the same. I wonder if James and Billy come here together a lot? Suddenly the best of friends, even though they never got on.

My attention is suddenly drawn by the sound of Dani murdering the Whitney classic, I Wanna Dance with Somebody. It's like she's trying to be bad on purpose.

She loves to sing, so she sings.

As bad as she is, you have to admire her confidence; that girl is fearless.

She's finally finished, six songs, yes, six songs later. Thankfully, it's over, and we can head back to our tiny, tiny room, that's unless Matt has locked us out, which I really wouldn't put past him.

Dani walks back over to me as the room applauds her; I'm pretty sure they're applauding her stopping.

'Right, chippy, then bed,' she states, banging her hand on the bar decisively.

'Babe...there is no chippy,' I tell her, breaking her heart.

'Excuse me...? I don't understand what you just said.'

'This is a tiny village. Why did you think there would be a takeaway?' I ask, confused as hell. Is she high?

'Everywhere has a chippy. What do people do after a night out?'

'They go home and eat some crisps.'

'Babe, I always have a chippy after a night out.'

I think she might cry.

'Well…not tonight.' I console her with a shoulder rub.

'How do people live like this? It's inhuman.'

At least she's not overreacting.

'Can we come back?' Dani begs.

'Absolutely; this is the only place that sells alcohol,' I inform her.

'Do we have crisps?' Dani asks me, linking my arm and walking me towards the door.

'I think Matt ate them all,' I lie; I did.

'Perfect…When will something go our way?' Dani huffs.

No time soon, I think to myself.

Chapter 10

The walk back isn't ideal, to say the least. I'm not even over-acting when I say we could die any minute.

It's pitch black; there's no pavement, and the odd sheep will just suddenly baa at you. Dani screamed so loud the first time it happened you would think she was face-to-face with a monster from Scooby-Doo. It was hilarious. We are using our common sense by using our phones as flashlights, which was great until both our phones died.

'Why the fuck do people live like this?' Dani complains, linking my arm.

'I don't know! It's peaceful, I suppose.'

'Peaceful? There's no takeaways, no talent, no pavements, no Primark,' She rattles each one off more dramatically than the last. 'There's no hope, babe; it's shit!' She does love Primark, to be fair.

'I could really go a Taco Bell right now,' I say unhelpfully. I'd settle for a Pot Noodle, I'm that hungry.

'It's not even like we can go home and make something... and I wouldn't eat anything that hard-faced cow made...it'll be laced with god knows what.'

'Do you think Matt got back alright?' Suddenly I'm thinking of poor Matt walking home alone in the dark.

'Stop trying to change the subject when I'm complaining… and no…we'll probs find him lying on the side of the road… He's a city boy, he don't walk,' she finishes right as she stumbles for the hundredth time. 'I HATE THIS ROAD!'

A sheep starts baaing right on cue.

'AW, FUCK OFF BEFORE I TURN YOU ALL INTO HAGGIS!'

'Not much further now,' I say as cheerily as I can.

'You've said that five times now…I'm really close to punching you in the face.'

She's not the biggest outdoor person in the world, but it's not like we have anything better to be doing, except maybe sleeping.

'I mean it this time. The other times, I was just trying to make you feel better,' I admit.

Her head turns so fast to face me that I swear she must have whiplash. She closes her eyes, takes a deep breath, and then whips it back around.

'How are you anyway?' she asks, still annoyed. 'You falling apart?'

'No! I'm good, cool as a cucumber me.'

Judging by those narrowed eyes, she doesn't believe me.

'I mean, it was a bit of a shock, seeing him for the first time.'

'Which one? Billy?'

'Both, but can you believe he just left?'

'I know! How do you feel about that?' she asks, concerned.

'Fine...I don't know, actually,' I say truthfully.

'By the sounds of him tonight, I would defo say that James is still interested.' She gives me the side eye, waiting for my reaction.

'Well, I'm defo not,' I inform her decisively.

As if.

'I don't get you. You make it sound like you've never liked the boy.'

I wouldn't go that far.

'But, you dated him for six years.' Dani puts a lot of emphasis on six.

'Well, it started when we were nineteen, and I wouldn't call it dating-dating.' It really wasn't. We were basically friends with some extras. 'We didn't start going out properly for like a year or two after that. Even then, we weren't very lovey. People used to always say, "You two seem more like friends," and they were right.'

'So why didn't you break up?' she asks like it's that simple.

'You know yourself; you get comfortable.' What a shit excuse.

'So you just stayed in the relationship? Unhappy.' She sounds very judgmental.

Dani doesn't understand that not everyone is as brave as her. I don't dive right in; I hesitate.

'James isn't a bad guy.' I suddenly feel the urge to defend him. 'He was always nice and decent.'

'You thought you would go for security over excitement?' She nods, understanding. 'Then why go with Billy?'

'He was...' How to explain Billy?

She's stopped; why has she stopped? She slowly turns her head to face me; she looks like she might cry.

'Right...tell me I haven't stood in shite...Have I stood in shite?' She asks with utter fear in her voice.

There is no good way to answer this because, of course, she has, indeed, stood in shite.

'Well...I'll just say, you haven't *not* stood in it.'

Dani was once told she could destroy a person's soul with just one look. Apparently, she has quite the bitch stare when she's upset. I thought they were overreacting. Now, in this moment, I completely agree with that comment.

I think I'd better stay quiet until the morning or until we're home.

After the longest twenty-five minutes of my life, we're finally back at the little house of horrors, and I've decided that I need a break. I need a little time by myself, without either Matt or Dani in my ear or in front of my face.

We've walked in complete silence since the incident, thank god.

'Babe, you go on up; I'll be there in a bit.'

'Couldn't care less,' she rages as she storms past me, heading upstairs.

Well, that's settled, then.

I always loved the garden here, and as I open the giant cast iron gate, I see that it hasn't changed one bit. It's like a picture right out of The Secret Garden. Completely enclosed, surrounded by trees, it's beautiful all year, but in summer, it's on another level. Kim does a fantastic job; she plants roses, daisies and sunflowers everywhere. Even now, with winter pretty much here, it's still stunning, with two cute red-painted benches at the sides; the grass is silently wild, which I love. There's the tree swing in the far right corner. It has artificial flowers around the handles, with a solid white painted plank as the seat, which I can't help but climb on. Swinging gently away reminds me of the good times.

This was always my favourite place to be. I would come over to hang out with James, and we'd spend the whole time in here. Reading by the sunflowers and picnics under the trees, it was perfect.

It's always peaceful here, and there is no better place to relax and be alone.

Oh my fucking god, it's Billy.

Why? Why is he here? Did he follow me in here? He's looking straight at me as he makes his way over from the gate. I'm frozen. I can't move my feet. I'm scared that if I stand up from this swing, I'll topple over.

Right, he's four feet away. I need to at least try and stand up. That went well; I'm still upright. Oh my god, why is he here? What will he say? What will I say? Two feet away; he's two feet away from me. He's stopped; he's looking me up and down. Why is he smiling? He looks good; his arms are so toned. I love a toned arm. His eyes are still so blue, ocean blue-eyed boy. He's wearing his leather jacket. What is it with men in leather? It does things to me. His hair is all ruffled, more dirty blonde than full-on blonde these days.

'Hi, polar bear,' he says in a low wanting voice.

That's what he calls me, or did call me; it's a long story. No, it isn't; it's an embarrassing story. I thought polar bears were albino bears. I blame the educational system; it failed me.

'Thought you would be hiding in here,' he says softly.

'Why are you here?' I said that strongly. I am strong. I will not play his games.

'I wanted to see you.'

I don't understand why he is still smiling. Does he not remember what happened the last time we saw each other?

'You saw me earlier...then you ran away like a little bitch.' Who am I right now? I'm so proud of myself. I'm a bad bitch; Dani is rubbing off on me.

'It wasn't the best time.' He doesn't look guilty, and he absolutely should.

'Because James was there? Best of friends, are you?'

I feel like I'm knocking this exchange out of the park. Even Billy looks taken aback. I have never been this bold, more shirking violet.

'Because you caught me off guard...because half the village was there.'

Who's he raising his voice at?

'I wanted our first time talking...to be just me and you.'

'Well, here I am...What do you want to say?' I feel less strong all of a sudden.

He better stop giving me that look. I know that look. There isn't a chance in hell I'm falling for that look again.

'I missed you,' he says, looking me straight in the eye.

Fuck. No one has looked at me like that in a really long time.

'I'm sorry,' he says, taking a step forward. 'I made a mistake.'

He made so many; I don't even know which one he means.

'Did you miss me?' he asks.

There's a hint of pain in his voice; well, I think it's pain. He moves within an inch of me.

'I'm here for the wedding.' Boundaries, I need to set boundaries.

'You just here for the wedding?' he whispers in my ear, placing one hand on my lower back, and the other makes its way up to my neck.

I can feel his breath on my neck, and I can hear his heartbeat, or is that mine? Mine is practically beating out of my chest. He pulls back a fraction, meeting my eyes.

'Yes,' I say in such a whisper that I don't even think he heard me.

I shouldn't be letting this happen.

'Really?' he presses against me as he strokes the side of my face, then starts kissing my neck.

'What are you doing?' I manage to say.

He pulls away to face me. 'I told you. I've missed you. You left before I had a chance to think.' His hand moves up my back, sending shivers through me. He places both of his hands on my face. 'I didn't know if I would see you again.'

'What choice did I have?' I whisper.

My resolve is breaking. By the second. I mean, what's one more time?

'You could have stayed,' he says as he tucks my hair behind my ear.

He pushes his body forward, and his lips are on mine. Every feeling I've ever had for him is flooding back through me in one huge wave. His lips feel the same, taste the same. He still knows how to use those hands, touching every correct spot. Now his lips are back on my neck, not gentle this time, wanting, needing.

Before I know it, he's pushed me up against a nearby tree, running his hand up my leg while I lift the other to wrap around his waist in one swift motion. He's pulling and ripping my clothes off as I return the favour. This isn't the first time we have had sex in this garden, but I can't remember it being this intense.

I shouldn't; I know I shouldn't.

Oh, who the fuck cares?

It's been two years.

Chapter 11

Ok.

I have no idea what that was last night; I'm still trying to work out if I dreamed it. Pretty sure I didn't, though, considering the grass stains, friction burns, and bite marks all over me.

Oh, the shame, not from the sex – that was needed – shame from letting him back in, literally.

Right, it's Sunday, four days until the wedding day. I can do this; I can handle four days, in this village, with these people.

Avoiding Billy.

And James.

And Kim.

Pretty much everyone.

Four days = 96 hours = 5,760 minutes. Oh my god, is that math right? Over five thousand minutes, I can't handle five thousand minutes; how many seconds is that?

What has my life become? In the last week, I've lost my job, been waxed of all my hair, faced my family, faced my ex, hidden under a table and slept with the only person

I shouldn't. Now, I'm lying in a broken, single bed, trying to work out how many seconds I have to talk to my family for. Oh, and I have Dani snoring on my right, in her broken single bed, and Matt watching Friends reruns on my left, in his not, broken, single bed. I need a shower, and I really need a bacon roll.

'What the heck is that smell?' Matt asks, sitting up in his bed, looking disgusted. 'Did she fart?' He points at Dani accusingly.

'It's the horses,' I tell him.

'The horses?' he asks, confused.

'There's a lot in the village,' I tell him. 'How many seconds are there in four days?'

'How the fuck would I know that...? Do these horses just shit all around this place? Does no one like...clean it?'

'No, not really.'

'What hell on earth is this place?'

He angrily jumps out of bed and goes into the bathroom, slamming the door behind him.

'WHY IS THIS TOILET SO FUCKING SMALL?' he shouts.

'It is tiny, to be fair,' Dani says, suddenly awake. 'Don't see why he needs to scream about it, though.' She sits up in her little coffin-looking bed and looks around the room with a complete look of disgust.

'It's a bit shit in here, ain't it?' she says matter-of-factly, casting a dirty look around the whole room.

'She never uses this room 'cause it's horrendous.'

'How nice of her to make an exception,' Dani sarcastically states.

'Yeah...I know.' I agree. 'Did you fart?'

'Yeah,' she says, without an ounce of embarrassment.

I sit up in my own personal coffin to take in our surroundings. Our three tiny beds sitting side by side, an inch apart is bad, the no storage is bad, the no heating is bad (we have no radiator), the smell is bad (we're next to the horses) and the no TV is soul destroying (I love TV). Together, all these issues make a shithole. The beds are also only a foot from the wall. Seriously, the whole room is like five foot total, and the bathroom is also a disaster; that's one foot total.

'Where are we eating?' Dani asks with puppy dog eyes.

'At this thing, I guess.' I'm dreading this day already.

'Aw god...can I patch it? I'm really tired,' she pleads.

'Absolutely not. Where I go, you go...plus, you said you really needed a rub down, preferably from a hot man with strong arms. A statement you made in front of my family, it was mortifying.' My mum has never heard such a sentence.

'I do, to be fair,' she says, ignoring me.

'I think we all do after a night in these beds,' I agree.

'What time is it right now?'

'Ten o'clock,' I tell her, through a yawn.

'When are we meeting them?' she asks.

'Twelve…We're meeting them there.'

She was there when we went over the details. She just clearly wasn't listening.

'How long does it take to get there?'

'It's about an hour and a half away.'

'So we have thirty minutes to get ready?' she asks, terrified.

'Yeah.' Plenty of time.

'Fuck's sake, Dotty. You know I need twenty minutes just to do my makeup,' she says, jumping out of bed.

'It's a spa; you don't wear makeup,' I tell her. 'How much do you think it will cost?'

'I'm more concerned about them fitting us in than the cost, to be honest…I mean, spas book out weeks in advance,' she says in a hurry, trying to find something to wear.

All our clothes are in one big heap on the floor. It was the only way to unpack.

'Well, I'm poor; I'm worried about the cost, just in case they can fit us in.'

Even if it is just the spa we go to, that will cost a good amount too.

'Don't worry, babe; I got you covered,' she tells me, waving away my concerns.

'Thank you, but no, that's too much.' I tell her. Better get myself out of bed.

'Babe! I'm not having you worrying about money on top of all the other shit...ok? So shut up.'

'Thank you.' I smile at her. 'But I can't take your money; I already owe you too much. Stop being so nice; you're too generous.'

'I know! But you're my best friend. This is what best friends do; we take care of each other,' she tells me forcefully. 'Babe, just let me take care of it. I got you.'

'But...' I start.

Matt comes out of the bathroom. 'Well, the shower is just as shit as the room,' he says, lying down on his bed.

'What's your plan for the day?' Dani asks him.

'Sleeping.' He huffs. 'You two both woke me up at different times through the night...thanks for that.'

'Come on; we were only like...what? Ten minutes apart, and I just walked in and passed out.' Dani says, making her way to the bathroom.

'More like an hour apart,' Matt says as Dani closes the bathroom door, which quickly opens back up.

'What!...An hour? What were you doing for an hour?' Dani asks, staring me down.

'Just...walking,' I tell her, trying to hide my blush.

139

'Walking? After we walked like a month home last night... you decided to walk some more? Bullshit,' she says accusingly.

'So...what were you doing?' Matt asks, sitting up on his knees, all excited.

'Or...who was she doing?' Dani accuses.

Now I have four eyes staring me down.

'It...it was a mistake,' I squeal, holding my face in my hands.

Matt gasps like we're in a Jane Austin novel.

'Who?' Matt asks. 'There are a few options here.'

'Was it James?' Dani asks.

What?

'What? No, why would it be James?'

'You being serious? With all that anger and frustration from last night. That's hot.'

'It was James, wasn't it?' Matt practically screams.

'No, of course, it wasn't. It was Billy,' I confess.

'Brother number two...interesting,' Matt says, nodding.

'The coward one, really...aw, babe. What we gonna do with you?' Dani says, inhaling slowly.

Great, I'll never hear the end of this all week.

Only 5,755 minutes to go.

Turns out the spa was two hours away, so we were late, giving my mother more reason to hate me and isn't that just perfect?

Since the rest of the party was on time (the receptionist's words), it's only me and Dani in the changing room getting ready. She's in a white swimsuit that is hugging all the right curves, and I'm in a black swimsuit that is suffocating my curves. I thought black was supposed to be slimming? This full-length mirror isn't doing me any favours, and standing next to Dani also isn't doing me any favours. She must be lying; there isn't a chance in hell we're the same size.

'You look fantastic, babe. Stop trying to pull it down, though...it can't cover any more skin...It's covering what it's covering,' she says, putting on lipstick.

Why is she putting on lipstick?

'Why are you putting on lipstick?'

'It's a pre-hen; they'll be pictures for sure,' she says like that was obvious.

Oh god, I'll need to run right into the pool to hide these extra rolls.

'Give me some for my lips,' I beg.

She hands it over.

'Did you shave your legs?' she asks with a grimace.

'I didn't have time,' I lie. I couldn't be bothered.

'Aw, babe...there's always time,' she says, looking at my legs in horror.

Just as I think about doing a runner, my mother storms in. Jesus, even she looks better in a swimsuit than me; how is that fair?

'How nice of you two to join us...over an hour late...but still time for makeup, I see,' she says, fuming.

'Sorry, Mrs Peters, that's my fault. You see, I had a dodgy stomach this morning and couldn't get off the toilet.'

My mother looks absolutely disgusted. She hates bathroom talk.

'Sorry, Mum, I thought it was the other one we used to go to.' I'm sure Jane implied that's where we were going.

'What happened to your knees? They're all marked,' she asks, looking me up and down.

'Oh...I fell.' Just once, I would love to be able to lie convincingly.

'Tell me, Dorothy...is it your mission to cause complete destruction this week?' she asks, hand on hip. 'Because you are off to a glorious start.'

'Course not...us getting lost was an accident...I didn't mean to cause any trouble.'

'You never do.'

The sheer disappointment on her face is enough to knock even the strongest person down.

'Come on; everyone is waiting,' she tells us before turning on her heel and storming back out.

'She is such a delightful soul,' Dani exclaims. 'At least she paid all of our entree fees.'

Thank god. I need all my money for drinking. By the end of this week, I will be an alcoholic for sure.

I'm trying to figure out if this is a pre-hen party for my sister or the 'I Hate Dotty Peters' club. The guest list includes my mother (A.K.A the president), Kim (A.K.A the founder), Sarah (my one-time best friend), Alisha (Andy's sister, I can't actually remember if she hates me or not) and finally, Chloe (Billy's girlfriend at the time of our affair). So yeah, basically, the people who hate me the most in the entire world.

I wish I was dead.

We're all sitting in the sauna together, except for my mum and Kim, so I'm overheated and half-naked, ideal.

Sarah is wearing a two-piece. She's still a size six; I'm so jealous. She hasn't changed much in two years, with the same short brown hair, shiny blue eyes and chubby cheeks that she's never been able to shake since we were kids. Alisha is the cutest thing ever; she's only five foot one and has hazel eyes, tanned skin and long black hair. She's a short Megan Fox lookalike. Then you have Chloe. She's stunning but a total bitch; she was even before I slept with her boyfriend.

She's five foot nine, has long wavy brown hair, green and hazel eyes, plus she also has the most beautiful, flawless skin.

I actually couldn't believe it when Billy came on to me. Why want me when he already had her? That's madness.

Me and Chloe never got on. She hated me the second she met me, but I never knew why. Her being a total bitch, did make the guilt easier to bear.

When she found out, she said her new mission in life was making sure my life stayed ruined. It's strange, knowing someone hates you more than anyone else in the world and actively wants bad things to happen to you. Lucky me, I have multiple people wanting that.

'So...Dot...how's life in the big city?' Chloe asks while looking me up and down and smirking.

The tone of her voice as she says Dot is something else. The venom in that one word is astonishing.

'It's...lovely,' I tell her, as I sweat even more than I already was.

'I couldn't live in a city,' Alisha tells everyone. 'It's so dirty and polluted.'

'Filled with dirty and scummy people,' Chloe adds in. 'No offence,' she says to Dani.

'Who would be offended?' Dani replies with sarcasm.

Looking at me, she tells me with her eyes that this bitch is on thin ice.

'So what's been happening here?' I ask anyone willing to speak.

'Well, after you slept with my boyfriend, we split up,' she tells me.

She's kinda stating the obvious, but I'll let her off.

'Then we got back together,' she tells me with a stupid grin on her face.

That wasn't so obvious.

'That surprises you?'

She must see the terror on my face. That absolute bastard. He has not done this to me again, made me a cheat – again.

'No,' I reply, deadpan. I catch Dani's saucepan eyes popping out of her head at this revelation, along with a slight smirk.

'That takes a big person...forgiving someone like that.' Dani says, clearly loving this.

'Well, after all the begging and pleading he did...plus the disgust in himself for what he did and at the person he did it with. I knew he was sorry.' She looks at me with pride.

No one's gonna say anything in support of me?

Guess not.

'What about you, Sarah...seeing anyone?' I ask my former friend. She never returned any of my calls or texts after I fled. This is our first time seeing each other. It's weird.

'Oh god, you don't know?' Chloe asks me with a giggle as the rest of the room stays quiet. 'Sarah is with James.'

'Damn.' Dani exhales.

'Oh.' That's all I can muster.

Sarah and James, what the fuck?

What is happening? Billy couldn't have filled me in on any of this last night? I'll kill him when I get a hold of him.

'Yeah...it happened a while back,' Sarah starts.

'He traded up,' Chloe interrupts.

While that was uncalled for, if I hadn't slept with her boyfriend last night, again, I would say something. No, I actually wouldn't.

'Like Billy tried to do,' Dani replies.

I love her so much sometimes. The look on Chloe's face is priceless; I wish I had a camera. What am I saying? I'm the bitch here. I slept with her boyfriend, like, twelve hours ago.

'It's getting a bit hot in here.' Alisha states, embarrassed and awkward. She gets up, making her escape.

'Yeah, I'm a tad hot myself,' Jane agrees, throwing daggers at me.

I didn't start this. Well, I suppose I did.

The rest of them quickly follow, leaving just me and Dani in the sauna.

'That was...something.' Dani says, trying not to laugh.

'I always hated Chloe...but I wouldn't have...last night... if I had known.'

'I know you believe that, babe.' She pulls me into a hug. 'But your history says otherwise.'

'I've grown,' I state.

'Course you have,' she says unconvincingly. 'Don't worry. We'll get through this, have a little faith.'

Is she for real? This is a nightmare. I doubt anyone will survive.

An hour later and we haven't tried another bonding session.

Me and Dani have taken shelter at the side of the pool, and the rest of them are taking Instagram pictures by the jacuzzi. We look like the creatures with no souls in the little mermaid, hiding in the shadows, watching the normal mermaids all play and have fun.

I want to go, preferably to the pub.

'Well, this is a barrel of laughs,' Dani says, kicking in the water.

'I never promised fun and games. I promised tension and insults.'

And tension and insults are what we have.

'So other than this and the future hen horror on Tuesday... what else are we doing this week?'

'I don't know...four days usually go fast...but I think these will go on forever...it'll be like watching Avatar again.' I realise in horror.

'It's five days, babe,' she tells me, looking at me like I've lost it.

'I'm not counting the wedding...I can't mentally go there. The thought of being in a room with everyone I fear is causing serious pain in my chest.'

'Right! Well...I think you should defo sleep with someone new. Get Billy out of your system.' She says this like we're discussing trying a new restaurant.

'I will definitely, not be doing that.' I tell her straight. 'Besides, like I've told you, there are no decent men in the village.'

'Granted, it's small, but you didn't only go to school with like five people. There must be a "one that got away."'

'Well. There isn't.'

'You hesitated,' she accuses.

'No, I didn't,' I protest.

'Who is it?'

'There isn't anyone. I'm very boring and have a boring romantic past. Billy and James. That's it,' I tell her.

Did she just snort at me? I bet she's doing that thing where she reads my mind, but I don't want to talk about it. It's a conversation I'm not interested in having.

'Fine. Don't tell me.' She huffs.

She'll get over it.

'Should we leave?' I ask her in the hope that she'll say yes.

'No, then you'll look weak and scared.'

'I am.'

'You absolutely are not. You are Dotty Peters, and you have every right to be here. Plus, I'm not friends with weak-ass bitches,' she says, completely serious.

'I made the mistakes,' I reason.

'Not just you.' She points at me. 'Mistakes are there for us to learn from. We live, we learn. I've learned that next time you have a family wedding. I won't be going.' She grins at me.

'Think I'll pass too.' I nod in agreement.

'You're doing good...taking it all on the chin...that takes a lot.'

'Thank you.' I smile at her in appreciation.

'Although, don't take it all on the chin, don't be a doormat,' she says, patting me on the shoulder.

'TREATMENT TIME!' Jane shouts from her lounge chair.

'Not a chance in hell...did you see those prices? I almost took a stroke,' I whisper to Dani, not making eye contact with the others.

'I think I did take a stroke...those are house deposit prices!' Dani exclaims.

'Dorothy! Are you and your friend coming?' Mum asks with little interest.

'We're good, Mum...thanks.' I give her a little wave.

'Yeah...we're just going to swim about a bit,' Dani tells her. 'And my name's Dani. Which you know,' she adds in a whisper.

'Fair enough, I'm sure we'll survive without your dazzling conversation,' Kim replies.

I see Chloe snigger out of the corner of my eye. They all walk away, towards a special treatment room door.

'This whole thing is weird,' Dani states. 'You sure you're related to these people?'

I take a deep breath.

'Yep.'

Although, a blood test couldn't hurt.

Chapter 12

I still wish I was dead.

Right now! There's nothing I wouldn't do to not be physically here.

We've only been sitting for twenty minutes, and in that time, I've been subtly called a tramp, a home-wrecker, soulless, heartless and my own personal favourite, a vulture. A vulture! Come on; these people need a hobby. Plus, my mum knows vultures freak me out, ever since I watched The Jungle Book when I was five. I still can't watch it.

The place is lovely, at least. I wasn't expecting much from a spa restaurant, but this is classy. There's cute pink flower walls all around, grand gold framed mirrors around the room, plush rose velvet seats and an actual harp in the corner. A harp, who has a harp? Who can even play a harp?

If it wasn't for the company, this would be a great girl's day.

'So, Dot...Selling shoes...that must be thrilling,' Chloe says, drawing out each word.

What does she know? It might be. Wait! How does she even know what my job is? Or *was*, I should say.

'Oh, please, for the love of god,' Dani says, exasperated. 'Would you give it a by?'

'It's only a question,' Chloe says. "Guess it's a sore subject."

'I sold shoes once,' Alisha tells us. 'It was alright.'

We all get back to eating our afternoon tea. My mum and sister haven't said a single word to me or made any attempt to call Chloe out. They've just sat there, pretending nothing is happening. Kim has had the biggest grin on her face throughout, bitch. As for Sarah, she may as well not be here. She's just sitting there, hardly moving, not speaking. It's all very strange.

'What about you, Dani? What do you do?' Chloe questions Dani.

Since she's looking for a fight, she'll find one with Dani.

'I'm a waitress.' Dani tells her proudly.

'How nice. You're in your thirties, right?'

Oh god, she went there. She brought up age; she's a dead woman walking.

'I am.' Dani says, a little less proud.

Dani hates being in her thirties. She's extremely sensitive about it.

'You not wanting to do more with your life?'

Chloe, darling, what are you doing?

'Dani's in uni, actually,' I tell the stupid bitch.

'No need to go there, babe...In uni or not, I have no issues being a waitress...I'm good at it, and I enjoy it. Actually, I'm great at it. So why wouldn't I be happy doing what I'm great at?' Dani replies confidently.

'For minimum wage?' Chloe asks, attempting to poke the bear.

'Chloe, what you wearing on Tuesday?' Sarah asks, changing the subject fast.

Chloe looks torn between taking this further or talking about clothes.

'I've got a nice little red dress.'

She turns to face me.

'Billy loves me in red.'

She smiles at me like the cat that got the cream.

If only she knew what her darling boyfriend was doing to me against the tree.

'What about you, Sarah?' she asks.

'I have a yellow dress; I thought that would work,' Sarah answers.

'What about you two? Something slimming?' Chloe asks me and Dani.

I don't know what is keeping Dani's temper in check, but I'm grateful.

'I'm wearing blue,' Alisha tells us.

I like this girl. She's nice and looks embarrassed every time Chloe speaks.

'Did you bring a date, Dot?' Chloe asks.

She's not laughing, but she's not *not* laughing – if that makes sense.

Can't I just eat my cucumber sandwich in peace?

'She did,' Dani answers her. 'Me and Matt, plus, weddings are a great place to meet men.'

Why say that?

Honestly, though, why?

'Ah, thought that was why you came,' Chloe declares, nodding her stupid head in understanding.

'Dani is kidding. We clearly didn't come here to meet men,' I clarify.

'Right! It's a coincidence, three weeks apart,' Chloe says, in her very best sarcastic voice.

'What are you talking about?' I ask, generally perplexed.

'Perhaps we should move on,' Mum tells us.

What is it now? Did James propose to Sarah three weeks ago? Did Billy propose?

You know what? I don't care. Whatever it is, I don't care.

Two years clearly isn't long enough.

I doubt a thousand years would be long enough for this cow. Why is she being such a bitch? Does she know about last night? That would explain a lot. Maybe he told her. No.

If he had, she would have totally shamed me by now and beat me senseless. It wouldn't take much. A fighter, I have never been.

When I started primary school, there was this older girl who made the omen seem like an angel. She targeted me from day one. She called me names, pushed me over a few times and once poured a carton of milk over me.

Then one day, I snapped and called her a stupid troll. That devil spawn slapped me so hard it knocked me over, right into a giant, manky puddle. I'm certain that's why I was in the green group at school, aka the dumb class. That was my first and only fight. There are still people who call me Soggy Peters.

'You know what, babe?' Dani announces. 'We shouldn't hook up with any men this week.'

Where is she going with this?

'Like any would have you,' Chloe whispers loudly.

'We shouldn't,' Dani loudly repeats, staring daggers at Chloe. 'Because you've done your bit for charity when it comes to the men in that village.'

I'm lost for words. Kim is fuming, judging by the look of outrage on her face. Dani is cheery and enthusiastic all of a sudden.

My mother looks disgusted, a common look on her face since I came back. Chloe is actually sitting open-mouthed, clearly also lost for words.

Jane looks defeated, and I feel bad. No matter what, she's my sister and this is meant to be about her.

'Maybe we should move on to the bars; get this night started,' Alisha says, breaking the tension.

'We're going to give it a miss tonight,' I tell my relieved sister. 'We need to get back to Matt. We should get an early night too.'

'Well, isn't that a shame?' Chloe fumes, composing herself. 'But, it's for the best.' Chloe stands up and motions for Sarah to join her. 'We'll go get the cars and see you all outside.'

With one last dirty look aimed at me and Dani from Chloe, she and Sarah turn and walk off.

'I don't know how your friend was raised, Dorothy, but you were raised better.' My mother berates me. She then stands, grabs her purse and leaves, quickly followed by Kim and my sister.

Alisha then stands up. 'I thought you were both quite right,' she tells us, smiling. She then walks away after the rest of the coven.

Well, to be honest, that's actually how I thought this day would go.

A hop, skip and a run later.

We are finally back at the house of horrors, safely in our room. Matt is in bed, as he said he would be; you would think he just completed a marathon. Dani is lying on her bed, staring at the ceiling. It's a bit creepy, like she is in some sort of trance. I'm doing my makeup, putting on my war face, because I will not be done dirty like last time. I'm having it out with Billy, once and for all. What's that old saying? Fool me once, shame on you. Fool me twice, shame on me. We're far past once or twice, but the sentiment is the same.

Two years ago, Billy swore to me that he loved me and that he wanted us to be together. Was I naïve? Yes. I love Drew Barrymore movies and thought I was starring in my very own. He said we had to break up with our significant others. He said we would let the dust settle, then be together properly. Well, I did my part; I broke James's heart, disappointed my family, and basically got shunned by the whole village. How dare I hurt poor James? Plus, people started whispering I must have someone new. He did absolutely fuck all; he just sat back and did nothing. Then Chloe found my underwear in Billy's car, and that was when things got really shitty.

'For what it's worth, I think you're being really stupid,' Dani tells me as she gets under the covers.

'I agree,' Matt says. His eyes are still closed, but I guess he's awake.

157

'Thanks, I'll take it under advisement.'

They are not wrong. Going to see him is stupid. I don't even know what he will say, but I need to have my say. I have to get it out. Get out how much I want to punch him in the face. I'm still in shock that he's done this to me – again. I know it takes two to tango and all that crap, and I know I didn't actually ask if he was seeing someone, but he could have brought it up.

How much of a coward is he?

When I asked him two years ago why he didn't break up with Chloe, he said it wasn't the right time; that we should take a few weeks between the dumping of our partners. I not only agreed with him, but I also kept sleeping with him for a month. Oh god, I'm pathetic. And when Chloe found out, she then told every human she met that I had been sleeping with her boyfriend.

Billy said I seduced him.

He said it wasn't fair for James to lose both of us, and again, I agreed with him.

God, I want to punch him in the face. I also want to punch myself in the face for being so stupid.

'Are we going out tonight?' Matt enquires, his eyes still closed.

'Well, I, for one, ain't staying in this room all night,' Dani announces as she throws off her covers and bounces off the bed over to me. 'You want me to come?' she asks, resting her chin on my shoulder.

'I can do it; I'll be fine,' I say a little high-pitched.

'I know you can do it alone...you just don't have to,' Dani reassures me.

'I have to, though,' I tell her, leaning in for a hug.

'Ok...but do your thing, then come meet us at the pub,' Dani instructs.

'You're making me walk another five hundred miles to that pub?' Matt bolts up like he's seen a bee. 'Are you trying to kill me on this holiday from hell?... Will your brother be there?' he asks, suddenly more interested.

Dani walks over to his bed, then jumps down next to him.

'Let's get super dressed up,' she says, all excited, a huge smile spread across her face.

'Love that idea.' Matt beams. 'Can we get a taxi, though?'

'There are no taxis here,' I say, breaking his heart.

'Does life ever go right for me?' Matt throws himself back under his covers.

Not for any of us.

I'm here.

It took three shots of Dani's emergency supply of gin, four pep talks and a literal push out the door by Matt. But I'm here, outside Billy's door. I look fantastic. I'm wearing my jeans that suck in my stomach to within an inch of its life, and I paired them with my leopard print silk top. It covers enough not to be too revealing, but shows enough to be sexy. I finished off with my cute leopard pumps. I would feel more pride in my outfit if I had chosen it, but Dani dressed me. However, this outfit isn't for him. It's for me – to give myself a much-needed boost.

Should I knock or just walk in? If I walk in, I'll look confident, but what if someone is in there?

As in Chloe.

Or James.

I should knock.

I should knock, like now.

Knock on the door, Dotty.

Come on, bravery time.

Knock on the door.

I might need professional help.

Fuck it.

Three overly loud knocks, and I hear footsteps.

Why am I nervous?

He should be nervous; he should be worried and feel shame.

Oh, Jesus, the door is opening.

There he is, standing in the doorway, looking all James Dean in his Levi jeans and baby blue shirt. That shirt is really bringing out his eyes.

'Hi, polar bear.' He looks nervous.

Yes, that's what I want; that's what I need.

'Get in before someone sees you.' He grabs my arm, nearly taking it clean off and rushes me inside.

Of course. *That's* why he was nervous; heaven forbid he is seen with me. His mum is still out, with the rest of the pre-hen party. What is he thinking? That a guest will tell on him to his mummy, and she'll throw him out.

His room hasn't changed; still a shitehole. He's the only man I've ever met who hoovers his room once a year. He chose brown and peach as his colours, controversial, and it looks horrendous. There is nothing on the walls, clothes everywhere, and an overflowing bin (clearly, Mummy hasn't cleaned in here recently). There is a big double bed that takes up much of the room.

'Missed you today.'

There's that lazy, crooked grin, looking down on me. Bastard.

'You did?' I say as sulkily as I can, without sounding twelve.

'Course, I've been thinking about you all day.'

He wraps his arms around my waist, leaning in for a kiss.

'I've been with Chloe all day. Your girlfriend, Chloe.'

He pulls right back up, still with his arms around me. I should hit them off, but it's nice to be held. It's been a long two years.

'I was going to tell you.'

'When? Tonight? Tomorrow? At the wedding?' I push him off, finding my inner warrior.

'I wanted to last night...but we got carried away,' he says with a pouted lip, looking like a sad puppy.

'There was time last night,' I point out.

'Ok...I didn't want to tell you...I wanted to be with you... and I knew if I told you...you would have run a mile.' He moves towards me slowly, like a hunter towards his prey.

'After everything that happened...you got back with her? If I meant...or mean, so much to you...Why?'

He looks away to the side, as if the answer is written on his wall, which means he doesn't have an answer.

'You weren't here. You left.'

Is he turning this on me?

'Come on; you know how I feel about you...you're my polar bear.' He moves towards me, but something inside me snaps.

'Don't.' I hold up my hand to emphasise my point. 'I'm not your polar bear...I'm Dotty Peters, and you; you are an asshole.'

He looks shocked, the wind taken out of his sails.

'So I hope you enjoyed last night...'cause you won't be back in my bed again...I mean garden...no bed.'

He's smirking at me.

'Whatever...you know what I mean. I'm done with you.'

'Me and you aren't done,' he says, with a hint of bitterness in his voice.

'We are Billy, trust me.' I tell him as I walk out the door, slamming it behind me.

That was a good last line. That was a banging last line.

I'm in a much better mood now.

I feel a new, thrilling sense of confidence as I walk along the corridor back to my room. I am a force of nature; no man gets the better of me. Is this how Dani feels every day?

This is what being on drugs must feel like, like you're on another level, at least, that's what I think. I have never done drugs. I watched Trainspotting when I was fourteen, and it scared the living daylights out of me. I didn't even try alcohol until my mid-twenties. I thought it was the start of a slippery slope.

'That was quick! You ready?' Dani asks me in a 'you better be' tone.

I was so lost in thinking how amazing I was that I didn't notice my two brightly-dressed friends coming towards me.

Dani is wearing a neon pink jumpsuit with a plunging neckline; lucky bitch has the equipment to keep it upright.

She's paired it with black high heels, clearly forgetting about the walk to and from the pub. Her flowing, wavy ginger hair is clashing somewhat, but she somehow pulls it off, just. Matt is wearing jeans and a bright yellow shirt; it's like I'm looking at the sun.

'We're very bright tonight.' I say, through a nervous 'please change' laugh.

'We want to make a statement,' Matt proclaims with a wave of his hand.

'Why are you suddenly acting more Graham Norton than Matt Bonner?'

Dani asks the question that I didn't want to because I thought it would be politically incorrect. I have been wondering the same since we got here, though.

'I'm putting on a show for the village folk,' he says innocently.

'We've had gays up here before, Matt; a couple of them even live here. We're not that behind in the times. Sorry, but Dani is creating more of a stir with her outfits.'

Dani has quite the proud look on her face.

'So, can you change your shirt?'

'No, we've waited long enough,' Dani declares, pulling me towards the front door.

'I was gone like ten minutes,' I protest.

'Felt like twenty,' she says, tossing her head back.

Great, a night out with the two Power Rangers it is, then.

Chapter 13

The thing with tiny villages is, no matter what day of the week it is, the pub is full. I suppose the same could be said for Glasgow pubs too. I don't think I've ever seen one of them empty, even in the morning. The other thing with tiny villages is that there only ever is one pub, meaning it's always the same people every night. With this being said, the long-term single Dani and newly single Matt aren't too happy with the lack of talent.

'This is bullshit,' Matt huffs, folding his arms.

'You can say that again,' Dani huffs, also folding her arms. 'There is no man here to stare at.'

There's me thinking we came out for a nice time together. We're sitting at the same table we were at last night.

'You were both here last night; you know there's no talent,' I say, taking a long, long drink of my gin.

'What a waste of an outfit,' Dani pouts.

'So, what's the plan for tomorrow, more Billy drama?' Matt asks, giving me a cheeky grin and wink.

'No...I was actually thinking...' I start, bracing myself for their over-the-top reactions. 'We could go a hike.'

'A what?' Dani asks, her eyes widening to the size of the moon.

'It's a really beautiful trail. I used to do it all the time... it's not too hilly.'

'Eh...I don't do outdoor exercise. I do indoor exercise, with cooled water and air conditioning,' Matt says, like I don't know that he only goes to the gym once a month.

'I'm with Matt. I don't do exercise; it wouldn't be fair to be this beautiful *and* skinny.'

Oh, I would love Dani's confidence.

'Why don't we go shopping?' she suggests. 'We could go into Inverness. How long does it take without the scenic route?'

'It's still two and a half hours,' I say with a whisper.

'Is that the nearest town here?' Matt asks.

I nod in answer to his question.

'Jesus, we really are in the middle of nowhere, aren't we?' Matt huffs.

He really can be such a huffy shit.

'I can't be bothered sitting in a car for most of the day.' Dani reasons with Matt.

'So we can hike?' I suggest again.

They are both sulking, but they both nod in agreement.

'Yay...this will be so much fun, I promise, and we can pack a wee lunch.'

'With what?' They say in unison.

This is a good point. We've officially run out of our Tesco snack stash. For dinner tonight, we shared two packets of squares and a packet of hobnobs. God knows what we're having for breakfast. There is one little shop half an hour away, but it is the biggest rip-off in the history of rip-offs. It costs three pounds for milk, seriously. If I take Dani and Matt there, they'll both have a stroke. To be honest, after living on a budget for the past two years, I might have a stroke. Unfortunately, it's our only option.

'There's this lovely little shop,' I lie; it's not even nice to look at. 'It has everything we need.' I lie a bigger lie as it has very few choices. 'We'll go tomorrow before we head to the hike.'

They do not look thrilled. Matt actually looks like he wants to punch me. Dani is distracted. What is she looking at?

Oh, this night has taken a turn.

Eight men, eight not-too-bad-looking men, have just walked in, each dressed in shinty jerseys. They are muddy, sweaty and bloody: precisely what Dani and Matt are looking for. Thank whatever god sent them; at least it will keep them distracted for a while. I sound like a harassed mother during the summer holidays.

Coming in behind them is Andy. He's played shinty since he was young; he tried to get James into it when they met. They played one game that ended with James needing stitches in his head, so he decided to stick to football. I always liked Andy; he was polite, sweet, and a decent guy. He is quite unique-looking with his red hair, freckles and dark green eyes. He towers over me at six foot four, but luckily Jane inherited Dad's height. The best way to describe Andy is like a huge teddy bear with the biggest, cheesiest grin.

'Who is that gorgeous creature at the bar...on the left?' Dani asks, practically drooling.

'I don't know.' I don't actually know any of the rest of them. 'But the one at the end, who just came in, is Andy.'

'The big mountain-looking guy? That's the groom?' Matt asks, shocked. 'Not what I was picturing; I thought your sister's type seemed more cardboard cut-out.'

'What are they wearing?' Dani asks, perplexed.

'Shinty jerseys,' I tell their puzzled faces.

I forget that shinty never took off down south.

'That game with the sticks?'

Matt clearly has a death wish, saying that loudly in a Highlands pub, but he is basically right.

'So he's a real man then,' Dani remarks, not taking her eyes off that poor guy.

'Ok, Dani, you're looking extremely desperate right now. If we could pull back the staring? Try and act cool,' Matt suggests, clicking his fingers and using them to draw her eyes to his.

She hits away his hand before reverting her eyes back to the bar.

Dani is sitting up like a meerkat staring at the very pretty boy. A pretty *young* boy, actually; he must only be early twenties. I turn back to face her. If she were a cartoon, her eyes would be popping out of her head.

'I thought there were only, like, five people in this village,' Dani says, as if accusing me of something.

'Well, he ain't one of the five that lived here, or lived here when I did, at least.'

'You said there was no talent. I thought you knew everyone.'

'It doesn't matter to me; they're all straight,' Matt says nonchalantly.

'How can you tell?' I ask.

'I have excellent gaydar,' he tells me matter-of-factly. 'I can still look, though.' He's looking at a drinks menu on the table. Pretending to be engrossed in its contents while sneaking looks at the bar.

'Let's go over and say hi to your Andy; he'll then introduce us,' Dani cheerfully suggests.

'He's with his team,' I tell her.

The truth is, I have no idea how Andy will be with me. I did cheat on his best friend, but he is a very nice guy.

'Forget him, Dani, the best-looking man that I've ever seen in my life just walked in.' Matt tells her. He's blushing.

'Oh my god!' Dani beams, clearly agreeing.

I turn back to the bar for a better look at this gorgeous man.

Holy mother fucking god!

Adam?

Adam is here?

Why is Adam here?

'Babe? Do you know him?' Dani asks.

Haven't I been through enough? Without having to deal with more embarrassing past mistakes?

'What's wrong?'

I can hear the slight panic in Dani's voice.

She must have turned away from him to look at me and see my face turn to ash.

'Is that Billy?' Matt asks.

Great, he thinks Adam is Billy. Probably 'cause I can't take my eyes off him.

'Is it?' Dani sounds shocked. 'Then I get it now.'

He hasn't seen me.

I can't let him see me.

I turn back around and grab the menu from Matt to hide behind it.

'That's *my* prop.'

'It's mine now,' I hiss.

'Babe, I'm concerned. Is that not Billy? Because you look terrified, and you are now hiding behind a menu,' Dani lists off.

'It's a step up from under the table,' Matt interjects.

'Is that Billy?' she presses.

'No.' My eyes are fixed firmly on the gin selection. They have quite a lot, to be fair.

'Then who is he?' Matt asks, confused.

'We need to leave,' I tell them.

'Why? What are we missing here?' Dani presses.

'Please, Dani. I know I've been dramatic the past few days, but I can't. I've hit my limit.'

'Ok, ok, we'll go,' she promises.

'There's only one door,' I inform her.

'Right. Erm. Well, they are all currently blocking the door,' she calmly tells me.

'Yes, yes, I fucking know that.'

I shouldn't take this out on them, but I'm freaking out. He's going to notice me. He's going to come over. I'm going to have to talk to him. Last time we spoke, it was a disaster. We got into a massive fight before he was a dick. He said things; I said things. It was bad, and it was also five years ago. I haven't seen him in five years, and I need another five years before I can handle seeing him.

'Dotty, relax. Breathe and count to ten.'

'I'm not in labour.'

'He's walking over,' Matt calmly points out. 'How's my hair?'

I shoot down under the table in one of the fastest moves I've ever made.

It's been said before, but I do not do well in a crisis.

'Hello. I'm Adam.'

I hear him introducing himself. Bastard.

His stupid English accent is still as strong as ever. He speaks so calmly and in control.

'I'm sorry, Adam, but due to a current situation. I don't think I like you,' Dani tells him.

'Understandable. This does look suspicious.'

He's mocking me.

'Care to shed some light on this matter?' Matt asks.

He wouldn't dare.

'Well, you see, the last time we were both here...' Adam starts.

And with that, I quickly get my ass off the floor and back on my chair.

'Found my earring,' I declare, looking only at Dani and Matt.

'Hi, Dotty.'

That's all it takes – Adam saying my name – to make every cell in my body shiver. What is it about this boy?

I turn to face him and find him looking down at me, smiling.

'Hi, Adam,' I say as coldly as I can.

He doesn't look much different. Still has his shaved dark hair. Same big, dark brown eyes.

He's bulked up; there's definitely more distinction under that shinty shirt. Not too much, though, stronger and firmer, without being over the top. It makes his broad shoulders stand out even more than before. I can see the familiar mole under his bottom lip and the tiny birthmark on his neck shaped like a C. Not obvious to everyone, only to those that know him.

'I'm Matt.' Matt smiles brightly at him.

'Nice to meet you, both of you.' Adam gestures to Dani.

'I'm Dani.'

Is she blushing now? Jesus!

'Well, I only wanted to come over and say hi,' Adam tells them.

He turns back to face me. 'Welcome home,' he says to me, giving me his signature side smile, before walking back to the bar.

'What the fuck was that?' Matt asks, shell-shocked.

'*Who* the fuck was that?' Dani demands.

'That was Adam. He's a friend of my brother, of the family. His mum and my mum grew up together,' I tell them.

'And?' Dani presses me.

'And nothing.'

'He's not an ex?' She gives me a look of disbelief.

'Definitely not. I told you, he's my brother's friend.'

'Come on, babe, there was clearly something between you two.'

'Nope. Nothing has ever happened between me and him,' I tell her firmly.

I'm basically telling the truth.

It's been around twenty minutes.

Twenty minutes of non-stop questions about Adam.

I also had a wave from Andy, which was nice.

'I'm going in,' Dani announces. 'Since you're not spilling any details, for now, anyway, I'm going to go find out that good-looking guy's name.'

Dani stands up, making her way over to the bar.

'Oh, I love it when she's forward,' Matt says in admiration as he downs his drink. 'I'm following her lead.'

'You can't leave me,' I tell him, panicked.

'Well, I'm going over. Either come with me or stay here.'

'I'll watch the bags,' I tell him, defeated.

He makes his way over to the bar.

Great.

I'm alone.

I should leave, but I can't let Adam think that I think that he was right. Which he certainly wasn't. He was such an arsehole the last time I saw him. I hadn't even done anything. Known him my whole life, and he treats me like

I'm public enemy number one. Adam's mum is from here, but she moved to Edinburgh for university, met a guy and then moved to England to be with him. When we were kids, Adam used to come up here all the time. For the summer holidays, Christmas, and even Easter. Then less and less as we got older.

Looking over, I can see Dani is doing very well with whoever that guy is. He is really pretty. He looks like Nathan Scott from One Tree Hill; tall, with dark hair and lovely green eyes that match Dani's. He's giving Dani the look, you know, the 'you've pulled' look. He has a lovely smile, innocent and cute. Oh my god, he has dimples; how adorable.

'Can I sit here?' Adam states from above me.

I was so focused on Dani I didn't even notice him walking over. He sits down, making himself comfortable.

'Since when do you play shinty? You hate sports.' I sound like a five-year-old.

'I was bored, needed something to do.' He goes to say something but stops himself. 'So what's the plan now you're back?'

He seems slightly annoyed; why is he annoyed? I should be annoyed. I am annoyed.

'There is no plan; I'm here for the wedding, that's it. What business is it of yours, anyway? You don't know anything about anything.' I can hear my annoying whiny voice. I don't love it.

'I see you're still in a mood with me.'

I want to smack him in the face. A mood! I'm livid with him.

'Yes. You acted like a complete bastard.'

'I wouldn't say I was a *complete* bastard. You weren't exactly a saint,' he says defensively.

'Don't-start-with-me-you-were-the-bastard-I-was-blame-less-I-did-nothing,' I say, taking zero breaths.

He goes to say something and hesitates again, leaving an extremely awkward silence. I should be used to these by now.

'I wasn't a saint;' what is he talking about? He called me stupid, a liar, a fraud, weak. Why? I don't know. All I did, was point out what a man whore he was.

'You're right. I shouldn't have said any of that shit.'

Wait. What? He knows I was right?

'Yes. Yes, you were wrong.' I don't know what to say now. 'Thank you.' Wait, he didn't apologise. 'And you're sorry, right?'

'No,' he states deadpan.

'Oh, very good, Adam; very funny.'

He grins at me. What he finds funny in this, I don't know.

'I'm sorry, ok? I apologise.'

'Well. Good.' I'm still annoyed.

'Oh, come on, eyebrows, I've said sorry, and it's been like ten years. Can we please move on?' He stretches out his legs and cracks his neck. Those are some strong-looking forearms he has.

'It's been five, actually.'

He would suit a sleeve of tattoos, like *really* suit a sleeve. I'm losing focus; what was I saying?

'Well, can we now move forward? How have you been?' he asks gently.

He hasn't taken his eyes off me this whole time. Which means I haven't taken my eyes off him or his arms. No, no. I'm not doing this. I do not fancy Adam.

Anymore.

I'm tired and stressed, that is all. I may have had a small crush once upon a time, but that doesn't count; childish crushes don't count.

'I've been good. Busy with work stuff,' I lie. 'What about you? Why are you back here?' I've been so focused on my anger that I don't know why he's even here.

'Grandad took a fall...' he starts.

'What?'

'He's ok.' He smiles at me. 'But he can't work for a while, so here I am.'

'What about your job?' He's a marketing director at some tech company. David told me about it in more detail when he got the job, but I only understood tech and company.

'It's Grandad,' he says, matter-of-factly, with no regrets showing. 'No job is more important than my family.'

Well, now I feel like a failure. Although, to be fair, I don't have his family.

Mr Fraser is the best; he's the sweetest old man, like Santa Claus. He was the best house to go to on Halloween; he bought the best sweets. After everyone found out about Billy, he told me that our mistakes don't define who we are and that I was a good person. I really needed to hear that. He has lived alone since his wife died ten years ago.

'And he's doing ok?' I have officially thawed. I need to know Mr Fraser is ok.

'He is; better than ok. He's now caught up on Yellowstone,' he says with a smile, a different kind of smile, one that beams across his face.

'So, you're only here until he's better?'

'Yeah, I guess,' he says, sounding unsure.

'Nothing or no one to get back to?' I ask, instantly regretting it.

'Nothing that can't wait.'

What the fuck does that mean?

'What about you?'

What is he asking? How long I'm staying? Or if I'm seeing someone?

He looks away and clears his throat. 'You planning on moving home anytime soon?'

Right! Course that's what he was asking.

'Well, as nice as it is here...' I hope that was as sarcastic as I was hoping. 'No plans to stay.'

'So you have seriously let those bastards run you out of this village? You actually care that much about what they think?'

'I've not let them do anything,' I say with no conviction. 'I'm not scared of them, and I don't care what they think.'

'You've always cared what *he* thinks,' he mutters under his breath.

'And you have always thought that you know everything,' I bite back at him.

'I don't get it.' He laughs, shaking his head.

'Get what?'

'What the fuck you saw in him for a start,' he tells me, turning away.

'Well, there was no one else.'

He looks back towards me.

I can't work out his mood or what he's thinking. He needs to not look at me like that, with those stupid eyes of his.

'You deserve better,' he whispers.

'Why?'

He looks towards the bar, but before he can say anything, something grabs his attention.

'Speak of the devil and his brother,' he says as I follow his gaze, dreading the sight I will see.

Yep, there they are, both standing at the bar, both staring at me. They then look at Adam, and everyone is looking raging. Guess the brothers aren't over Adam being a complete dick, either. Aren't men meant to just have a beer and let bygones be bygones?

I mean, Chloe will always be after my blood, but no one holds a grudge like a woman. Not that I blame Billy for being upset. Adam did sleep with Lindsey, Billy's girlfriend, once upon a time. Which, of course, wasn't nice, but it's not like Billy can take the moral high ground. By the look on his face, Billy is definitely still upset about it. He looks like he wants to run over here and strangle Adam with his bare hands. Although, judging by what happened last time, I don't think Billy could. I wasn't there when they fought, but Billy's face looked like a swollen tomato for about two weeks.

Adam was only visiting for a week. This is what he does; he makes you think he's this great guy who would do anything for you, and then bam. He causes destruction. When I was nineteen, he hadn't visited for three years, then he came up and was sweet and full of compliments. Then he went and slept with Sarah. Sarah! Another three years pass until he shows his face again. He was as charming as always, then slept with Lindsey. He can't help himself.

'Still fighting then?' I ask him.

'Who's fighting?' he says, his voice dripping with contempt.

'You serious? You're all giving each other daggers. This still about Lindsey?'

'Who?' he asks, looking confused.

Typical! He's bedded so many women he can't even remember their names. I can't help rolling my eyes at him.

'You still haven't changed, then?' There's that whiny tone in my voice again.

'What's that supposed to mean?'

'Nothing.' I don't want another fight.

The last one was bad enough; I hit him pretty hard. I have never slapped anyone in my entire life, but I was so pissed off at him.

'This looks friendly.'

I turn to see that James has found his way over to our table. Crap, I forgot that they were here.

'James,' Adam says with disdain.

I'm not used to seeing Adam so uncomfortable and angry.

I also don't understand why he's angry. He slept with Billy's girlfriend and battered him. So what's his problem?

'Sorry, Dot, should I move my leg? Let you get under the table.' James smirks.

'James. Go away,' Adam tells him forcefully. It's a demand, not a request.

'I was only saying hello,' James claims.

'We're having a conversation that doesn't include you.' Adam is seriously mad.

James looks slightly taken aback as he holds his hands up and walks back to the bar. Billy is still there but has his back to us.

'I don't want this turning into a thing. I'm going to go.' I tell him.

'I'll drive you. My car isn't too far,' he says.

'It's fine; I'll walk.'

'You're not walking home alone.'

'I'll get my friends.' Who I can't see.

'Your friends are having fun.'

'Well, I'm a big girl.'

As I stand, he stands.

'Maybe I'm scared.' He grins at me.

'Fine, but no fighting,' I say, giving him a small smile.

As we make our way to the door, I catch Billy looking our way. He doesn't look happy.

We've been walking for about twenty minutes in complete silence. After living with Dani for nearly two years, silence isn't something I'm used to. We're on the same road that me and Dani were on last night, but we have the added benefit of rain. It's not torrential rain, but it's not ideal. Basically,

I'm walking in the pitch black, I'm wet, and I'm cold, and there's a weird silence.

I can't handle much more, to be honest. I have no idea what the hell is happening with Adam. I hate how he always manages to make me feel like this. He's turned his head around a few times to say something, then changed his mind and looked back ahead. He had a look of pure confusion on his face. I wouldn't know where to start in guessing what's wrong with him. I've been wrong many a time when it comes to this boy.

To top it off, I have a stone in my shoe.

'Are you going to say anything? Or are we walking the whole way like this?' I demand. I've hit my limit.

'You haven't said anything either,' he accuses.

'You're the one that insisted on taking me home!' I shout.

I stop walking. One, to remove the stone shredding my tiny left foot, and two, to emphasise my annoyance.

'What are you doing?' He stops a few feet in front of me.

'Removing someone annoying,' I say, shaking my shoe in the air.

'I apologised; why are you still annoyed?'

'I'm not annoyed,' I say, annoyed.

'What do you want? Should I beg for forgiveness? Grovel at your feet?' He smirks.

I wouldn't mind that, actually.

'Don't do that.'

'What?'

'Act all charming and innocent. You are anything but innocent.'

'I am extremely innocent, Dotty Peters.' He playfully skips over, getting closer to me. 'Well, not completely innocent.' There's his cheeky grin again.

That grin and flirty banter. Classic Adam. He knows the effect he has on women. On me. I need to change the subject.

'Have you ever apologised to Billy?'

That was a mistake.

'Have I what?'

Yep, definitely a mistake. He's annoyed.

'It would ease the tension; you did batter him and...'

'And what? He attacked me!' he rages in bewilderment. 'What is wrong with you? How can you still be hung up on that prick?'

'I'm not hung up on him,' I angrily tell him.

He snorts, rolls his eyes and then charges ahead. Bastard.

'Don't storm off ahead of me. This is all your fault.' I shout, storming after him. 'What makes you think that you get to act indignant?'

'What!' he exclaims, spinning around. 'I didn't do anything, and where did you learn the word indignant?'

Cheeky bastard.

'I know words, and you did plenty. You came up here, slept with anything that moved and knocked the shit out of Billy,' I scoff. 'Didn't do anything? You also said nasty things to me. That is clearly the main reason I'm upset.' God, my hands are sweaty.

'What the hell are you talking about? Sleeping with anything that moved? All I'm guilty of is defen...' He stops mid-sentence and looks to the side before turning back to me. 'All I'm guilty of is doing absolutely NOTHING!' he shouts before storming off. Again.

He's kicking stones like an actual five-year-old.

'This is why I wanted to walk home alone.' I exclaim, storming past him this time.

I don't know why he's pretending he wasn't bed-hopping. He came up and started flirting with every woman he could find. God only knows how many he slept with.

'So what? I flirt with a few people, so I must have slept with them?' he shouts from behind me. 'By your logic, that means you'll sleep with any and every person from any family.'

I spin around so fast that I almost fall over. Did he smirk at my near fall?

'That is idiotic and makes no sense. Alright, I made a mistake.'

'What mistake is the mistake?' He cuts me off. 'Cheating on James? Or sleeping with Billy? Because cheating is one thing, but Billy. You no standards?'

I'm starting to get very offended. What is everyone's problem with Billy?

'Both! Ok? Both were mistakes.' I shoot him a dirty look, then turn and start walking ahead.

He rushes to catch up to me; I'm pretty fast when I want to be. He walks beside me in silence. Guess that argument is over since neither of us is talking. I have plenty to say, but I don't want to fight.

'You seeing anyone in Glasgow?' he asks, unbothered.

Talk about a change in tone and conversation. Suddenly he looks sheepish; he must be feeling guilty for being a dick.

'Not really.'

As in, nothing, zero interest from anyone.

'Not while you're still pining after Billy,' he whispers, staring at the ground.

'I'm not pining after anyone. I have no interest in Billy. I'm going to this wedding, then going home.'

I look over at him. No reaction.

'I'm taking Dani and Matt on a hike tomorrow. To the grand trail.'

'Do you remember when we went on our great adventure?' he asks.

'Course,' I say, smiling at the memory. 'That's where I got the idea to go. I was thinking about it the other day.'

'You sure you can all handle it? You almost cried last time.'

'I was fourteen! And I didn't almost cry. You and David walked it like it was a race.'

I can totally handle it. It's only walking; I do that every day.

'You nervous about the wedding?'

'No. Yes. Well, wouldn't you be?'

'Remember, this is your family. It's your sister's wedding,' he says firmly.

'They are the ones making me nervous. My mum is the most angry and disappointed in me.'

'That's more to do with her past than with you,' he reasons.

'Mmmm. Actually, I think Chloe is the most angry with me.'

'What a bitch she is.' He rolls his eyes in acknowledgement.

'Right! I know I slept with her boyfriend, but she is the worse. Actually, I felt very little remorse towards her, to be honest.'

'I heard Kim threw eggs at you.' He smiles broadly.

'She may have.' I smile back. 'Fucking ten of them.'

He starts laughing.

'Oh yeah, it's funny now. But it took two bottles of shampoo to get it out.'

My hair was silky smooth, though. Hopefully, my embarrassing egg history has brought our fighting to a close.

The walk and drive back to the bed-and-breakfast have actually been really great. We laughed and talked about everything. I told Adam all about the scandal from my point of view. He agreed my mum overreacted; he disagreed that my leaving was the best choice. We managed to talk about Billy as little as possible, thank god. Now we're parked outside.

'What are your plans tomorrow night? If you're not traumatised after the hike.' He grins his stupid gorgeous grin at me. Not gorgeous, pretty. Not pretty, sweet. It's a nice grin. 'Back to the pub?' he asks, tapping the wheel.

'Maybe.' I hit his arm. 'My friends will likely need a drink afterwards.'

'Guess I might see you there then,' he remarks, locking eyes with me.

'Guess you might.' I literally can't look away.

I don't know what this is; I can't take my eyes off him. Did he just look at my lips? Does he want to kiss me? No, no. I can't do this again. This always ends the same way. I think Adam feels something, and it turns out he doesn't because it was all in my head. He doesn't and has never liked me that way. He's made it clear we are only friends.

Yet he is looking at me in that certain way that makes my heart stop. Should I kiss him? Absolutely not, not after last time.

'So-I'll-see-you-tomorrow-or-the-next-day-or-someday. I'll see you.' I rush out my words faster than Dani does and practically bounce out of the car, giving him no time even to say goodbye. As Dani would say, what a brass neck that was.

Chapter 14

I've been back in this room for three hours. It's safe to say that my roomies aren't worried about me since they're still not home. Meaning now, I'm the worried one. I've wiped off my makeup, changed into my jammies and been sitting in bed doing nothing except playing Project Makeover on my phone.

It is only one in the morning. They probably stayed until last call, and with that long walk, they'll be ages yet, which is rather annoying when I want to talk through my feelings.

Who's knocking at the door?

It can't be them; they have a key. Adam? No, he wouldn't. Would he?

I jump off the bed and walk over to the door. I shouldn't have opened it; it's Billy.

'What?' I demand.

He stands there, looking sheepish and guilty, tapping his hand against his leg. He goes to move forward into my room.

'No.' I hold out my hand, emphasising the point of no entry.

'I only want to apologise.'

'Ok, apology not accepted. Goodnight, Billy.'

Just as I'm about to close the door in his face, he stops it with his hand.

'I'm sorry. You were right; I've treated you like shit.'

'And Chloe?' I might not like her, but he's doing her dirty.

'And Chloe. It's been hard without you; why do you think I sent you the invite? I missed you.'

'*You* sent the invite?' I thought it was David. He can definitely see the surprised look on my face.

'Of course I did. I love you. Do you still love me?'

It's too much; I can't deal with this right now.

'Polar bear! Do you?'

'You need to leave.'

'Why? Is Adam in there?' He straightens up, looking behind me.

'What? No, Adam isn't here,' I tell him.

'Course he isn't,' he says, relieved. 'Sorry, I saw you leave with him and...'

He goes to touch my face, but I smack his hand away.

'Go, Billy. I mean it.' I manage to shut the door in his face this time.

What the hell was that?

An hour later, I'm still up, still thinking about Adam, Billy, my family, and this whole messed-up situation. Who does Adam think he is? Not kissing me. Who does Billy think he is? Telling me he loves me. I hate men.

I can hear Matt. Finally! I need help with all this drama.

The door opens, and he stumbles inside. Great, he's pissed.

'There's the dirty stop out.' Matt points his finger at me, smirking.

He collapses on the bed face down.

'I was home before you,' I say.

'Only because I had to trek through the Wicker Man hills,' Matt mumbles. 'I got lost. It's a miracle I'm alive.'

'Where's Dani?'

'Went home with Jake,' he mumbles again before turning over to face me.

'Who the fuck is Jake?' Why is he letting her go off with a stranger? Hasn't he ever seen a Netflix documentary?

'The rugby boy with the nice legs.' He gets up and stumbles over to the toilet. 'What about you? Where did you and Adam sneak off to? You lucky bitch!' he shouts from the toilet.

'He only brought me home.' I've decided it's too late to go into specifics, and he's too drunk.

'Really?' He walks back in, stripping off his jeans and shoes. 'Well, Billy and James will be relieved.' He can't quite get those shirt buttons undone. 'They were not happy when you left with him.'

'Really? How? What did they do?'

'Well, their faces fell off their faces onto the floor for a start.'

What?

'Then Billy went on about how Adam was a whore, or did he say poor?' He gives up on the buttons and gets into bed. 'David kept rolling his eyes. I don't think he likes Billy very much.'

I don't know why he's closing his eyes. We aren't done here.

'My brother was there? What else did Billy and James say?'

'Dani knows more than me; she was the one giving him abuse,' he rattles off through a yawn.

'Abuse? What did she say?'

'Dot, darling, this isn't twenty questions. I'm drunk and tired. It's time for bed.' He blows me a kiss. 'Goodnight.'

'Just tell me, did James say anything to Billy? About me?'

'Don't quote me, but I think so.'

Oh, that's interesting. I want to know what James is thinking about all this insane crap.

'So you don't know anything?' I huff.

'No.'

'Right.'

'Are we done with this episode of The Chase?' he begs; he's such a child.

'For now. Goodnight.'

'Night.'

How do I sleep now?

Chapter 15

I was blissfully sleeping, dreaming about my own wedding day, when I heard the room door slam. Not close, slam.

Matt shot up like we were getting invaded, screaming, 'DOTTY! DOTTY! Get them!' while he hid under the covers.

He'll be great if anyone ever tries to kill us.

Dani then threw her high heel at him, told him to shut the fuck up and started slamming anything slammable.

I think I was in a state of shock. I kind of just lay there, making no attempt to help or run away. I also won't be great if someone tries to break in and kill us all.

Dani was in a state, throwing stuff, shouting at nothing and really just looking raging. It all put me in a bit of a panic. I had all these horrible thoughts running around in my head; she's been attacked, someone's died, she's found another white hair.

She said everything was ok, that everyone was alive, and no one had hurt her or anything. She didn't tell us why she was in a rage, just jumped in the shower and still hadn't come back out after about twenty minutes. She does keep shouting, 'Fucking embarrassing,' and 'Fuck my fucking life.'

Me and Matt are sitting in silence, anxiously waiting for her. It's nice, Matt not talking. He keeps looking over at me, all wide-eyed and stressed-looking, though.

Finally, the bathroom door is opening.

Dani storms out, still in a rage. 'Why are you both staring at me?'

Oh, that was a bitchy tone, and her hand is on her hip, all I'll slap you, with one wrong word. Maybe she's just hangry? We'll get some chocolate in her as soon as possible.

'We're waiting on you, so we can use the bathroom.' Matt hurries a reply, then jumps out of bed into the safety of the toilet, coward.

Dani huffs, rolls her eyes and starts getting ready.

'We going on this hike or what?' she demands to know. ''cause you need at least an hour to fix yourself. You look a riot, and I can't be arsed waiting around.'

Mean. True, but still unnecessary.

'Yes,' I say, keeping my words short.

'Well, get ready then,' she aggressively demands.

Oh, we need crisps, too, and a can of Coke to appease this demon bitch fit.

'Ok.' I jump out of bed, looking for anything to wear, before she makes me leave half-naked.

'Hurry up, Matt. Dot needs to wash her face and get some makeup on; she looks half dead.'

Well, again, that may be true, but it didn't need saying. Twice.

Well, we're now at the shop, washed and dressed. Dani's mood hasn't changed, and Matt has the same look as me: that we want to deck her.

'How much?' Matt shrieks, holding up a packet of Hobnobs that are three pounds fifty. 'What kind of scam are these people running?' he demands.

I did pre-warn both of them that these were village prices, but I don't think they knew what that meant. Since Dani is in a bitch fit, I haven't been able to ask her about last night, which is driving me crazy.

'How can this packet of Walkers be one pound seven-ty-five?' Dani is asking Julie, the shopkeeper, who doesn't look impressed by the angry Glaswegian.

''cause that is the price of them,' she replies deadpan.

'It's daylight robbery,' Dani informs her.

Julie shrugs in response. 'Free free to shop elsewhere.' Julie is clearly taking none of our shit.

'You know, Julie...' Dani starts.

'We'll take the Walkers. Matt, give Julie the rest of our shop, please.' I manage to jump in before Dani gets us barred. I ain't driving to Inverness today for a packet of Walkers.

'Can I get these shortbread slices?' Matt asks like he's asking his mother for a treat.

'Yes. That's us, thank you.' I give Julie the best smile I have; she isn't impressed.

Alright then. I don't know Julie that well. She's forty and has lived here for about ten years, I think. Moved up with her husband.

I remember when me and James were younger; we always said we would open our own local shop and call it The Tuck Shop. It would be fairly priced and have everything people needed. Then we got older, decided it would be too much hassle and patched the idea. After school, he became a policeman, and I went to university to be a teacher, but that didn't pan out either.

'We leaving or what?' Dani huffs as she storms out of the shop.

What fun today will be.

A small, thankfully quiet car ride later, and we are at the start of the trail. I can't be bothered, truth be told.

Surprisingly, Matt looks keen; he's doing stretches. Dani is looking ahead; I think she's trying to work out where the end is. We look the part, all of us dressed in running shorts, T-shirts and even backpacks. Dani's even wearing a skip hat.

'Before we start....' Matt is standing in front of us, making a statement. 'Dani, why are you in a mood? We should start this thing mood-less.'

'I don't want to talk about it.' Dani throws her head to the side like she's on Dallas. Very dramatic.

'Was it Jake? Was he shit in bed?' Matt asks, screwing up his face.

'I don't want to talk about it,' she repeats, with a more forceful tone. 'But I'll try not to be a moody cow.'

'Can't ask for more than that,' I say, aiming to be diplomatic. 'Shall we start?'

'Fine,' they say in unison.

I'm supposed to be the main point of focus right now. I have gossip and drama, which they are ruining.

I need a break, my legs are on fire, and I'm sweating everywhere. I forgot how tiring this was, and I'm not the only one feeling it. Matt looks like he's about to die, and Dani looks like she's about to cry. Perhaps this wasn't the best idea.

The last hour has given me time to think. I have concluded that I'm still confused. I don't know what to believe or what is real.

'What the hell is that?' Matt stops in his tracks, looking mortified at the sight in front of him.

Fuck, I forgot about this. I wonder how adventurous they are feeling. You see, the track isn't the smoothest; there is a small bed of water to cross without a bridge or a boat.

'So, are we done then? This the end?' Dani remarks.

'Well, no.' I turn to see four angry eyes on me. 'You see, it's pretty easy to cross; you just take off your socks and trainers, then use the rocks in the water to...hop across.'

Silence.

'She taking the piss?' Matt asks Dani, who looks still with shock. 'You taking the piss?' He then asks me.

'Seriously, it's easy, trust me.' I flash my trustworthy smile.

'Trust you? You are taking the piss. Dani, would you shout at her?'

'I'll go first,' I offer.

I take off my socks and trainers to the horror of Matt. Dani looks around, I think, trying to see a way across that doesn't involve water. I put my stuff in my backpack and make my way to the water. This seemed less daunting when I did it last time; I'm a little scared, actually. I think the water has risen quite a bit, and I feel like there were more rocks before.

I said it was easy, so now I have to do it; perfect. The water is moving fast, like a waterfall speed. Come on, Dotty, you can do this. You *have* done this. Just bend down and put one hand on that big rock. The big, slippery rock covered in moss.

I'm going to die. One slip and my head could smack off a rock.

Although…that would mean I wouldn't have to go to the wedding. It's the perfect excuse; breaking a leg would work too.

Shut up, Dotty; you are going to do this like a pro. One step at a time.

'You going across or what? You look pathetic!' Dani shouts, finding her supportive voice.

'Yes, just planning my route.'

Ok, now or never.

I did it; well, I've got one hand on the big rock. Now time to move my foot across; it feels lovely and moist on this rock, ew. Right, I now have two hands and two feet on the rocks, and my breathing has increased greatly, as has my sweating. If I move my left hand there and then my right foot there. I'm basically playing Twister, Extreme Twister.

'See? See how easy this is?' I shout back at my audience.

'Yeah, babe, you look real graceful!' Dani shouts back.

I can't see her face, but I know her eyes are rolling.

'It's like watching the Olympics,' Matt shouts sarcastically.

I can sense his eyes rolling too.

One more rock move, and I'm across.

I did it! Oh my God, I'm so proud of myself.

'I did it!' I call over.

I get a head nod and a thumbs up from Dani, which I appreciate, even if it is sarcastic.

'I'm still not doing it,' Matt calls back.

'Come on, Matt, think how proud you'll feel.'

'I'm thinking how cold I'll feel when I fall in!' he shouts.

'Dani, you come first, then he'll have to do it,' I reason.

'Who do I look like to you? Mowgli from The Jungle Book?' Dani shouts, folding her arms in a huff.

'It's only jumping a few stones. I'll tell you a secret if you come over.'

'What secret?' Dani asks, her interest piqued. 'An Adam secret?'

'You need to be over here to hear it.' I don't know what I'll say, to be honest. I have a few details to share with her about last night.

I can see the hesitation, with Dani at least. Matt is still a strong no. He's clearly telling her they shouldn't move. The thing is, Dani loves gossip. Even if she doesn't know the people, it'll be eating away at her. She can't not find out.

'Fine, fuck it!' Dani shouts, dramatically kicking off her trainers.

Matt shakes his head in disappointment. 'You're going to fall in.' he shouts after Dani, who's making her way to the water.

How is she getting across so much faster than me? I've done it before.

She's already across, the bitch.

I mean, I'm happy for her and all that.

'You didn't even stumble.'

'Try not to sound so disappointed.' She narrows her eyes at a guilty-looking me. 'Don't worry; Matt will fall for sure,' she reassures me.

'If he comes over,' I add doubtfully.

We look over at Matt, who's staring back at us shaking his head no.

'Matt, if you don't come over, then we need to leave you here,' I warn him.

I can see the cogs turning in his head. I mean, we wouldn't actually leave him; but he doesn't know that for sure.

'Fine,' he calls back.

Stubborn git.

'What's the secret?' Dani asks.

'I'm not telling without Matt,' I shout over.

'Just leave him; he'll be fine, happier even,' she reasons.

'It's another two hours to the end. We can't leave him here for two hours.'

'What are you saying right now? Two hours? We've already walked like three hours.' She's not best pleased with this new information.

'Fifty-five minutes, actually,' I tell her.

'Don't move, Matt. I'm coming back over.' She shouts at Matt, moving back to the water.

'Don't you dare!' I pull her back. 'We're a united front.'

'I'm not with you on this. I'm already having a bad day, Dotty, and this isn't helping.' She draws her eyes off me, and I feel like I'm pushing her too far.

'Why, what happened?'

'Nice try.' Dani looks back at Matt. 'Matt, this walk is another two hours.'

'Fuck that!' he shouts back.

I just realised something.

'Matt! I have the food.'

If looks could kill.

Is it this village? Does it turn people against me?

'Fantastic! Fan! Fucking! Tastic!'

I also think I'm pushing Matt too far.

Clearly, he's hungry because before I know it, his shoes are off, and he's halfway across. How is he getting across so easily as well? This is bullshit!

'Right, I'm across. You happy?'

I wouldn't use the word happy.

'It'll be worth it in the end.'

Yeah, they don't agree.

I can't go on. I won't make it. These two whinny brats will be the end of me. It's been an hour since the great leap across the ocean, an hour of them bitching constantly. I feel like a single mother of two toddlers.

At least the scenery is beautiful; the Highlands are truly stunning. I know I grew up here, so I'm technically biased, but it's the most epic place in the world. Living in Glasgow definitely has its perks, but you can't find untouched nature like this.

There are animals of all sizes everywhere; we've passed dozens of sheep and deer; the deer are adorable, but the sheep are intimating. They glare at you like sociopaths; I fear for my safety. There's nothing quite like being in the mountains; completely peaceful and calming. It's like we're the last people on earth, although next time, I'll pick my company more carefully.

'Next time you have an idea of how we should spend our free time, keep it to yourself,' Matt scoffs, casting me a dirty look.

'I agree with that statement,' Dani replies firmly, like we're in a courtroom drama.

It's one walk through the mountains, one *beautiful* walk through the mountains, I might add. Ok, it's a little hilly with a bit of an incline, but it's fine. Dani might be breathing a bit heavier than usual, and Matt's T-shirt is a tad wet from the sweat. Overall, though, we're doing great.

'I wish I was dead,' Dani mutters.

Talk about a drama queen.

'It's one walk, Dani; get a grip,' I tell her.

'I'm dripping in sweat, and I'm surrounded by every insect known to man. My thighs are chafing, my legs are aching, and I really need a pee...It isn't just one walk; it's a nightmare!' Dani shouts, rattling off each issue one by one. She kicks a patch of mud. All she did was make her shoes dirty. So more fool her.

'I'm also starving and need a drink, but I'm scared to have one in case I need the toilet. God knows I'm not peeing outside,' Matt warns.

Why? He's a man.

'I think we should stop for food, actually,' I suggest. 'I'm a little peckish.'

'Yes, let's sit on the sheep-shit-covered dirt, have ourselves a picnic and then get back to our car,' Dani cheerily suggests. 'I think we've all had enough fresh air for one day.'

'I agree,' Matt says deadpan, looking up at the sky like a great depression has befallen him.

Something snaps in me.

'YOU PEOPLE DON'T APPRECIATE NATURE!' I scream out of sheer frustration.

'Alright, Dotty, calm yourself,' Dani says calmly.

'DON'T ACT LIKE YOU'RE THE ONLY ONE WHO'S SUFFERING!' Matt screams back at me.

Dani looks shocked and concerned by our sudden outbursts.

'I DIDN'T ASK YOU TWO TO COME HERE,' I scream back.

'YES, YOU DID!' Dani joins in on the screaming.

'FINE, I ASKED YOU, BUT I DIDN'T ASK *YOU*,' I throw back at Matt.

'WELL, THAT'S GRATITUDE FOR YOU,' Matt hits back.

'GRATITUDE? YOU'RE JUST HIDING FROM YOUR EX WHO CHUCKED YOU.' Dani shouts.

Are we on the same side then?

'IT WAS MUTUAL,' he declares, taking a seat on the grass.

It's more grass than dirt.

'LOOK WHAT YOU'VE STARTED, DOTTY.' Dani turns on me.

Not on the same side, then.

'SHUT UP.' I take a seat next to Matt. Calming slightly, I say, 'You're the reason we're in a bad mood because of your bad mood. Your bad mood put us in a bad mood.'

'Yeah, what's wrong with you anyway?' Matt demands.

'I said I didn't want to talk about it.' Dani sits down next to us. 'It's embarrassing.'

'Sex injury?' Matt asks, screwing up his face in disgust.

'Matt, shut up. Is it?' I ask, looking at her legs. I don't know why I'm looking at her legs. I've never had a sex injury; I'm extremely vanilla.

'No, it's Jake.'

'The guy from last night?' I'm struggling to picture him in my head.

'Yes, he was very charming last night. Had the best chat, and sweet too. Did you see his legs?' Dani asks.

Matt nods with wide eyes.

'I know! His eyes are incredible, and his lips are...something else. He did this one thing with his tongue...'

'We get it, Dani, you're not in fifty shades right now.' Matt cuts her off. 'Get to the scandal.'

Dani looks at him, narrowing her eyes and biting the inside of her mouth. She does that when she's guilty.

'It's not a scandal; I didn't break any laws.'

'What! What law? What did you do?' I ask, suddenly very concerned.

'I did...Jake.' She looks to the side.

'Is that it? Jesus, Dani, not like it's your first one-night stand. Why are you being a drama queen?' Matt says as he grabs my bag. 'We eating?'

Matt takes out the Hobnobs and starts eating away; I've gone straight for the Dairy Milk myself.

'He's twenty.' Dani whispers.

'What, babe?' I thought she just said twenty.

'Jake is twenty. I slept with a twenty-year-old,' Dani confesses.

Me and Matt sit there, stunned, food hanging from our mouths. Matt spits out the remains of his Hobnob.

'Does he know? That you are thirty-two,' he asks.

'I'm twenty-nine,' Dani states firmly.

'Dani, for the last time, lockdown years count as real years. You are thirty-two,' Matt tells her sternly.

I personally let her be twenty-nine; what's the harm? She looks twenty-nine anyway.

'How old does Jake think you are?' It needs asking, so I asked.

'It didn't come up.' There's that guilty look again.

'Then how did his age come up?' I question.

She shakes her head innocently.

'Wait, so he was born in the two thousands? That's horrible; I feel old.'

Poor Matt. Although he's right, people born in the two thousands should still be in primary school.

'Dani, tell us what happened,' Matt presses.

She hesitates. Fidgeting with her hair.

'Well, he said something about not knowing who Usher was, what with him being a toddler at the time...which I thought was a joke...It wasn't. Then I asked his age and nearly died when he told me. Then he asked mine. This was in the morning...we had already had sex, so what was I supposed to do? I couldn't tell him the truth...so I lied a little, only took off a few years.'

'How many?' Matt asks.

'I said I was...twenty-two.'

Matt bursts out laughing, which is a little insensitive, but I can't help laughing too. Dani does look young for her age, but you would have to be blind to think she was twenty-two.

'I can pass for twenty-two,' she rages. 'He totally believed me. Until he asked what year I was born...In my defence, I can't do math that fast in my head.'

'What year did you say?' I can't wait for this answer.

'I went in the wrong direction. I thought to be older you went up. I panicked...and I said two thousand and...six,' she confesses.

'So...you made yourself eighteen,' Matt says before he bursts out laughing again.

'No...I made myself seventeen,' she says, her head hanging low in shame.

I can't not laugh. This is hilarious. We can't breathe from laughing. Me and Matt are literally rolling around on the ground.

'Do you both mind? I'm humiliated over here,' Dani says while hitting us.

'What happened? When the wee boy did the math.' I ask.

'He said that my math didn't make sense. So I grabbed my bag and ran away.'

'Oh god, Dani, that poor boy will be scarred for life,' Matt howls.

Dani scowls at us while grabbing and then eating a Snickers. Matt wipes the tears streaming down his face. Twenty? God! Looks like we are definitely the talk of the town now.

'Can we change the subject? We've spoken enough about me. I want to talk about something else,' Dani demands.

'That'll be a first,' Matt sarcastically remarks.

Followed up by a death stare from Dani.

'What happened with Adam?' Dani diverts the attention onto me.

I won't go into the history, that'll take too long, but I can talk about the end of last night.

'It was so strange; I thought we were having a moment. I thought he was going to kiss me. Then he didn't. Nothing.'

'Well, you can't blame him,' Dani tells me.

'Why?' I ask, wounded. She's meant to be on my side.

'Because he knows all about how obsessed you were with Billy,' she says matter-of-factly. 'I mean, it was a bit pathetic, babe, with the poems, letters and gifts. I'm not judging, but. What was wrong with you?'

'You gave him gifts?' The look of disgust and shame on Matt's face is priceless. 'Like what? You didn't go full bunny boiler, did you? Give him a lock of your hair?'

'Of course I fucking didn't.' I didn't give Billy anything. 'Who the fuck said I gave him poems?' Poems! I can't even rhyme.

'Who cares about the poems? Did you write him letters? Did you basically stalk the boy?' Matt asks in a way like I'm a mental patient.

'I didn't give him anything.'

Did I? Did I have a nervous breakdown and block it out? No, I would have blocked out much more than that.

'Are you trying to remember if you did or not?' Dani tenderly asks.

'No, I am not. Who even said this crap?'

'James told me last night. He said you were chasing Billy for years,' Dani sweetly says with a smile, patting me on the arm.

'Babe! I didn't do any of that, and I was not obsessed with or stalked Billy,' I tell them both forcefully.

211

'I'm fucking confused!' Matt shouts. 'Who do you fancy, Adam, Billy or James?'

'No, first. Who *did* you fancy? 'cause didn't you grow up with Adam?' Dani quizzes me.

'Yeah, kind of. Adam grew up in Kent, but he came up most summers, every other Christmas and for, like, weddings and stuff.'

'And Billy?' Dani presses.

'He lived with his dad; he only came up a few times here and there. Then when he was like, I think nineteen, he moved up here permanently.'

'Why?' Dani eagerly asks.

'He had this fight with his dad's new wife. She said he should move out and get a real job. He disagreed.'

'Right! And what's the crack with Billy and Adam? 'cause he seemed to fucking despise Adam last night. Didn't he, Matt?'

'I don't even know anymore. I'm losing the will to live over here. I can't keep up,' Matt moans, throwing himself back onto the grass.

'What did Billy say?'

'He wasn't saying much, but when he did, it was about you not being safe with people you don't really know. Said

Adam was a whore, how he was a charmer and wasn't a good person.' Dani finishes with an eyebrow raise.

'He also said Adam couldn't be trusted and was only after you to get to him,' Matt adds.

'You never said that last night,' I accuse him.

'I forgot; just remembered talking about it.' He sits up, brushing off the dirt now all over him.

'How the fuck do you forget that?' I rage at him.

He replies with a shrug.

'James said that Adam wasn't your type. Then he said you wouldn't know if he was playing you because you just love attention,' Dani casually remarks.

I hate that expression. We all love attention.

'Did anyone stick up for me? My brother? Either one of you?'

'Of course I did. I always have your back, you know that, but I was also busy with the twenty-year-old. They didn't say anything when your brother showed up and waited until he wasn't there to say anything again. I mainly heard them as background noise. I did say they should spend more time thinking about their own girlfriends than about you.'

'So they should,' I retort.

I look towards Matt's direction.

'What?' he asks, annoyed. 'I didn't need to defend you; that Ally girl did.'

'Who?'

'He means that chick from the spa,' Dani offers. 'She turned up during.'

'Alisha? Alisha stuck up for me? Alisha was there? What did she say?'

'Oh my god, next time I go out, I'm wearing a tape recorder,' Matt says, with another eye roll. 'She was saying how you were too savvy to fall for bullshit, and that it wasn't anyone's business. Although she was dead wrong about you being savvy.' He laughs.

This is a lot of information. Why is Billy being a dick? Why do they think Adam is up to something? Adam might sleep around and every now and again play with my emotions, but he would never intentionally hurt me. I would hope.

'Billy said he loved me last night,' I blurt out.

'And you've waited all this time to tell us? What happened when he told you, did you kiss?' Dani asks, sitting up very straight, mouth ajar. 'What about Adam?'

'I slammed the door in his face, and Adam is complicated.'

Dani slumps down, looking confused.

'Do you love him?' Matt asks tenderly.

'No.' I think I meant that.

'At least you have men interested,' Matt says sadly, looking up at the sky.

I look at Dani for some hint of what to do. She shrugs.

'Didn't you just shout about how it was mutual?' I ask.

'Well, he said he didn't love me anymore and that he was moving out...so I mutually agreed that, yes, he should move out.' He shovels in another two Hobnobs; he has almost eaten the whole bag. How selfish is that?

'I never liked him,' Dani confesses.

She sits up and grabs the last two Hobnobs. Bitch.

She didn't like him. They all went out one Friday night, and the next day, all I heard about was how rude the guy was. I never met him; I'd seen pictures, though, and he was hot. The Duke from Bridgeton hot.

'I know, but I did,' Matt bellows before throwing himself back onto the grass. 'I'm getting older and fatter by the day. Everyone I went to school with is married and having babies. Where is my happy ending? Don't I deserve some happiness?'

'You're not old,' I offer.

'I'm not Dani old, but I'm not young free and single anymore. Only single.'

I'm not old,' Dani responds in annoyance. 'Cheeky bastard.'

'Well, you're the closest to forty.'

Does Matt want to be punched?

'And you have chin hair, babe. That's old.'

Yeah, he wants punching.

'That means I'm unfortunately hairy, not old.' She automatically touches her chin. 'Look, Matt, you're handsome, smart, and have money. You'll be fine,' Dani sternly points out. 'I'm the one who can only pull a twenty-year-old.'

'At least he was hot,' Matt reasons. 'Can't believe you ran away.'

'Well...' she starts, with an embarrassed look. She is suddenly taking great interest in her trainers. 'I didn't get far...I ran out...realised I didn't know where I was...so I went back...to ask for a lift...but he doesn't drive so...his mother drove me home.'

She looks up, and I am biting my lip so hard not to laugh that I draw blood. Matt masks his laughter with a cough. As far as embarrassing stories go, this is her new top one. She looks mortified.

'Was she younger than you?' Matt asks, grinning from ear to ear.

'OF COURSE SHE FUCKING WASN'T!' she screams, smacking him on the arm. 'Dotty, lighten the mood. What was this moment with Adam?' Dani asks with a pleading look.

Finally. I didn't think they were going to ask.

'Well, after we fought, we had a good time, talking about the past and what we've been up to, etc. Then we were back at the B&B, and we looked at each other. Then nothing. It was weird...' I ramble off.

'You looked at each other?' Matt asks through narrowed eyes.

'You know what I mean; the look. The *I might like you look*,' I tell his confused face.

'I know that look,' Dani says, nodding with her hand on her cheek.

'Right! I don't know why I'm even surprised; this always happens.'

'What happens?' Matt asks, still confused.

I didn't want to go into this, but I need to vent.

'He visits; I think he likes me. Then it turns out it was all in my head,' I confess, embarrassed.

I don't know what's wrong with me. I get to the point where I think I'm completely over Adam. Then he shows up, and it turns out that no, no, in fact, I still have my childish crush.

'Walk us through this, babe. When did this happen?' Dani asks.

'Well, like last time. When we had the fight, basically, Adam came to visit, and I thought we were, I don't know, feeling something for each other. Then he slept with Sarah.'

'Who's Sarah?' Matt asks Dani.

'Dot's ex-best friend, who now dates James,' she tells him.

'I'm in an episode of Dallas,' he exclaims.

'He also battered Billy,' I add.

'Aw, you said battered; we've turned her Glaswegian,' Dani proudly declares.

'Why did he batter Billy?' Matt asks. 'For you?'

'No, Adam also slept with Lindsey.'

'Who the fuck is Lindsey now?' Matt asks Dani.

'I don't know,' she replies.

'She was Billy's girlfriend,' I tell them.

'So how did Billy get battered?' Matt asks; he is completely lost.

'He hit Adam first.'

'You were there?' Matt asks me.

'No, no one was, except James; he broke up the fight.'

'Mmmm,' is all Dani says, nodding some more.

'Interesting,' is all Matt has to offer.

I mean, I expected more, to be honest.

'Let me run through this 'cause it's getting confusing.' Dani starts. 'You grew up with Adam...'

'We spent summers together,' I interject.

'Right, since you were five.'

I nod in agreement.

'James moved here with his mum when you were ten without Billy...you didn't meet Billy until you were, like, a teenager when he visited?'

I nod in agreement.

'And you thought he was cute?'

I nod again.

'But you didn't become obsessed?'

'Absolutely not. I thought he was cute, then he left, and that was that.'

'Then Adam grew up and stopped visiting.'

Another nod from me.

'You then started seeing James when you were, what, nineteen?'

'Kind of. I was twenty, almost twenty-one, when I got with James properly. Adam stopped coming up when he started college, and he came back up when we were nineteen. I started spending more time with James then. But we weren't together-together. Me and Adam fought, I didn't see him again until I was twenty-three, and then we had the big 'fight.' Even I'm getting confused, and it's my life.'

'Then Billy moved here. You fell in love with him while seeing James, but nothing happened?'

'No, Billy moved back when I was eighteen, but we didn't get together until I was, like, twenty-three; it went on for a few years before it blew up.

'And you were eighteen when you saw Billy again?' Matt is lost.

'Yes,' I tell him.

'What took so long then?' Dani asks, puzzled.

'What?' I'm confused.

'You and Billy, what took so long?'

'I don't know. He wasn't interested.'

'But you were?' she presses.

'No. I don't know.'

I've never given it much thought, to be honest.

'So it wasn't until after Adam showed up the second time that you got with Billy – when Billy said Adam slept with his girlfriend, causing you two to have another 'fight,' then Adam left, and you started the affair with Billy?' Dani finishes.

'Yes, but you forgot Adam sleeping with Sarah.'

'When was that?' Dani asks, confused.

'When we were nineteen.'

'When Billy and Adam met?' Matt asks, invested.

'Yes.' I smile proudly at him for keeping up.

'They hadn't met before?' Dani enquires.

'No, Billy hardly ever visited.'

'And that was the other fight when Adam slept with Sarah?' Dani questions me.

'Yes,' I reply, angry at the memory.

'Was this another time when you thought he liked you?'

'Yes.' I fume.

I still understand it. They weren't even friends; he didn't even know her that well. I never took Adam as a sleep-with-strangers type of guy. I thought he hadn't slept with anyone; I hadn't.

'I have a theory,' Dani says, clucking her tongue. She has the same look she did when she won against me at the Friends quiz. Smug.

'Me too,' adds Matt, equally proud of himself.

There are no theories. It is what it is.

'I believe that you have never actually loved Billy,' she softly says, inhaling through her nose and breathing out slowly. 'I think you had a fight with Adam four years ago, then latched onto Billy when he left. I'm guessing Billy made you feel better and gave you attention,' she tells me, placing her hand on my shoulder.

It was not as simple as that. She's making me sound weak and desperate for attention.

'No, I didn't. I liked Billy. I still remember when I first saw him.'

'Yeah, when you were a young teenager,' Dani points out. 'You had a crush on Billy, probably out of boredom and frustration because Adam wasn't here.' Dani says this like it's not my life we're talking about here. 'I mean, why didn't anything happen until after Adam visited?'

'With James and Billy. You said you didn't get with James properly until after Adam slept with Sarah.' Matt butts in again.

'It wasn't like that. We were kind of dating.'

'So when Billy moved back when you were eighteen. Why didn't anything happen?' Dani questions. She's looking intently at me; not one feature on her face is moving.

'What?' I understand the question but have no idea how to answer.

'It was the perfect opportunity. You were single, not with James yet.' She reasons. Where is she going with this?

'I don't know.'

'He didn't show interest? Make a move?' she presses.

Ok. I don't know what to do here. Technically, he sort of did, but I was young and didn't want anything to happen. I mean, I still liked him, but not like that, not yet, anyway. If I tell them this, they will only take it the wrong way.

'No. I was still young in his eyes,' I lie. Badly.

Dani and Matt share an extremely annoying look of amusement between them.

'You didn't fancy him anymore, did you?' Dani asks with an even more annoying raise of her eyebrow.

'It wasn't as simple as that. I was young, I was confused, I was finishing school, and One Tree Hill had finished. It was a trying time,' I ramble.

They're staring at me. Looking mighty pleased with themselves. I'm getting angry now.

'So after Adam slept with Sarah and went back home. James picked up the pieces?' Dani asks rhetorically. 'Then, with Billy, you weren't interested. Until Adam came back, and you had another fight?'

'Only that time, Billy picked up the pieces,' Matt adds.

'No. No. You don't know what you're talking about.'

Is that right? Did I basically use James and Billy?

For some crazy reason. I have started crying. I think hearing it out loud makes it ten times more upsetting.

'Aw, babe, don't cry.' She pulls me into a hug. 'I'm sorry, we got carried away; we don't know what we're talking about. Let's talk about something else. Like your dad. When are we getting to meet him?'

'Tomorrow, I think, before we leave for the hen. He's supposed to get back tonight from Aberdeen,' I sniffle.

'Well, that will be lovely.' Dani kisses my forehead. 'Let's get back to the tin can. Yeah?'

I nod in agreement.

I have many emotions and thoughts going through my head. So I push them deep down. Right now, my only focus will be making it through this week.

'Fuck. We need to jump that pond again, don't we?' Matt kindly points out.

Change of plan. I have two things to focus on. The other is getting across that pond.

I'm upset. Actually, that's an understatement. I'm inches from a mental breakdown. We're back at the water. Matt was first to cross, and he fell in. Dani was second to cross; she also fell in. You see, we spent so much time walking and talking that it then started raining. The rain meant that not only did we all get wet, but the water level raised. The patch of water that was easy enough to cross before is now impossible to cross. The rocks are submerged in the water, making them extra slippery and dangerous.

I wish I could say I didn't laugh at Matt, but I did. I didn't laugh because he got soaked in manky water. It was the smugness he had; he was bragging about being amazing and the next Double O Seven. He spoke too soon, though; he still had one rock to jump. One rock too many.

I didn't laugh when Dani fell, mainly because it happened so quickly. She put one hand on the rock, took one step, missed it and went straight in. Amazingly, neither of them got hurt. I will, though, either by falling in or by them killing me when I get across.

I've been standing here for five minutes now, frozen in fear. Dani and Matt are standing directly across from me, soaked and murderous. I have never been looked at with such hatred, which is really saying something.

'IF YOU DON'T GET ACROSS THIS FUCKING WATER RIGHT FUCKING NOW, I WILL FUCKING KILL YOU!' Matt screams support at me.

'SERIOUSLY, DOROTHY, I'M FUCKING FREEZING AND WANT TO GET FUCKING HOME!' Dani screams more support my way.

She was hugging me not that long ago.

I'm going to die. I can feel it. Death is near.

'DOT, WE'RE LEAVING IN FIVE FUCKING SECONDS.'

Oh god, she will as well. She has the car keys.

'I'M COMING.'

Oh god, oh god, oh god.

I have the speed of a snail; I'm literally moving in slow motion. One movement at a time, one movement at a time. I have one hand on the rock, freezing disgusting water running over it. Now I have one foot.

Fuck.

I've done a Dani; I'm in the water. Hypothermia, here I come.

'SERVES YOU RIGHT!' Matt shouts.

Yep. It does.

Chapter 16

Now everyone in the village hates me.

I have no allies.

We have been back at the bed-and-breakfast for three hours; we have showered and are now dry. We haven't spoken one word to each other since I fell into the water, and Dani shouted, 'KARMA!'

Dani is lying in bed under the covers, watching Scrubs. By under the covers, I mean completely under; I can only see a tiny patch of ginger hair. Matt, I can see. He's sitting up in his bed playing Farmhouse or Farming Town; it's got Farm in the title. He's wearing four jumpers. Why he brought four jumpers is beyond me, but whatever keeps him quiet. He does, every once in a while, look round at me with a thunderous look.

It feels lovely.

This time not talking to each other has given me time alone with my thoughts. I have come to the conclusion that I want to go home.

Dani moves from under the covers and emerges all messy hair and annoyed.

'When are we heading to the pub?'

Oh, I don't think so.

'I didn't think we were.' It feels weird to speak. You know, when you don't speak for a while, and then it feels like you're doing it for the first time.

'Well, I'm not sitting in here with you two all night!' a horrified Dani tells me.

'If we go three nights in a row, we'll look like alcoholics.' I try to reason with her. The main reason is me not wanting to see anyone. Mainly Adam. No, mainly Billy. Both, really, in equal measure.

'We're on holiday,' Dani firmly states, sitting up. She rests her head on the backboard, staring up at the ceiling.

'She's unemployed, not on holiday,' Matt adds, still playing Farm World. 'I am, though, so I am up for the pub.'

They are on their own. I ain't putting myself through any more emotional torture.

'You two head over. I'm going to stay here. Get an early night.'

'Stop being a complete wimp. You're going.' Dani points more aggressively with each word in my direction. 'You are Dotty Peters. I am Dani no-last-name-needed, and he is Matt Owen.'

'Why is my last name needed?' Matt asks, clearly offended.

'You asking that question is the answer to your question.'

That was a great response from Dani, actually.

'Dotty! Glam yourself up. We're going to show these fuckers who we all are and how they shouldn't even think of fucking with us.'

Scrubs has had a profound effect on her. Seems like we are going to the pub tonight. I'm guessing this means we're all talking again. That's nice, at least.

When no one else is in this room, it's actually alright. Matt and Dani have been gone an hour, and it's been blissful. I definitely wasn't up for the pub tonight. I need space to handle the many emotions running through me. Guilt, frustration, embarrassment, and, let's not forget, the crippling anxiety.

I've been replaying everything in my head over and over again. It's depressing how pathetic my love life has been. I mean, come on. I was so fixated on Adam, a guy who has never shown actual interest in me, that I fucked over two other guys. Actually, I'm not taking all the blame for Billy. He caused his own drama; I only helped.

What makes it all the more pathetic is the fact I didn't even realise it. Talk about living in denial. I knew I was hurt and heartbroken when Adam slept with Sarah, but I didn't realise I was latching onto James as a life raft. I did care about him, but not enough, though. I wasted years of his life. I am a bad person. Oh god. I don't want to be the bad guy, the villain.

All I need is a couple of eels, and I'm Ursula from The Little Mermaid, destroying other people's happiness because I'm a lonely, old sea witch. I should have gone to the pub 'cause I need a drink.

It's not only my love life that is depressing me. I've been home for three days now, and my family haven't reached out once. Why am I still here? They clearly don't want me here. I'm putting James through torture. I'll ruin any event I go to. I should go, let everyone enjoy themselves. Matt and Dani won't mind; country living certainly isn't for them.

I do want to see Jane walk down that aisle, but maybe that should be my punishment. Missing it.

Maybe it isn't too late? I make mistakes, many mistakes, but I could make things right. It's never too late to make amends. Isn't that what they say? Or is that only for people with addictions? 'cause the way I've been drinking, I think I classify as an alcoholic. Adam is right about one thing; this is my family. I can't run away again.

Is that my phone? Since I've been with Dani constantly, and she's the only person who ever texts me, I forgot what it even sounds like. They probably want a lift home. It's from Jane.

Just so you know, first activity has been changed to paintball tomorrow. Wear warm clothes and comfortable shoes, but bring a change of clothes. NICE clothes. I'll forward the address x

She gave me a kiss.

She could have not told me or let us go to the wrong place, but she didn't. That's it; I will put things right. I will stop acting like a teenager from one tree hill. I will put Adam to the back of my mind and focus on my sister.

That's a plan.

What does she mean, "nice?" I wear nice clothes.

Chapter 17

I've been awake for ages, thinking of every possible scenario that could happen today. I've also been trying to work out how I will cope with these scenarios. I have come up with nothing. I can't handle another day with a bunch of women who hate me. I haven't even spoken to my mum since the Sunday disaster. Then there's Chloe. There is also Sarah. Surely Kim isn't going; actually, she will. She would never turn down an opportunity to shoot me with something.

Dani's alarm starts ringing, quickly followed by Dani's loud moans of protest.

'GOD, why am I still tired?' she screams into her pillow.

'It's the country air; it knocks you out. If it wasn't for my complete state of panic, I would be exhausted too.' I groan.

'Babe, it's three more days, chill.'

Easy for her to say.

'Maybe we should leave, head home.' I hear the desperation in my own voice.

Dani turns round to face me. 'I don't think you're done here. Not yet.'

She holds out her hand for me to take, which I do, and I instantly feel like crying.

'If today gets too much, we'll leave early, I promise. But, babe, this is your family, your home; you have every right to be here.'

'I want to be strong and not run away, but I don't think I can take it.' I was much more confident last night.

'Course you can, we can. You're just tired,' she calmly tells me.

'*You're* tired? I'm absolutely exhausted,' Matt announces, awoken from his deep sleep. 'When we leaving for these hen/stags?'

'We have an hour,' Dani tells him as she jumps up and rushes to be first in the bathroom.

'Bitch, you better be no more than ten minutes,' Matt demands.

Three more days.

Well, this is familiar; the three of us sat in this car outside my family home. Me, frozen in fear, like a coward.

'Dotty, and I say this with love, could you get a grip of yourself? You're getting more pathetic every hour.' This is why I don't count Matt as a good friend.

'Leave her alone; she'll move when she can.'

'She's proved already that isn't the case.'

He's sassy in the morning without coffee.

'I'm fine. It's just that my dad's car isn't here. Which means he isn't home yet.' I sigh, disheartened.

It's not that it's unusual that he's away. Growing up, he always worked away. I was only hoping that he would be here this week. Like, for the whole week.

'I know you want to see your dad, babe, but he'll be back for the wedding,' Dani reassures me.

'I know, it's just Dad's the nice one and the only one to call me these past two years,' I add, annoyed.

'Yeah, I know, and no offence to your dad, but it's not like he would defend you or go against your mum.'

Bit far, Matt.

'You don't know my dad.' I can't help sounding annoyed and offended.

'No, I'm just going by what David said,' Matt says in his defence.

'David? As in my brother?'

'Yeah, he said the other night that your dad would never do anything to upset your mum and stays out of all arguments.'

'Why would David say that?'

'That was my fault, actually,' Dani interjects. 'I asked David if he sent you the invite.'

'Why? He already said he didn't.' I mean, she was there.

'Yeah, but that was in front of your mum,' Dani reasons. 'I thought it had to be him, but it wasn't, so I said it must have been your dad then…That's when he said it couldn't have been your dad 'cause blah blah blah. Sorry if you're upset, babe; it was an innocent conversation, promise,' she adds in a worried tone.

'I know…and he was right. Dad wouldn't go against Mum.' So Billy was telling the truth. He did send the invite.

'Now that that's cleared up. We going inside?' Matt asks, impatient as always.

'Yes.' Let's get this over with.

It's only been five minutes, and I already want to kill sixty percent of the people in here, starting with Chloe, the stupid cow. She laughed at my outfit (they said to dress comfortably; what is wrong with joggers and a hoodie? Ok, they're bright blue, but it's all I had. She called me Cookie Monster. She then recommended an acne cream to me; I have one spot on my chin. She called Dani's hair 'brave' and asked if her outfit didn't come in a bigger size. Her tank top and leggings are slightly tight, but her jumper is kind of hiding her assets. She then asked Matt why he was there – three times. It's a miracle none of us have punched her in the face.

My mum and Jane have hardly looked in my direction, let alone spoken to me. After Chloe ran out of insults, she and Alisha went to the corner in the living room with Jane, probably saying only nice things about us. Matt is in the kitchen with David. I would rescue my brother, but my mum is in there, too, with Andy, so I leave them to it. As usual, I'm with Dani, alone in the other corner of the living room, and of course, we, too, are only saying nice things.

'I swear if we were back home, I would kick the living shit out of the bitch,' Dani spits.

'I know, babe, and I would totally be your alibi.'

'One more insult, and I say we tell her about you and Billy having sex in the garden.'

'Absolutely not,' I tell her, panicking.

'Course I won't, but I really want to.' She shoots Chloe another couple of daggers.

'Yeah, me too.'

'Right! We getting this show on the road or what?' James asks, making his arrival known.

He's followed by Sarah, standing firmly behind him. Then, of course, we have Billy standing beside her. All my favourite people in the same room.

Let the fun begin.

Considering the cost of petrol these days, the decision is made to only take two cars. In car number one there is Billy, James, Chloe, Sarah and Jane. In car number two there's me,

Dani, Matt, Andy, David and Alisha. Since car number two is one heavy, the back is tight. Since Andy and Matt are tall, they get the front, whereas the rest of us get to get comfy in the back. From left to right, it goes David, Alisha, Dani, then me. I'm sweating like no one's business; I can't handle the body heat.

'So. What's happening? Why are we all going together?' Dani asks.

Thank god someone has finally asked; we've just been going with the flow. They said what time to be at the house, and that was about it.

'They didn't tell you?' Alisha asks, slightly shocked.

Why would they? We clearly don't matter to this wedding in any shape or form.

'Well...' Alisha hesitantly starts. 'It was meant to be that we all went into Inverness together, then split up into hens and stags.'

'What do you mean "meant to be"?' I ask, panic-stricken. Don't say it, don't say it.

'Well, the hen's day got cancelled; I think it was over-booked, so...' She looks between me and David.

Poor thing shouldn't be the one to have to give the bad news.

'So, now it's a joint hen and stag.'

'Stop the car!' I shout.

'Don't stop the car,' David warns.

'Shut up, David. Andy, stop the car.' I put on my best teacher voice.

'Andy, don't listen to her.' David also seems to have a good teacher's voice.

'Why are you doing this to me? I can't spend all day with them. No offence to whoever's friend or family I'm insulting.' I think it's only my family I'm insulting, actually.

'Look, Dotty, I agree it's weird, and to be honest, David was supposed to have told you,' Andy explains, giving David a stern look in the mirror.

'What! You were supposed to tell us?' I reach over past the girls to smack him in the arm.

'Yes, but I knew you would cancel like a weakling.' He reaches over to smack me back, turning it into an actual fight.

'OH, MY GOD!' Dani screams, throwing herself between us. 'You both look ridiculously childish. Babe, we're in this situation now; we need to deal with it. Although, David, that was a dick move. Even if you are right; she totally would have cancelled. Now, where are we going?'

'Paintballing.' Alisha sheepishly says.

'Paintballing?' Matt asks, horrified.

'Yes,' Alisha whispers.

'Stop the car,' Matt tells Andy.

'Matt, grow up,' Dani snaps, annoyed.

'I can't go paintballing; I still have PTSD.'

'You'll be fine,' Dani says dismissively.

I don't know what he's talking about, and I don't actually care. I told Dani it was paintballing, and she said, 'Don't tell Matt.' So I didn't. Judging by the fact that no one else has asked, I don't think they care either.

'I'm not taking part,' Matt huffs.

'Is it just us going then?' Dani asks Alisha, changing the conversation.

'Pretty much, it's all of us and the shinty team,' Andy tells us.

'The what? The shinty team? All of them?' Looks like it's Dani's turn for fear and panic.

'Yeah, the whole team.'

Oh, Andy.

'Stop the car,' Dani demands.

This is turning into an actual nightmare.

'Alright, I don't understand what's happening.' David sounds angry.

He's clearly had enough of our bullshit.

'But this car ain't stopping. Dot, you are dealing with your past. Matt, you're dealing with your fear or PTSD, and Dani, I'm guessing by the look on your face that you did, in fact, sleep with Jake, which means I owe him 50 quid. But it doesn't matter; you are dealing with him too, ok? Ok.' He sits back, taking a deep breath.

Normally, silence makes me uncomfortable.

Not today, though.

Chapter 18

I'm twelve years old again. We're standing in our paintballing attire, about to pick teams. Jane and Andy are clearly the team captains, they haven't started picking yet, but I know I'll be last; I just know it. I was always picked last in gym class at school. Being small with no natural athletic ability will do that. Yet today, not only will I be picked last, but most of the people here will probably be aiming towards me more than the others. I'll be a bloody, bruised mess by the end of the day.

Matt and Dani look as livid as hell. Matt wasn't going to partake, but David said he had to, and that was all it took. The shinty boys are getting ready in the changing rooms, but the rest of the gang are all here waiting. Dani hasn't stopped looking at the changing room door; she is absolutely about to shit a brick. Chloe is literally hanging off Billy and keeps pulling him in for some serious public displays of affection. Even Kourtney Kardashian would call it a bit much.

Sarah hasn't left James's side, which is a tad creepy, but you do you, babe. Alisha is standing with Jane; she's probably saying she ain't driving home with us. David and Andy are talking with the instructor. They were talking to Billy, but, well, it got uncomfortable. I'm not surprised it's the three of us standing together alone; we're pretty tragic.

'God save me.' Dani pleads beside me.

I turn round to see six shinty-playing men walking towards us.

'Quick, Dotty, make me invisible,' Dani pleads. She grabs my arm and holds on so tight that I already feel the bruise forming.

As they walk over, I can see Jake grabbing a quick glance at Dani. Aw, that was quite cute.

'Babe, it'll be fine. He's not walking directly to us; in fact, he's heading straight to Andy,' I reassure her. 'Plus, you're braver than this. Where's that badass attitude?'

'You're one to talk, Dotty Peters,' Matt interjects.

'I'll think you'll find I'm dealing with my situation very well right now,' I tell him proudly.

'Really, babe?' Dani asks. 'cause isn't that Adam?' she asks, nodding over to the changing room door.

Yep, that is, in fact, Adam. How did I forget he was on the shinty team?

'Maybe paintballing won't be that bad after all,' Matt smugly adds.

'Shut up,' I hiss at him.

Adam nods in my direction before joining the rest of the boys.

'Time to pick teams,' David shouts to us all.

We all walk over and form a tense circle. Dani is looking firmly at the ground, I'm looking firmly at Dani looking at the ground, and I don't know what or where anyone else is looking.

'Ladies first.' Andy gestures to his future wife, smiling proudly.

'Thanks, bae.' She sweetly blows him a kiss. 'Alright, I pick...'

It's like watching The X Factor; she's doing that long pause crap.

'Chloe.'

I mean. Seriously! Look at her smug grin walking up there. Cow.

'I pick James.'

Andy is loyally sticking with his best man.

'Alisha.'

'Lucas.'

This is going to be boys versus girls at this rate.

'Sarah.'

'Jake.'

I seriously want to be on the boy's side.

'Ryan.'

Jane just stopped the girls versus boys.

'Darren.'

'Steven.'

'Adam.'

Oh fuck. Adam's on Andy's team.

'David.'

Ok, now it's the three of us, Billy and one shinty boy, so being last would put me on...

'Dotty.'

What? Andy picked me!

'Matt.'

Oh no, we lost Matt to the dark side.

'Dani.'

Andy just picked Dani. Although since Jake is on our team, I don't think she's as happy as me.

'Greg.'

Poor Billy, he's last. Fuck poor me; he's on my team.

'Billy.'

'May the best team win.' Jane winks as her team walk off to plan their attack.

Chloe is fuming.

'Right, team, let's win this mother!' Andy declares, leading us to our team camp.

'If you want to run, I will totally run with you,' Dani whispers in my ear.

'What did you say our motto was? Fuck them. I think it's time I grew up and stopped being scared.' If I say it out loud, it might help me feel brave.

'Of course, you would choose today, the only day when I need you to be a coward,' she hisses.

'Like this situation isn't much worse for me,' I hiss back.

'Yeah, babe, but you caused this situation,' She fires back.

'That's neither here nor there. And no one forced you to lie about your age.'

We funnel into a makeshift cabin bunker thing and wait for Andy's instructions. Dani pulls me over to the back of the group.

'Right, strategy time,' Andy announces. 'We are playing capture the flag now, but they can be eliminated, so hit hard to eliminate them all.'

He's clearly in his element. He might love Jane, but he definitely isn't going to let her win this.

'I think we should split into three teams of two and one team of three. We need one team of two to stay here and guard our base. That way, if anyone needs a rest, we have a safe place to go.'

'We'll do that.' Dani volunteers us.

'I like the enthusiasm, but we need at least one good player to guard the base.'

'How do you know I'm not fantastic at this thing?' Dani questions him.

'You said you've never played before,' Andy reasons.

'And? Doesn't mean I'm not amazing.'

I see Jake and Adam grin at her remark.

'Isn't the dead zone a safe place?' I ask, already confused.

'Yes, but then the other team can see you and know where you are,' Andy tells me, taking all this very seriously.

Alisha walks through our door thing on the left, followed by a grinning Matt.

'What are you doing? The buzzer hasn't sounded yet.' Andy isn't impressed by this ambush.

Alisha doesn't look impressed, either, actually.

'We need to swap players,' she tells him, annoyed.

'What? Why?'

I can guess why.

'Because Chloe is having a bitch fit, and Sarah is mid-breakdown.'

Judging by her tone and body language, she's unimpressed by the girls' reactions. I like her.

'James, Billy, you're both swapping with me and Matt.'

Adam turns round to me and smiles, and then he raises his eyebrows. I can't help but grin back at him. It is funny to think of them having meltdowns over their boyfriends being in the same room as me. It's also great for my self-esteem.

'Are you serious? I'm not swapping; this is the winning team,' James whines.

'I'm just the messenger, but I'm not going back there so.' Alisha walks in and over to us. Bold choice. 'Fucking ridiculous,' she whispers to us.

'James, do me a favour and swap, please.'

Poor Andy.

'Fine. Come on, Billy.' James snaps, annoyed.

'I'm not swapping,' Billy tells him.

'Come on, Billy, don't be a dick.' Andy pleads.

'I'm not dealing with her when she's in a mood.'

'Billy, move your arse.' James warns.

Billy looks at him and must realise he's not leaving without him because he quickly gets up and heads for the door. Dani, being Dani, makes a loud whipping noise, which is then followed by the rest of us laughing. They leave, closing the door behind them, and Matt then makes his way over to us.

'Oh my god, that was hilarious!' Matt tells us.

'Really?' Dani gleams, loving the drama.

'That Chloe bitch lost her shit,' he starts.

'Right, back to the plan!' Andy shouts, reclaiming our attention. 'Right, me and Lucas will take the lead, followed by Jake and Darren.'

This is sounding very sexist.

'Some of you won't know this, but Adam is by far the best shot here, so he'll set up high and cover us. Alisha, you'll stay and guard.'

'Guarding? That's a shit job,' she complains to her brother.

'I need someone good to guard,' Andy explains.

'I'll guard,' Matt offers.

'Already offered.' Dani tells him.

'Fine, but for game two, I'm not guarding.'

Game two?

'Fine. Matt, you stay with Alisha. Actually, Adam, you'll be better off working alone. Which then leaves Dani and Dotty together.'

As he finishes, everyone looks at us, clearly saying, "They're too shit to go together." They're right, but I'm still offended.

'Actually, why doesn't Dotty go with Darren, and Jake with Dani?' Andy then suggests.

I very nearly burst out laughing. Matt does.

'What?'

Clearly, the rumour mill hasn't reached Andy.

The buzzer suddenly sounds.

'Fuck! Right everyone, get your team member!' Andy shouts.

I feel terrible; I've been so busy focusing on who I'm avoiding that I have no idea who Darren is. Although the tall, pale, ginger guy in the corner, staring and now walking towards me, might be a clue.

'Don't worry; I'll protect you.' Darren says with confidence. Famous last words.

It turns out Darren can protect me in the wild jungle. Seriously, I have no idea what's actually happening. All I see is wildernesses, and all I can hear is shouting and fake gun sounds. It's been twenty minutes of us running around and ducking every now and then. I'm completely useless, but somehow I'm still in the game. Not only have I not been shot, but we've managed to shoot someone. Alright, *Darren* has managed to shoot someone, but I was right there beside him. He eliminated Sarah; it was fantastic.

'Right, we're going to head towards those bushes, ok?' he explains slowly.

'Ok.' Like I have a choice.

He signals for us to move. I try to keep up, but my tiny legs won't allow me to. We pass the bushes, but he keeps moving forward. I think he's aiming for their base. He's a good five feet in front of me.

Shit. Fuck. Darren's been shot. I can hear the victory scream coming from somewhere.

Great, I'm fucked.

'Aw, well.'

Darren is taking it better than me.

He looks at me like I'm stupid. 'You need to run now,' he shouts to me.

Or I could wait here and be shot, have this be done and over for me. The competitor in me suddenly awakens, and before I can even think, I'm running back towards our base.

I don't know why I'm running back to the base. I don't even know if I am running back to the base. It all looks the same. One big forest maze.

Jesus, I think my heart stopped. Someone just grabbed my arm and pulled me behind a tree. Adam.

'Shhhshh. Sorry, didn't mean to scare you.' He lets go of my arm, leaving an unnerving, tingling feeling.

Didn't mean to scare me; he basically gave me a stroke.

'You scared me half to death.'

'I had to. You were running right to them,' he impatiently whispers before grabbing my arm again and pulling me over to a hideout.

We kneel down in actual dirt; why do people enjoy this?

'Where's Darren?' he asks, letting go of my arm, giving me that tingling feeling all over again.

'He got shot.' I feel like they're all taking this a tad too seriously. 'Who else is dead?'

'I don't know anyone on our side, but I shot Steven and David.' He's trying not to smile, but the pride is written all over his face. He turns round to keep a lookout.

'Darren shot Sarah, so at least three of theirs are dead.' Look at me doing math in my head. 'How do we know when one team are all dead?'

'You've played before, badly, but you've played.'

I suck air in through my teeth to show he's pissing me off.

'Oh, come on; you know you're shit.'

'I'm still alive.' I defend myself. 'And last time, we didn't play the flag game. This is easier.' I'm getting pins and needles from kneeling.

'Did Jane upset you by not picking you?'

'No.' I lie. He's not looking at me, so hopefully, he can't tell.

'Did it annoy you that she picked Chloe first?'

'No.' He doesn't need to look at me to know that one's a lie.

'She clearly doesn't trust Billy around you.'

Why did he say that?

'No, she clearly doesn't. Can't blame her, though.'

'Why? Because you're still interested?'

What? How many times do I need to tell people?

'No, I'm not interested,' I say.

'Is that right" He doesn't sound convinced.

'Yes, I mean it; I have no interest.' Has he heard about the other night? Did Billy say something?

'Glad you're finally seeing the light.'

'That's not patronising at all.'

'Well, it has taken a while,' he remarks, annoyed.

'Said by someone who wasn't even there. You don't know the whole story.'

'I know you.'

'Is that right?'

'Yes.'

'Alright then, tell me about myself,' I challenge him.

'Well, for starters...' He grins, looking me over. 'You're not an outdoor girl.'

'Well, I have been in the city for a while,' I tell him.

'That's not why; you were always a city girl,' he tells me.

'No. I lived the village life for most of my life,' I state.

'Yeah, but it never suited you,' he says matter-of-factly.

'Why? Because I don't do outdoor sports.'

'No, because village life bores you; it always did.'

'Is that right?' I challenge him.

We haven't spoken in years, but he thinks he knows all about me.

'Yes,' he whispers, moving closer towards me. 'That's right.'

I'm breathing heavily, but I can't seem to control it. He really does have the most incredible eyes.

'We should shoot someone,' I say, breaking the silence.

'We should.' He agrees but doesn't move an inch.

'Andy really wants to win.'

'He does.'

'I don't care either way.'

'Neither do I.'

Suddenly, James is in my head. Perfect timing.

Now the image of Adam and Sarah is in my head. I don't know why, but I can't get rid of it. I look away, finally breaking eye contact and feeling a little sick.

'I'll head back to the base, see what's happening. Leave you to it; I'll only hold you back.' I get up, and without looking back, I head towards the base. If I get shot, I get shot. I need to get away from here and that image.

Well, I didn't make it back to base, unsurprisingly. Greg came out of nowhere and shot me in the chest. I didn't care to be honest; I needed a pee. Me, Matt and Alisha are sitting on a bench, defeated. Alisha isn't impressed and completely blames Matt. Apparently, when they got 'ambushed,' Matt held up his hands and said, 'Cool.'

The only people still out fighting the war are Andy, Adam, James, Billy and, amazingly, Jake and Dani. Everyone else is sitting away from us, having a drink and talking about who knows what. Alisha is clearly over them by the sound of it.

'Another two bite the dust.' Matt points out Andy and James walking over.

'Doesn't that just leave Billy for their team?' Alisha asks.

Nope, 'cause Billy is close behind them. Since that marks the end of Team Bride, a horn sounds out, signalling the end of the match/game/war. Andy looks ecstatic, and Billy and James look livid. I can see Adam making his way over; he doesn't look nearly as ecstatic as Andy, considering he must have shot Billy. My other teammates cheer him on proudly, though.

'Thank god, now we can go.' Matt sighs in relief.

'Isn't there another game?' I ask Alisha, my go-to for information.

'Yeah, but not paintball.'

The look of horror on Matt's face at this new information is a picture.

'Great! More fun for me,' Matt says sarcastically.

'Where's Dani and Jake?' I ask, looking all over.

'Don't they know that sound means it's over?' Matt questions.

'How are they not shot?' I add.

'Right, time to change and move on to the next phase.' David calls out, clearly not noticing we are missing two.

I catch Chloe snickering with Jane and follow her eye view.

Perfect, it's Dani and Jake walking over, dishevelled as fuck. She literally has twigs and shit in her hair. They are both covered in dirt. It's very Gavin and Stacy. Dani quickly abandons Jake and rushes over to us.

'Don't say it, don't ask it, don't even think it.' She warns.

At least she's taking some of the focus off me. I look over at Adam; he's either trying hard not to look my way or is highly focused on whatever Darren is saying. I still can't get him and Sarah out of my head. I need a drink.

'Where are we heading next?' Dani asks. She's looking very flush.

'In the woods, Dani? It's freezing.' Matt berates her.

'What did I just say?' she snaps back at him.

'Can't we just go home? No one here even likes us,' Matt points out, sighing heavily.

'I like you.' Alisha smiles. 'Next stop is laser tag.'

Laser tag! That's another form of paintball.

'That's just another form of paintball.' Dani huffs, unimpressed.

'I know.' Alisha agrees. 'The boys couldn't agree on anything.'

'Then what are we doing?' I ask nervously.

'Then food.'

Thank god.

'Then bar crawl.'

My liver will never recover from this week.

'So it was the hen night that was overbooked,' Dani points out.

'Yeah, we were meant to go to an Alice in Wonderland-themed garden party.'

Alisha doesn't sound too disappointed that we didn't. Neither am I, actually.

'Right, well, let's head on over then.'

We reluctantly start making our way over.

'Dot, Adam will take you, Alisha and Dani to the next stop,' David shouts over to us, clearly not realising the torment he's putting me through.

I look over to Adam, who glances at me for a second, then heads towards the changing rooms.

'What did I miss?' Dani whispers to me.

'Nothing, literally.' I whisper back.

Chapter 19

How many car trips filled with tension and animosity can one person take in a week? Adam hasn't said one word. Not a single noise has left his mouth since we got into the car. I beat Dani to the back seat, putting her in the front, something that clearly confused her.

It's been thirty minutes, Dani and Alisha tried a few conversation starters, but Adam wasn't having it. I have one idea on how to get him talking.

'Dani, what happened with you and Jake on the battle-field?'

Alisha snorts at my question, and Dani whips her head around to face me, furious.

Did I just throw my dear friend under the bus? Yes. Do I regret it? No, and I doubt I will later.

'Babe. Really?' Dani asks through gritted teeth and knitted eyebrows.

'I was wondering too.' Alisha says, offering me assistance.

'I'm not talking about this.' Dani turns back round, facing forward.

Adam is still mute, which means I must persist.

'Well, it was obvious to everyone. That something happened.' I look towards Adam for a reaction or hint he's listening. Nothing.

'Maybe I'm innocent and naïve. But I thought you fell.' Alisha shrugs.

'Only because you don't know the full story,' I tell her. Wow, I have no morals.

'Dorothy Peters, me and you are going to fall out,' Dani warns me, turning around and throwing me a dirty look.

'What story? What happened?' Alisha presses excitedly.

'Adam, what about you? Why are you in a huff?' Dani asks, irritated.

Dani also doesn't seem to mind throwing me under the bus.

'I'm not in a huff. I'm not ten years old.' He replies huffily.

Alisha's eyes are darting rapidly between the three of us.

'Well, that's just not true. You haven't said a word since we got into this car, and you are gripping that wheel tighter and tighter by the minute,' She tells him without looking in his direction once. 'You would think that you would be all happy and high on adrenaline after winning the game.'

'Didn't you and Jake win it too? You weren't shot either,' Alisha points out.

'Alisha, me and Jake are off-topic,' Dani tells her.

'They clearly weren't playing the game,' Adam sarcastically remarks.

'We were playing,' Dani spits back. 'Look, I am not talking about this with people I barely know, no offence.'

'You know us better than Jake.'

Alisha's sarcastic side is starting to show, and I'm here for it.

'Alisha, me and you are also going to fall out,' Dani warns. 'Back to you, Adam. What's with the mood?'

'There is no mood. Why would there be a mood? Dotty, why would I be in a mood?'

Ok, two points. One, he called me Dotty, and two, is he trying to start a fight?

'I don't know why you're in a mood.' I can feel my temper starting to flare.

I mean, what is he trying to say? That I did something wrong? I didn't do anything wrong.

'No? You can't think of anything?' he presses.

'Not a thing. Are you saying I did something?' I fire back. I'm getting fucking annoyed now.

'I'm not saying anything. I'm asking if you can think of a reason why I could be annoyed.' His heckles are clearly up.

'No, I can't think of a thing,' I spit.

Alisha and Dani are clearly taken aback by this sudden back and forth.

'Well, Adam, since you clearly think Dotty did do something, why don't you tell us what it is?' Dani innocently says to him.

Awkward silence time.

'What the actual fuck is wrong with you?' Adam shouts; I'm thinking, at me. 'You went to his room last night. Are you really that stupid?'

'Whose room?' I'm confused, and who's he calling stupid?

'Whose? Whose do you think? That absolute prick of a man: Billy,' he rages.

'Billy? You actually think I went to his room last night?'

'According to him,' he shouts.

'He said I went to his room?' I'll kill that prick.

Alisha's mouth is hanging open, and Dani's eyes are like saucepans as she looks at me.

'You saying you didn't?' he asks, softening. Slightly.

'No, I fucking didn't, you arsehole,' I rage at him.

'I'm an arsehole?' He's angry again.

'Yes, you're an arsehole. Going in a huff with me, calling me out in front of Alisha and Dani. Accusing me before finding out the truth, or even just simply asking me. Not to mention, even if I had gone there last night, that's my business.'

'You tell him, babe.' Dani shouts in support of my rant.

'I'm in charge of my life, mistakes and all.'

I honestly don't know where that came from, but I feel like a goddam queen.

Another awkward silence. I'm losing my queen feeling.

'You're right.'

Too fucking right I am.

'So, you didn't go to his room?'

'No, I didn't,' I tell him, catching his small smile at my reply.

'Out of curiosity, when did Billy tell you that shite?' Dani asks, turning to look at his face as he responds.

'In the changing room.' He looks nervous. 'He told everyone.' He catches my eye in the mirror.

'He told everyone in that changing room that I went to his room last night?' I slowly say, trying not to go insane.

'Everyone except David and Matt; they were already changed and outside.'

Now he sounds sheepish.

As he fucking should.

'Well. Isn't that fantastic? Dani, don't you think that's fantastic?' I'm trying to keep my tone cheery and carefree.

'Yeah, babe, it's fantastic, alright. So, Adam, what did Billy say happened? After Dotty turned up?'

Dani is clearly pissed off too.

'That he turned her down,' Adam whispers reluctantly.

'I'm sorry,' I say. 'He said what?'

That fucking motherfucker. Not only has he made me out as a desperate stalker, but he also has the nerve to say that he knocked me back.

'Don't worry, babe. I'll deal with this fucking dick,' Dani tells me, full of venom.

She has fire in her eyes.

'I'm going to drive home with the two of you; these journeys are entertaining as hell.' Alisha gleams.

We've pulled up outside the laser tag place. Everyone's outside talking and laughing; I feel like I'm about to explode. No one has left our car yet, clearly waiting for me to decide the next move.

'I know this is a stressful and complicated matter, but I'm really excited and loving this.' Alisha grins like a child.

I mean, I get that. As an avid EastEnders watcher, I would be loving it, too, if it wasn't my life. I like that we can count on her for honesty.

'How are we doing this takedown, verbal or physical?' Dani asks, looking outside the car for Billy. She cracks her knuckles like a mobster out of The Godfather.

'I vote physical,' Adam says, raising his hand.

Of course he would. I feel so pent-up and rage-filled. How could Billy say that? Humiliate me like that in front of all those people, some I don't even know. If I didn't feel stupid before, I certainly do now. Is this a pride thing for him? Or is this who he's always been? And I was just tricked into thinking he was something more. To think I was feeling guilty, that I was the only villain. Either way, what should I do now? Lose my temper in front of everyone, cause a great big scene?

'Neither,' I say.

I'm certain Dani just got whiplash turning around to look at me, shocked by my answer.

'This day isn't about me; we go in there and act normal. I'll deal with him later.'

'Seriously?' Adam isn't impressed.

'Yes. Let's go,' I say, climbing out of the car.

I won't let him get away with it, but I also won't let him make me the bad guy – again. This day will be a success, even if it kills me.

'Great, everyone's here!' Andy shouts over the chatter as our little car gang walk over to the crowd. 'Teams will be slightly different. Here, we'll be in four different teams.'

Andy is adorable. He's so excited, like a five-year-old at Christmas. I can see James looking at me from the corner of my eye. I can only imagine what he's thinking about me right now. I have no doubt he'll tell Sarah, who'll then tell Chloe, and won't that be perfection?

'Babe, one look from you, and I'll take the prick down,' Dani whispers in my ear.

I smile at her in appreciation.

'Me and Jane will be team captains, and then, I guess, James, since you're best man. Jane's maid of honour isn't actually here until tomorrow, so who should be the fourth?' he asks Jane, who's looking at him adoringly.

'Chloe. She's acting maid of honour for the day.' Jane smiles at Chloe.

The butter-wouldn't-melt look on Chloe's face is making me want to destroy something – like her face.

'Cool.'

Was that annoyance in Andy's tone?

'Ladies first, as always.'

How has this happened? How am I in a team with Andy, Dani and Alisha? It's a miracle. Jane's team is her, Sarah, Darren, David and Matt. James's team is him, Lucas, Greg and Adam. Then Chloe's team is Billy (her first choice), Lucas, Ryan, Steven and Jake. I'm not overly competitive. I enjoy winning, but I don't care enough to go above and beyond. That being said, I ain't losing to that bitch.

Everyone will be scored individually, and each team will have an overall score. I need to have a higher score than

Chloe, and I need our team to beat hers. I don't care about winning overall, but I must beat her and Billy.

It's about to start, and my adrenaline is pumping. The four of us are huddled in the corner.

'Right, I won't lie. Everyone thinks we're the losing team.'

Andy's motivational speaking could use some work.

'But I believe that the three of you hate enough of them to go fucking mental.'

'This is true,' Dani rages. She is bursting to let out some aggression.

'We can do this.'

He's getting better; I feel more motivated.

'Right, that's us. Good luck, team.'

With that final statement, he runs out.

We have a minute to get out of the room and hide before the buzzer goes off. We all flood out, heading in different directions. It's a fucking maze and a half. It's hardly been two minutes, and I have no idea where I am. The whole room is dark, with fluorescent lights everywhere. I can hear shouting and fake gun noises.

Ok, breathe. I can do this; I just aim for the buttons on their vests.

I have a good aim.

I can hit a target.

Ok.

I got this.

It turns out I'm amazing at laser tag. Who knew? I didn't. We're about ten minutes in, I've only been hit three times, and I've managed to hit multiple people multiple times. Me and Dani met up for a few minutes and destroyed Chloe's base; it was marvellous. I've shot Billy three times, which was also marvellous. I've hit Adam a lot and Jake; all is fair in love and war, though. I love this game. Was that the buzzer? Oh no. Oh, the scores. We all make our way back to the room and go straight to the leaderboard. Team scores: Jane's team came last, and James's team were second to last.

This is amazing, we won!

'Oh my god, we won!' Andy shouts, jumping up and down. 'What was that you were saying, James? No chance, my team has no chance.' He gloats, rubbing it right in. 'Where's my team? Dotty!' He runs over, picks me up and spins me around. 'You came second, you little natural, you.'

Second, I came second. I love this pride feeling. It's so usual and amazing.

'Babe, I came fourth, can you believe it? 'cause I can't.' Dani grabs me, hugging me tight. 'We need to do this more when we get home.'

'Who won?' I'm buzzing for second place, but I still want to know who beat me.

'Lucas,' Andy tells us before walking over to his stags.

Everyone is taking off their vests and heading out the door. 'Well done.'

I hear Adam before I see him. I turn round to find him standing behind me, smiling.

'Thank you,' me and Dani say in unison.

'You two better take your vests off and get your coats. It's food time.' Alisha shouts over to us.

'Thank god. I'm starving.' Dani says, taking off her vest.

'I'll get yous at the car,' Adam says, locking eyes with me before he turns and walks away.

'Hurry up, babe. I told you, I'm starving!' Dani shouts.

I see no one else congratulated me before they left. Sore loser bastards. Whatever. I came second. I'm a fucking machine.

Chapter 20

Something has become apparent to me today. Billy and Chloe aren't as popular as I thought. In fact, I would go as far as saying that they are very unpopular. The guys have completely patched him. At paintballing, I thought they were all just focused on the game, but no. All through the meal and at the first few bars, they didn't say a word or go near him. Then there's Chloe. Other than Jane, no one's talking to her either, not even Sarah. They're like pariahs.

Our first stop at bar number one wasn't for us. It was stylish, filled with posers and overpriced, not quite the right destination for some hens and stags. We gained some new gang members there, though; Darren, Lucas and Greg's girl-friends have all joined in on the fun.

We're now at a club called Yellow Hood (fuck knows who named it), which is surprisingly busy for a Tuesday night. The clientele is a mix; there's the young, the kinda young and the not young. It pains me that I'm in the last category. It's pretty cool inside, though it has a techno, 80s warehouse look. There are arcade games, posters of 80s movies and pop stars. The chairs and couches could be more comfortable; they've gone for style over comfort with a metal steelworks look. They're pretty shit and kinda hurt.

I've somehow managed to avoid everyone other than Dani, Matt and Alisha. I've stuck to them like glue, determined to stay drama free. Until now. Now I'm alone, waiting in the queue outside the toilet. I tried to get Dani to come with me, but she just had to dance. Madonna was calling.

We're definitely overdressed. Dani is wearing a low-neck, black maxi dress with black platform heels. Matt is wearing dark grey suit trousers and a white shirt. Then there's me; she said 'nice,' in my defence. I'm wearing a high-waisted, flared pink skirt and a black crop top. I look ridiculous.

'Finally left your bodyguards then.'

I hear that familiar, arrogant tone that I know so well. I used to think it was charming, but no, it's an annoyance. It's coming from behind me. Yep, there's Billy.

He must have a sixth sense when it comes to me, like a lion pouncing when a gazelle separates from the herd.

'Go away,' I demand. I couldn't be less bothered with him right now.

'I need to talk to you.'

His tone is now soft, with a hint of wanting. Prick.

'About what? Me coming to your room last night.' I turn round in time to see the look of disbelief on his face.

The thing with my village is that people may always be gossiping and know everything about you, but they never say anything to your face. If you hear a rumour about someone, you don't tell them. If you hear someone has been bad-mouthing you, you don't confront them. It's who we are, but it's not true for Adam; he always tells you.

'What are you talking about?' he asks, looking confused over the question.

'Cut the shit, Billy. I know what you said; I just don't know why you said it. I don't know why you would do that to me. As if my family and the rest of the village don't think little enough of me already.'

I'm searching his face, but I honestly don't see any emotion I recognise.

'You really are something else. As if all the shit you've already done wasn't bad enough, you try to drag my name through the mud some more. You know how hard it is with my family. How hard it must have been for me to come here. Classy move.' I turn back around, away from him, hoping he gets far away from me.

'I don't know why Adam is talking bullshit, but I wouldn't do anything intentionally to hurt you.'

I turn back around.

'You know I wouldn't.' He tries to take my hand, but I pull it away. 'Adam can't be trusted; you know that. He's using you to get at me.'

I nod in agreement. 'Yeah. But I didn't say Adam said anything.'

He pauses for a second. 'You didn't have to. Of course it was Adam. He's always doing shit to get at me.'

It's always about Billy.

'So if I went and asked James, he wouldn't know what I was talking about?' I challenge.

'No,' he says with such confidence.

He knows I wouldn't ask. He knows how to play me. Looking at him right now, I feel like the biggest idiot. What was I thinking? I don't think I was.

The bathroom door opens, perfect timing. I jump inside before he can try and stop me. If he knows what is good for him, he won't be there when I get out.

He wasn't waiting for me when I left the bathroom. So he isn't a complete moron. I made my way back to the booth I had left Alisha and Matt in, but they were gone. So now I'm sat by myself, looking like a reject. I can't see anyone.

Oh great, there's James, walking straight towards me. I'm definitely going to need to start therapy again after all this.

I wonder how likely it is that he just wants to congratulate me on my laser tag performance. Unlikely.

I'm cornered, trapped alone in a booth, with nowhere to run. I wasn't up for a drinking night, so I'm stone-cold sober; that was a mistake.

'First time I've seen you alone,' James states as he sits down beside me.

He doesn't seem drunk, a little tipsy, maybe.

'Dani's at the bar,' I lie.

'You having a fun night?' His tone is sarcasm-filled, and his body language is seething. He's scanning the room, probably looking out for Sarah. I can't see her taking it well, us being alone together. 'I'm guessing, since you've been avoiding everyone but the Glaswegians and look utterly embarrassed and ashamed, that Adam told you that Billy told us about last night.' He still hasn't looked at me. He downs his drink, waiting for my reply.

I'm not responding. I'm not defending myself over something that didn't even happen.

'Silence, is it? I mean, I wasn't surprised. When it comes to Billy, you've always been pathetic and desperate.'

Who does he actually think he's talking to?

'You probably weren't expecting rejection, though; that must have cut deep. You've probably been crying over him this whole time, probably thought he would tell you he loves

you and what a huge mistake he made. Pretty sad, actually.'
He pats my leg and sighs.

I stare at my leg in shock. I could literally kill him with
my bare hands.

'You could always try Adam. He might do his bit for
charity.'

Oh. Oh. Well. What a fucking fuck face.

'Here's the thing...' I start.

He turns round to face me. My voice is low and calm.

'Your brother is a lying bastard. My best guess is that his
ego is wounded after my rejection of *him*.' I scan his face for
a reaction, but he's just smirking. I don't care what drama
this starts. Whatever happens, it's on Billy. 'I am really sorry
I hurt you, but I am done being made to feel like shit about
it. It's time to move on, and for the record, I wouldn't touch
your brother ever again.'

The other night doesn't count.

'That's your story? That Billy lied?' he snorts, rolling his eyes.

'There's a lot you don't know James.' I shouldn't have
said that.

'Like what?' he asks menacingly.

His eyes are burning a hole into me now.

'Doesn't matter.' I turn away from him, but he pulls my
arm back around so I'm facing him. Not too forceful, but
he's on the edge.

'It matters to me,' he says.

I can hear the frustration in his voice. I get it, but I don't understand what the purpose of bringing up painful memories would be.

'Why? It's in the past. It's been two years. Time to move past this shit,' I practicality beg.

'You're right! It is in the past. I'm not wanting a fight here, Dot. It's just difficult to have closure when we've never actually had a proper truthful conversation.'

That is complete bullshit. We had multiple conversations, all of which included him shouting and calling me a slut. As for his 'I don't want a fight,' if that was true, wouldn't he be acting like less of a dick?

'Are you fucking kidding me right now?' I rage, clearly taking him aback. I've never lost my temper with James before, but a girl can only take so much. 'We spoke, James, and I took all your insults, bad mouthing and general prick-ness. You were hailed the poor, hurt, lovely man, and you had no problem letting me be treated like utter shit by everyone.'

'You slept with my brother. Remember?'

'Yeah. I'm not pretending that I wasn't in the wrong, James. But you knew I was having a hard time when we got together and that I wanted to get away for a while. It was never right; it was never true love. I tried ending us before Billy. I know you remember that.'

He suddenly looks slightly shocked and a little guilty, if only for a second.

'I cared about you; you were one of the most important people in my life, but...'

'You never wanted to be with me,' he says, cutting me off.

'I didn't know what I wanted,' I confess.

'Doesn't mean you had to go after my brother.'

'I didn't.' I'm done protecting Billy. 'He went after me.'

'He wouldn't do that. You always wanted him, don't lie about it,' he scoffs, turning his back to me.

'Yeah, I thought that too, but I didn't want him. He chased me, and he had no shame in it.' I stand up and walk over to his side. 'And never fucking touch me again.'

I turn on my heel and get the fuck out of the club.

Alright, I shouldn't have walked out of the club. It's cold, and I have nowhere to go. It felt like the thing to do, though, a strong walk away, like in the movies. I have two choices, walk back in and look for Dani, or wait outside in the cold for her to come and find me. Since I'm in no danger standing outside (there are two bouncers and a few smokers out here with me), I decide to wait.

On second thoughts, it's freezing.

I walk back in to see Sarah and James talking by the bar with Andy and Greg. Dani is sitting at our table with Alisha.

The pride I felt about five minutes ago is long gone, replaced with utter fear and dread.

'Hey, babe, where did you go?'

She's acting normal, so clearly, World War Three didn't start yet. Sitting down beside her, I feel the urge to run and disappear.

'I need to go. What's the plan for getting home? I'm sober; I only need a car.'

Dani and Alisha share a look, then turn to me with concern.

'We're having an after-party at Andy and Jane's. There are four designated drivers: Lucas, Adam, Sarah and Steven.' Alisha says. 'The plan is for us all to leave together. Although if you're sober and it's me, you and Dani, then all we need are two more, and we could leave now. I'll go ask around.' She quickly squeezes my hand in sympathy before heading off on her mission.

I'm guessing that James is trying to get Andy to bring the after-party forward, and then he can go home.

'What's going on, babe?' Dani sounds worried. She's looking at me like she's waiting for me to tell her who to kill. She may have had a few drinks, but she's still ready to have my back at any minute.

'I'll tell you when we get home.' I smile. 'But I'm ok. I promise.'

Dani knows when not to push, so she nods in agreement. 'I'll find Matt.'

She goes to stand up, but I pull her back down, causing her to land a tad too aggressively on her ass.

'No, babe, I need you to stay with me.'

'You could have just said that, babe; you didn't have to rugby tackle me.' She pulls her arm away from me, acting all wounded.

I can see Alisha walking back over with Jake, Matt, David and Adam. Jesus, I didn't need a small army.

'Found a car and four more people. I don't mind waiting for the next lift.' Alisha answers my question before I ask it. She really knows how to read my emotional state.

'Is everything alright?' Adam asks me. He's searching my face, probably for a clue on what's happening now.

'Yeah, course, we're just tired. Right, Dani?' I nudge her.

'Exhausted,' she replies, backing me up.

'David.' Andy starts making his way over to us from the bar. 'We're going to head to the after-party now.'

'Er, yeah, we were just talking about that,' David answers, his eyes darting between the rest of us, confused as to what to say.

'Right!' Andy isn't stupid. He immediately looks at me, knowing I've started something. 'Sarah's heading with James, and they need three more.'

'Me and Jake will head back with them,' Dani tells Andy. She turns around and pulls me into a hug. 'Don't worry, babe; I got this,' she whispers in my ear.

Got what? What the fuck has she got? What is she doing to me?

'Ok.' Andy agrees, looking heavily concerned. He can't argue with her. What would he say? Maybe you shouldn't 'cause you're best friends with Dotty, who Sarah and James can't stand. Awkward.

'Well then.' Adam shouts, breaking the awkward silence. 'Shall we go then?'

At least Adam seems to be back on my side. I think.

Chapter 21

Apparently, I'm going for the hat trick of embarrassing and awkward car journeys. We've been sat in almost complete silence for the whole forty-five minutes we've been driving. Alisha purposely jumped into the back seat, clearly wanting another back-and-forth between me and Adam. Matt and David are in the back with her; they've been sitting on tenterhooks, wanting to say something but holding back. In fact, everyone's on tenterhooks; we all look uncomfortable and scared to speak. Alisha's been on her phone practically the whole time; I have a sneaking suspicion she's texting Dani. I saw them sharing numbers earlier, but she hasn't asked for my number. I don't know why she hasn't, though.

I'm not certain why no one is talking. I mean, me and Adam kind of ended our argument, or whatever it was. Matt and David, as far as I'm aware, don't know anything about what Billy said, and Alisha doesn't have any clear issues that I know about. Maybe they think I'm having a breakdown; maybe they think I don't want to talk. Maybe I should talk.

'So...' I should really have thought about what I was going to say. 'How good was laser tag?' Adam gives me the side eye. I don't know what else to say.

'You mean laser tag was good for you,' Matt retorts.

I turn round in time to see David nudging him and widening his eyes in a, shut up now way.

'What was that?' I demand.

'What was what?' David innocently replies.

'You nudged him to shut up,' I accuse.

'No, I didn't.'

'Yes, you did.'

'No, I didn't; you're seeing things.'

'You nudged him.'

David glances in the mirror at Adam.

'Why are you looking at Adam?' I spin back round to look at Adam. 'Why did he look at you?'

'I don't know,' Adam lies.

'You're lying.' I spin back to look at David and Matt. 'Matt, what's going on?'

'I don't know.' Matt lies badly; he's gone all red.

I'm not loving all these people keeping things for me.

'Matt! Tell me right now, or I'll tell everyone in this car about our trip to Liverpool.' I warn.

'You wouldn't,' he challenges.

'I've lived with Dani for two years. She's taught me to be ruthless. So I will.'

He looks between me and David, torn. His hesitation doesn't last long.

'They made you win the game.' He confesses.

'Fuck's sake, Matthew.' David shouts in disappointment. Matthew?

'It was to make her feel good. What's the point now?'

'Let me win?' I ask, confused. How can they let me win? I spin back around to Adam. 'What did you do?'

'I didn't do anything. It was Lucas, if anyone,' Adam confesses. 'He felt bad about...' He stops himself. 'He thought you needed a pick me up, so he told the boys not to shoot at you.'

That must be why Andy picked me first. He wanted to win.

'We didn't want to tell Andy. He had already said he would pick you and Dani, to make sure you weren't stuck with anyone else, and we didn't want him to think he won by default. So no one tell him,' he warns Alisha.

Andy wanted to protect me; I'm both touched and confused.

'I thought it was Steven's idea.' David thinks out loud.

'I thought it was Lucas's,' Matt says, disinterested.

'It was a group decision,' Adam says, settling the conversation.

'So we didn't actually win,' Alisha says in sudden realisation. She looks totally crestfallen.

'Did you actually think you had?' Adam asks her, looking at her in the mirror, knitting his eyebrows in disbelief. 'Dani shot like one person, and Dotty hid for most of it.'

'Er, I shot a few people, actually,' I tell him indignantly.

'Yeah, 'cause they let you,' Matt snorts.

Well, don't I feel like a moron? I proper thought I nailed that as well. Wait...

'Does Chloe know this?' I dart between all three of the boys, dread filling my soul at the thought of that bitch knowing I was pitted.

'Are you being serious?'

I lock eyes with Adam as he asks, turning quickly to me before focusing back on the road.

'Everyone fucking hates her.'

'Well, that's not exactly true, is it?' I state.

'No, it's true, Dotty,' Alisha tells me.

I turn back round to face her.

'I mean, the guys don't have anything to do with gossiping or any of that, but they all agree they can't stand Chloe,' she states firmly. 'Or Billy. Actually, they hate him more. He was only invited because James is his brother, and Chloe was only invited because she's his girlfriend. I told Andy not to be polite, but he's too soft.'

I can't say I already thought this, 'cause then it would look like I was keeping tabs on them all night. I should leave this information as it is, but I won't.

'Why?' I'm not asking because I care; it's interesting and gratifying.

'What? Why? Seriously?' Adam says, shaking his head at me. 'Because he's a dick.'

'Yeah, pretty much.' David agrees. 'And Chloe's seen Mean Girls too many times; she thinks she's Regina George.'

'Jane seems to like her,' I add.

'Does she fuck.' David laughs. 'She's only being nice to her to annoy you.'

I don't know how to react to that. I turn back around and face forward. It does make me feel better that people aren't blind to Chloe, but it makes me feel like an idiot that I was the only one blinded by Billy. I always knew he wasn't perfect, but I thought he was just misunderstood.

'I know you're probably going to beat me up for this, but what the hell did you see in Billy?' Alisha asks me.

Suddenly the car gets extremely tense, and I think I could hear a pin drop; it's that quiet. No one is looking at me; I think that's on purpose. Adam is gripping the wheel a little tighter. David looks like a statue; he's not even blinking.

'It's complicated.' Well, what else can I say?

'Aw, come on, Dotty, you can do better than that,' Alisha demands.

'Look,' I hiss, turning around to face the three of them. 'I was hurt and emotional. I felt very unwanted, and he was there, saying all the right things. He can be charming when he wants to be.' I spin back around. 'And for the record, for whoever cares, I now realise what a dick he is.' I glance at Adam, but I can't tell what he's thinking.

I want my bed.

Chapter 22

The second half of the journey was much better than the first. The silence was replaced with small talk, thank god. Before I knew it, we were at the house. We only got here about five minutes ago, but as soon as I walked in, I went straight to find Dani, which I haven't yet been able to do. Since the house party is in a tiny 'old school' cottage, I managed to make eye contact with everyone from today as I came through it. I'm now hiding in the toilet. I couldn't get more pathetic if I tried.

Even though I basically ran through the cottage, I noticed how stunning it is. It's incredibly warm and cosy. Jane's style is everywhere, from the soft colour tones to the modern décor. The bathroom has been painted eggshell. It has the fluffiest grey towels I've ever felt, and the whole room smells incredible; I think it's jasmine. They've put out fancy soap and hand cream; it's the same one my mum buys. I'm guessing they've done this for the group. Surely they don't use this stuff all year; it costs a fortune.

I've sent Dani three texts, but still no reply. I can't stay in here much longer, but I can't walk home because it's a two-hour walk. Great, now someone's knocking on the door.

'Dotty, open the door; it's me.' Dani knocks again impatiently.

Thank god she's finally here. I jump up, open the door, pull her inside and quickly lock it again.

'Where have you been?'

She walks over to the mirror to check her makeup.

'Babe, guess what I found out.' She takes my seat and sits on the toilet, leaving me to stand.

'If it's that they let us win, I already know.'

'No, I already knew that. Jake told me.' She bats away the information.

'Course he did. You've spent most of today with him. Doesn't he care you're old?'

'Calm yourself with the old,' she says, standing up. 'Or I won't tell you what else Jake told me.' She gleams.

'What did he tell you?'

She looks very proud of herself all of a sudden.

'Well, you see, it turns out Jake has a big sister.' She pauses, looking at me, grinning. 'Guess who she is!' she enthusiastically asks, grabbing my arms and literally shaking me.

She's like a Duracell bunny, her heads bobbing back and forth. She looks like she's about to explode.

'I don't know.'

'Lindsey!' she squeals. 'As in the Lindsey who Billy dated. As in the Lindsey who Adam supposedly slept with.'

'Lindsey is Jake's sister?' I ask, surprised.

I don't know why I'm surprised. I never actually knew anything about Lindsey.

'Yeah, but babe, Adam didn't sleep with her. Not only did Jake say that definitely didn't happen, but he phoned her for me to hear for myself. Am I right in saying that Billy told you that?' she asks me with widened eyes.

I don't get it. It doesn't make sense. Why would Billy say it? And why did they fight?

'What did Lindsay say?'

'She said automatically that Billy must have told you that. She said he was really jealous of Adam and all the attention he was getting, especially from you.'

She points in my direction as if I don't know who I am.

'She then said she dumped him because of how much of a waste of space he was. Which makes complete sense to me.' She screws up her face in distaste. 'So, you going to go confront him?'

'And say what? Tell him he's a lying, disgusting, pathetic waste of a human being,' I rage.

'Yeah, pretty much. Is that the only reason you and Adam fought?'

'No, that just blew it up more. We fought because he said I was...' I break myself off. 'It doesn't matter,' I mutter.

'Babe, I can't help you fully if I don't know the whole story.' She looks annoyed.

I sit on the edge of the bath as she sits back down on the toilet. I hate telling people things that make me look stupid and pitiful. I take a long deep breath.

'Ok, so after Adam, I went off university; I started and then dropped out. Adam came up after three years...' I turn away from her. 'Looking extremely...'

'Look at me,' she demands.

I reluctantly look back. 'Good, extremely good. Everyone was flirting with him; I was jealous,' I admit. 'And I may have gone a bit overboard in making him feel unwelcome.'

She narrows her eyes at me.

'Not in a huge bitchy way or anything. I just didn't talk or spend any time with him. I may also have gone heavy on the flirting with James and Billy in front of Adam.'

She closes her eyes and shakes her head.

'Well, he started it; I only...encouraged it. Which led to Billy trying it on and me telling him I wasn't feeling it. I then felt stupid and realised I was acting like a bunny boiler. It wasn't like it was Adam's fault he didn't like me.'

'So you rejected Billy?' Dani looks slightly shocked.

'Well, when he came back up, I didn't like him anymore. He seemed different; I don't know. Anyway...I was going to go and see Adam, say sorry for ignoring him, but then

I found out about him sleeping with Sarah.' I wince at the memory. 'So I was upset, and when he was leaving, he came to see me. We had a fight; he said I was different, I said he was the one who had changed, and then he left.'

'And you started seeing James?' She looks sadly at me.

'He was really sweet, genuine. I thought, why not give it a try?'

'Then Adam came back?'

'Yeah, a few years later. When he came back, I just wanted to spend time with him. I missed him. Didn't care about Sarah as much.'

It feels so strange to go through all this; I think I buried it so deep I blocked it out.

'I'm guessing that's what Lindsey was talking about, why Billy was jealous.' Dani says, putting the pieces together.

'I thought Adam seemed off about me and James when he was here...we spent some time together and...I thought something was happening between us...I even thought he was going to make a move at one point...but he didn't. Then one day, he started a fight out of nowhere...he said things, I said things...but I thought it was because he had feelings for me, so I decided to go see him and have an honest and upfront conversation.'

Dani moves over to the bath and wraps her arm around me.

'Before I went to see him, I saw Billy, all bruised and bloody, and he told me about Adam and Lindsey. I was so mad, I went straight over to Adam's and went off on him.'

'What did Adam do? Or say?'

'Nothing really, I shouted and screamed at him, then left.'

'And that was the last time you saw him until this week?' She asks, suddenly realising my living nightmare.

'Yeah.'

'Fuck! So what are you going to do?'

Like I know.

'Nothing. Why say anything?'

'Come on, babe, the boy clearly likes you.'

'This is the thing, though, Dani. I always think me and Adam are on the same page. I think he's feeling a certain way then the rug gets ripped beneath me. I seriously don't want to do it again.'

She puts her head on my shoulder. 'I know what you're saying, but it sounds like a lot of crossed wires. If it is crossed wires, don't you deserve to know the truth? Whatever that is.'

She kisses my forehead, stands up and reaches out for my hand. I take it and pull myself up. We nod in unison, and I reluctantly leave the bathroom.

Heaven help me.

After leaving the bathroom and walking around the house twice, I finally see Adam through the living room window, making his way down the road.

This probably isn't my smartest decision, following someone into the darkness on a deserted road, but here I am. How fast is he? I've totally lost him. I feel like I'm in a horror movie. The only sound I can hear is harrowing wind, my feet crunching on sticks, and god knows what. The only thing I can see is utter darkness, and it's freezing.

'Where are you going?'

'FUCCKK! Jesus Christ.' Oh my god, my soul has left my chest.

I turn around and can just about see Adam sitting on a fallen tree trunk, I think. It's pitch black out here. As I walk closer to him, I can see that it is, in fact, a tree trunk.

'You ok?' He laughs at my fear-ridden face.

'Oh yeah, I love getting scared half to death,' I remark as sarcastically as I can.

He stands up and makes his way over to me.

'Then you shouldn't walk around country roads alone at night. Why are you walking alone down here?' He seems disconcerted or put out.

'I was looking for you.'

'Why?'

Does he have to sound so suspicious?

'I have a question for you. And I really want you to tell me the truth.' Guess it's now or never. 'Why did you fight Billy?'

He moves closer towards me until we're hardly three feet apart. He's looking at me as if he's trying to figure something out. It's not a difficult question.

'Why?'

Oh fuck off and tell me already.

'Because I want to know if it had anything to do with me,' I tell him.

He pauses, clearly debating with himself.

'Yes, it did.'

'It did?' I ask, slightly shocked. I mean, I thought as much, but having it confirmed is a whole other thing.

'Of course it did. He wasn't going to get away with disrespecting you.'

I feel completely out of my depth. The sudden desire flowing through me is something else. My mouth has gone dry, my legs feel like jelly, and my heart is going ten to the dozen.

'Because we're friends?'

It's an exceptionally loaded question. A make or break, final decision question. That he better answer. He's hesitating. Fucking brilliant.

'No, not because we're friends.'

If he doesn't kiss me, I swear to god I'm going to scream. Seriously, what is he waiting for? 'cause I'm not kissing him; it's totally up to him. I'm not that much of a feminist. He's taking too long.

'I should head back; Dani will be getting worried.'

'I don't think you should leave.'

'Why?'

He moves within an inch of me, and I see it, even in the darkness. That wanting look. There's no mistaking it.

Finally, his lips find mine. Starting with such tenderness, cupping my face with his hands. Is this actually happening? Slowly more power and passion come into his kiss. His hand moves down onto my neck, stroking my chin and lower lip. The other is on my lower back, pulling me closer, sending electric shocks through me. I have one hand on his chest; I can feel his heart racing as fast as mine. My other hand is clutching his arm. I'm holding on for dear life, in case he thinks of letting go. I've never felt this feeling for someone. It's intoxicating.

His lips slowly pull away from mine. Both of us are breathing heavily.

'What do you want to do?' he whispers, still holding me.

Well, I definitely don't want to stop kissing him.

'It's very cold tonight; we should probably get indoors.'

'We probably should.'

'Then you should be a gentleman and get me warm.'
'I can do that.' He smiles, suddenly looking nervous.
This day has definitely taken a turn in the right direction.

Chapter 23

I hope I'm not the only person in this car feeling nervous. We rushed to the car and said a total of four words to each other on the way. Now here we are, driving on our way to, I hope, Adam's, in silence, but not an awkward silence or even an uncomfortable silence. It's a knowing silence, if that even makes sense. We both know what's happening, what we want and how the other is feeling. Even with that, I still feel nervous. I wish I had drunk something earlier. Having sex with anyone for the first time is hard enough, but this is Adam…

I've thought about this happening many times over the years, but now it is happening, I'm terrified I won't be able to measure up. Adam is charming, funny, good-looking, successful and basically perfect. I doubt he's had trouble with women these past years. Me, on the other hand, well, I'm a fucking disaster, aren't I?

It's as if he senses my self-esteem plummeting because he takes my hand in his. I don't look at him. I can't right now; the butterflies in my stomach have taken over my body.

I always wonder if the other person feels the same electric bolt you feel when you touch.

He's pulling over; why is he pulling over?

Oh, wait, we're here.

I was so caught up with the hand-holding thing that I didn't realise we had pulled into the farm. It hasn't changed one bit. The same old Land Rover is in the drive; there's the same adorable cottage that looks like it's about to fall down, and the same old incredible early eighteen-hundreds Victorian-looking house. I used to come here and pretend I was a witch in Charmed. It looked close enough to their house for me to make-believe.

'What you thinking?' he nervously asks.

'Honestly? About when I used to come here and play witches.'

He laughs lightly at my reply before gazing right at me, into my soul. He has amazing eyes filled with such sincerity.

I take the lead and open the car door; I've waited long enough.

I make my way across the gravel towards the cottage. The cottage was always Adam's, ever since he turned eleven. His grandad fixed it up for him. He walks over until we're walking side by side. He grabs my hand again, opens the door and leads me inside.

With the closing of the door, he takes my other hand in his and gently pushes me against the wall. His face is inches from mine; I can feel his breath, hear it quickening. I look up to meet his eyes, which bore into mine. He lets go of my hands. He places one hand on my jawline, stroking gently as the other runs down my left side, moving under my skirt. His eyes are still on me. His lips finally touch mine, but only for a second, before they make their way to my neck, then my throat, to my chest, to my stomach, to my...

Oh. My. God.

I'm terrified to move even a fraction of an inch. It's spectacular, marvellous, incredible. I don't have enough words. All I know is that right now, this moment is complete perfection.

Three hours. We had sex for three hours. I didn't even think that was possible, to be honest. James never lasted longer than fifteen minutes, including foreplay and after cuddling. Once a week. Billy, well, Billy was shorter than James.

Three hours! I'm absolutely shattered, and my whole body is in pain. I was in positions I didn't even think my body could get into, but my god, it was worth it.

It started off slow and tender, then went into utter passion. I have bruises, and he's covered in my claw marks. I now know what Rachel meant in Friends by "animal sex." We did stop for about ten minutes to hydrate, and then it was right back to it. It has been years of pent-up sexual tension, well, for me, at least.

Now here we are, lying in his bed. Well, actually, I'm more lying on top of him than the bed. He's circling my back with his hand, sending goosebumps all over me. I've already literally kissed every part of his body, yet it's the only thing I want to do right now.

There's so much to talk about, to clear up. I want to know about the fight; I want to know what he's thinking and, more importantly, feeling. I'm sure there's also plenty he wants to know, but I'm tired and very comfortable.

Everything can wait until morning.

Chapter 24

How disorienting is it, waking up in a strange place? Not that I do it often; I've just done it enough to know it's disorienting. It's even more disorienting and downright confusing, waking up alone in a strange place.

After I woke up, I waited in the bedroom for about twenty minutes before working up the courage to go into the living/kitchen room. Where he also was not. As much as this cottage is clearly a health and safety risk, it's also cute as hell. It's just like the cottage from The Holiday, complete with its own good-looking Jude Law character, when he actually bothers to be here.

Adam might not live here permanently, but this cottage is all him. The shelves are filled with his books on history, and the walls are covered with his many photos and all the random crap he bought at markets while he was travelling. I recognise the Cheers sign he found in Germany and that weird portrait of Albert Einstein he bought in Italy. Yet the most heart-warming thing is the terrible clay plant pot I made him when I was ten. He kept it. It's an ugly yellowish colour, is completely uneven, and you can't put water in it 'cause it's full of holes. But he kept it.

I did find a note on the kitchen counter, saying he had to go somewhere early, but that he'd be back as soon as possible. So here I am, sitting on his brown Chesterfield, contemplating my next move. I want to see him, wait for him, but Dani has called me twenty-two times and keeps texting me to move my arse and get home, even after I texted her saying I was alive and would be back soon. There is also the issue of me not having a car, and the bed-and-breakfast is an hour's walk away.

Great, there she is again. May as well answer this time.

'Hello, I'm still here and haven't left yet.'

'Babe, that's not good enough; I need you back here now.'

'Well, Adam's not back yet, and I don't want to walk.'

'WhatsApp me your location, and I'll come and get you.'

'Why you so desperate for me to come back?'

'I'll explain when you're back. WhatsApp me right now.'

And with that, she hangs up on me. I do as I'm told and head back to the bedroom for my clothes. I can't walk out of here in just Adam's T-shirt. I'm such a cliché, but I'm totally taking it with me. It's a cliché for a reason.

I feel like such a dirty stop out, waiting here on the side of the road in yesterday's clothes. I thought it was better to wait for Dani here, rather than have her tearing through the farm with her music blaring.

Finally, she's here. Why is Matt in the passenger seat? I thought she would have left him at the bed-and-breakfast.

She pulls up a tad, too aggressively for my liking. Matt gets out and climbs into the back, giving me a worried look and sucking in air through his teeth. What is happening? I climb on in and wait for the sky to fall.

'What's going on?'

'Babe, you won't believe what I've found out.'

I look round to Matt for a hint. He shrugs, not having an idea.

'What is it?'

'Not here, we need privacy, and I need to not be driving.'

She pulls away and drives on, to I have no clue where.

I haven't heard her correctly. What she's saying can't possibly be right. It can't be true; it is not possible. It is not possible that James and Sarah were seeing each other when I was with him. That didn't happen, because if it did, then that would mean they've allowed me to bear the brunt of something that we all did.

'Babe, you still breathing?' Dani grabs me by the shoulders and looks at me, full of concern.

We're back at the start of the hiking trail, standing outside the car. Matt is standing open-mouthed. He's leaning on the bonnet with his arms crossed, shaking his head, looking back and forth between us.

'That's not possible,' I insist.

She lets go of my shoulders and joins Matt on the bonnet.

'Sorry, babe, but you got well and truly shafted.'

'Don't sorry me, you don't have to sorry me because it's not true.' My voice is shrieking more and more with every word.

'They started sleeping together about a year before everyone found out about you and Billy.'

'Dani! No, it's not true; it can't be. He wouldn't...she wouldn't...'

'Did Jake tell you?' Matt asks, finding his voice.

'No, Alisha did. She wanted to tell you herself, but she thought it would be better if you heard it from me.'

'Well, as much as I like Alisha and think she's nice and that, I'm not about to take everything she says as law,' I shriek.

I mean, what would Alisha know? She wasn't even around; she was at university the whole fucking time.

'Andy told her.'

'What? Andy knew?' Matt gasps.

'No, no, he wouldn't do that to me. He wouldn't let that be done to me.'

'He's James's best friend, and there's no secret I wouldn't keep for you.' Dani said. 'Alisha said Andy told her this week after you came back. She said that he felt guilt-ridden.'

'But, they all turned on me. How could they all do that? Sarah didn't say anything. Like nothing.'

Perfect, tears are forming. Dani moves towards me, but I wave her away.

'Did you tell Sarah? About you and Billy?' Dani asks.

'No, I never told anyone.'

My friendship with Sarah was nothing like the one I have with Dani. We grew up here together and went drinking together, but we weren't close-close. Although I thought we were good enough friends for her not to sleep with my boyfriend.

'And I'm guessing she never knew about how you felt about Adam?' Matt asks.

I feel like I'm living in Hollyoaks.

'She must have. It's clear as day,' Dani corrects him. 'Sorry,' she adds. 'But it is. Speaking of Adam, I'm guessing things went well last night?' Dani asks with a great big grin.

'Yes.' I can't help but smile and feel instantly better at the mention of Adam. 'Things went amazingly.'

It doesn't last long. I'm back to feeling pissed.

'No, babe, stop the rage face. Tell us about last night.' She demands. 'What was said? Did you ask him about Lindsay or the fight with Billy?'

'No, we didn't talk at all.' I can't help the now humongous smirk on my face.

'You lucky bitch, I love it.' Dani gleams with pride.

'It was amazing. Completely and utterly amazing.'

'As happy as that makes me, and as much as I want happy Dotty, what are you going to do about this whole James and Sarah thing?'

On the one hand, I want to shout and scream and have a massive argument. On the other hand, it's still Jane's wedding.

'Nothing,' I reply.

They both look at me like I've said I thought Theresa May was a great prime minister.

'What the fuck did you just say?' Matt demands.

'It's Jane's wedding.'

'Fuck Jane,' Matt bursts out. 'Sorry.'

'And then there's Adam. I don't want to have a big thing about the past when we're doing whatever we're doing.'

'I get that.' Dani nods in agreement. 'But if you want to blow things up, babe, I will blow shit up with you.'

'So will I; I will totally blow shit up with you two bitches,' Matt adds.

'Thank you, I appreciate it.' I make my way over to them and slide in between them on the bonnet, putting my arms around them. 'Let's just have a normal rehearsal dinner tonight and a drama-free wedding tomorrow.'

Then maybe I'll blow shit up the day after that.

Who am I kidding? I totally won't do shit.

Chapter 25

It's been three hours. Three hours since we got back to the bed-and-breakfast. Three hours, and I have had one text from Adam.

I'll see you tonight.

What the fuck is that?

Do I answer that?

I didn't just leave; I left a note saying that Dani needed me and that I had to get ready for tonight. Then I left my number so he could call me.

I'll see you tonight. Yeah, no shit, Adam. I'll see many people tonight.

'I'm starving,' Dani groans. 'If I don't eat soon, I'll faint.'

I feel that. None of us have had a meal since last night. It's now one in the afternoon, and all we've had are some crisps and a third of a chocolate bar each. Usually, I can wait a little longer in the day to eat, but I partook in a lot of physical activity last night. Much more than usual.

It's also not helping that we're in this shit room with nothing to do. We're currently lying on our own beds, staring at the ceiling.

'Dani, could you stop saying you're starving? We know you're starving; you've told us many times now that you are starving. Not only that, but we are also starving. We're aware of the starving situation, and you talking about it isn't helping; it's making it fucking worse.'

Matt is clearly hangry.

'Don't worry; there will be plenty of food at the house. Mum always over orders.'

'Dotty, don't go making promises that you don't know you can keep,' Matt warns.

'When can we leave? Now? Can we leave now? I want to leave now,' Dani pleads.

'It doesn't start until five.'

'What about the pub? Can we go to the pub and eat their nuts?'

'Why don't we do something? Take our minds off the food.'

'Like what?' Matt says, deadpan.

'What about a puzzle? There's a few downstairs; I could run and grab one,' I offer.

'What is it with you and fucking puzzles? Puzzles are long, boring and pointless. I'm not doing a jigsaw puzzle of a stupid, pointless dog or cat.'

Yep, Matt is hangry.

'We could take a nap,' I suggest. 'Then we don't have to talk to each other anymore.'

'I like that idea,' Dani says, in support, I guess.

'Fine.' Matt agrees.

Great, I'm not even tired.

Turns out I was tired. I was actually the last one up, woken up to Dani and Matt screaming at each other over a razor. Apparently, Dani used Matt's razor, and now he has a rash. When they woke me up, Dani was already half ready, and Matt had just showered, putting me under immediate pressure.

I caught up quickly, though; that was thirty minutes ago, and look at me. I'm showered and almost ready to go. I only have the finishing touches to my makeup and then my outfit to put on. I didn't bring an outfit for the rehearsal dinner, so I've had to borrow one from Dani – again. Not to be ungrateful, but it wouldn't be my first choice. It's not my colour, for a start. It's green, lime green. The material is extremely unforgiving. It is silk, so it showcases all of my lovely lumps and bumps that I would rather hide.

Dani is wearing black, which she's worn a lot on this trip. It isn't her usual colour, but it's a stunning dress, velvet and booby. She's finishing off her hair; she's gone for loose waves, which are carrying a full bottle of hair spray in them.

'Dani, could you please stop spraying that for two minutes? I'm choking to death over here,' Matt huffs.

Matt is wearing black, too, a very smart and sophisticated suit/shirt combo. They look like they're going to a grand ball, not my mum's garden.

'Are we overdressed?' I ask.

'What? No, Dotty, we are not,' Matt scowls, shaking his head at me.

'Babe, we never get to dress up; we need to take full advantage,' Dani explains. 'I'm ready.'

'Same. I've been ready for ages,' Matt huffs.

'I only need to put my dress on.'

If I can get into it.

'Perfect, we all need to down a gin before we go.' Dani pours, by the look of it, very strong gins and hands us one each. 'Here's to a drama-free, fun and amazing night.'

We clink our glasses.

What could go wrong?

Chapter 26

'Ok, everyone clear on the rules?' I ask.

We're sitting outside my family home, still in the car.

'Yes, we get it. Basically, don't talk to anyone, and don't leave you alone with anyone. Can we go in already?' Matt rages in the back.

'No, no, that's not what I'm saying.'

'We get it; we know the list,' Dani says. 'Adam good, brother's bad, David good, Sarah bad, Alisha good, your mum bad. Need I go on? Because, like Matt, I want to go in already and eat. I need to eat.'

'I know, you're not the only person wasting away. I only want to know that you both know the rules.'

'How about if someone starts anything, we attack them?' Matt suggests.

'Let's call that Plan B.'

'I don't care what we do – after I've eaten,' Dani warns.

'Fine, yes, we can go in.'

As we make our way out of the car and along the drive, I feel that familiar feeling of dread wash over me. My mother has that effect on most people. She wasn't always so stern and cold-hearted, or so I'm told. Legend has it, she was once very well-liked, funny and adventurous. That was until she fell pregnant with me, causing quite the scandal and shame.

'What about Jane? Is she in the good or bad category?'

'I don't know.'

'I would say good,' Dani offers.

'Maybe. Right, here we are, we ready?'

'Honestly, babe, I just want to eat and get drunk. Then maybe find Jake at some point.'

'He's still too young; he's hardly even a man, Dani,' Matt warns.

'I'm aware of his age, Matt, alright? Is someone going to knock on the door or...?'

I hesitate, causing Matt to roll his eyes, huff and bang on the door.

'I was going to do that,' I say.

'Yeah, 'cause there's lots of evidence to back that up.'

There's that eye roll again, which is getting old.

I feel a lot better now that I've eaten. It's amazing how you can feel like you're about to murder someone one minute, then feel completely calm the next, all because of a mini burger. Ok, maybe it was five mini burgers. I needed the pick me up, Adam still isn't here, and I'm surrounded by bitches and assholes.

The set-up is incredible, though; Mum always could throw a party. The garden, which was already impressive, now looks like a royal garden event. We're all standing in a huge white gazebo. It has a bar at the back, and an impressive buffet to the left, filled with mini everything, burgers, cakes, canapés and macaroons. The DJ is set up on the right, next to the dance floor. There are five tables with silk tablecloths decorated stylishly with white rose petals and tall vanilla-scented candles. One of which is hosting me, Dani, Alisha and Matt. Alisha is wearing a dark blue maxi dress. She looks beautiful and comfy; I'm very jealous.

It looks like an actual wedding, so god knows what tomorrow will look like.

The usual suspects are here, plus Mum's friends and Andy's mum and dad. I think there's about thirty of us in total. The good thing is, probably the best thing actually, is the open bar.

'I'm in such a good mood,' Dani announces, eating her third macaroon.

'Me too, but isn't this all a tad extravagant?' Matt says, giving the room a suspicious look. 'I mean, I thought it would be a lot more chill than this, as in seven of us round a table eating a roast or something. Do we even have rehearsal dinners in this country?'

'I think you do if you're rich,' Dani says before eating her fourth macaroon.

I've been scanning this room the entire time we've been here, but no, still no Adam. Where is he? He knows I'm always early at parties, which is either sad or polite.

'How's the outcast table getting on?' David smirks before sitting down with us.

I can't even deny it; we are clearly the loser, outcast table.

'No longer hungry,' Dani says through a mouthful of food. You would think we've gone days without food.

'Still not getting fed at hotel horror?'

'No, brother, we are not.'

'Dotty, I'm confused...' Alisha starts.

'Why?'

'Well, everyone you're scared of is already here. So why do you keep looking at the door? You're constantly looking at it.'

'First of all, I'm not scared of them. I would just rather never speak to them ever again.'

She's right; everyone is already here that I'm scared of. We have Andy, Jane, Sarah, James, Lucas and his girlfriend at one table. There's Chloe, Billy, Steven and Steven's girlfriend on the table next to them. Then we have the family table, made up of Andy's mum and dad, my lovely mother, a few of her friends and some grandparents on both sides. My dad still isn't here; his stupid flight was cancelled. The fourth and final table is basically the extras, consisting mainly of Jane's actual close friends, who have finally arrived.

'Babe, you going to answer the question?' Dani asks, breaking my train of thought.

'Yes, I was, I am. I'm looking for…my dad.'

'No, you're not.'

'Shut up, David; I *was* looking for Dad.'

'I already told you that he wasn't getting in until late.'

'I can still look, in hope.'

'She's looking for Adam.'

'Fuck's sake, Dani.'

'You are?' David asks doubtfully.

'I'm not looking for Adam.'

'Really?' Alisha asks.

'Really.'

'So you don't want to know that he just walked in,' Dani adds.

'Seriously?'

I spin my head so fast I think I now have whiplash. Which wasn't worth it since he's not here.

'That wasn't funny, Dani.'

'No, it was.' She chuckles away at herself.

I can see the curiosity boiling over on David and Alisha's faces. Matt couldn't care less; he's inhaling a mini pizza.

'Why you looking out for Adam?' David asks.

'I'm not.'

'Babe, that denial isn't working.'

'Did something happen? Have I missed something?' David presses.

'Yes,' Dani and Matt say in unison.

'Did you finally admit you like him? Seriously? Well done, sister. I never thought you would.' He smirks.

'What? I don't even know what you're talking about.'

'Oh come on, you've been in love with him since we were kids.'

'Really?' Alisha asks, all excited.

'No.'

'Yes,' Matt, Dani and David say in unison.

'What would you even know?' I direct my anger towards David. 'You don't know me.'

'You don't own me,' Dani starts singing.

'Not right now, babe,' I beg.

'I know that.'

'Come on, Dotty; you're not exactly cool and aloof,' Matt points out.

'Anyone with half a brain can see it. Except for the dumb and dumber brothers,' Dani adds in.

'I'm going to need you to lower your voice.'

'This drama gets deeper and deeper,' Alisha gleams. 'Seriously! I can hardly keep up. Is that why Adam and Billy can't stand each other?'

'I have no idea. I thought it was cause Adam slept with Billy's girlfriend.'

'He didn't?' David asks, confused.

'No.' My turn for a unison reply with Dani, Matt and Alisha.

'James said he did,' David points out.

'Lindsey's going to be raging when she finds out that's what everyone thinks,' I say.

David takes a second to register that information.

'They why did they fight?'

'Jesus Christ, I feel like I'm in the twilight zone. I'm getting more food,' Dani announces. She heads back towards the buffet.

'We don't know,' I tell my brother.

'I need a drink. You want one?' Matt asks David.

'I'll come with.'

In a matter of seconds, almost everyone's gone.

'So, do you love Adam?'

'Alisha, after these last few days and hearing all the information I've been told. I don't even think I'm sure of my own name.'

'Well, not to confuse you further, but...'

'Stop right there. I don't want to hear any negativity or rumours, especially about Adam.'

'I wasn't going to say any. I was going to say that, in my personal opinion, Adam really likes you.'

'You think?' I ask, suddenly very into this conversation.

'I do, but you could always ask him since he just walked in.'

I get the same whiplash I did the first time. Although this time, it is worth it, because he has just walked in.

With his mother.

Kate is the nicest, warmest and most stylish person to ever leave this village. She's also beautiful; she has long wavy brown hair, bright green/hazel eyes and a Julia Robert's smile. We were always close, but that was before all this drama. I was already nervous to see her, and that was before I slept with her son. I'm absolutely bricking it now.

Oh god, she's seen me.

'DOROTHY!' she screams in enthusiasm.

So she looks excited to see me, which is a good thing. Although, the volume of her excitement has drawn attention to us from the whole room, which isn't a good thing.

I get up to greet her as she comes rushing over, arms open and ready.

'Dorothy, my little cherub.'

She pulls me into a huge bear hug.

'You look incredible, stunning. ADAM! Have you seen this vision?'

I'm overwhelmed; all I can do is stand here, grinning like I'm high. Dani's the only person who compliments me like this usually. It's refreshing.

'Mum, you're embarrassing her.'

'No, you're not, not at all,' I tell her.

I catch Adam's eye; he looks shy and bashful. He gives me a quick half grin. It's adorable and sexy. He also looks incredible. He's wearing a navy blue suit; I've never seen him in a suit. He wears it well.

'How's it been?' she whispers.

Kate has never been one to shy away from an awkward question.

'It's been fine.'

'That's a complete lie, Dorothy. Let's cut that out right now,' she warns me.

She's also never been one to shy away from telling people off.

'Babe, how many macaroons can you eat before you're sick?'

Dani appears back at the table; she has seven macaroons on her plate.

'I would say four,' Kate offers. 'Who's the gorgeous redhead?'

'Whoever you are, I love you,' Dani tells her.

'Kate, this is Dani, my roommate. Dani, this is Kate, Adam's mum.'

'I was Auntie Kate for her first seven years, but she outgrew me.'

'Katherine.'

My mother has made her way over and is now standing two feet away from me. This is the closest she's been to me since I got back.

'When did you get in?'

They do a nice quick hug.

'Adam picked me up from the airport this morning,' Kate answers.

This morning makes sense now.

'I would have been here earlier, but my dad would not stop talking my ear off. He's worse than an old woman, telling me all the village gossip. It was good, though.'

'Well, come on over and see the bride,' Mum instructs.

'Yeah, of course; I just had to see my favourite girl in the world first.' She pinches my cheeks and heads off with my mother in tow.

'That was like a parallel universe, where people are nice to you,' Dani says. 'Adam, your mum is amazing; I love her.'

'You didn't tell me your mum was coming,' I say to Adam.

'Of course she was coming; she wouldn't miss Jane's wedding. I need a drink; you want one?'

'No, I'm good,' I answer.

Does he mean for me to go with him? Should I have said yes?

'Dani? Alisha?'

'I'm good, thanks,' Alisha answers as Dani shakes her head.

He nods, smiles and leaves.

Ok.

I don't get it.

Chapter 27

I'm slightly intoxicated. I'm also infuriated. Every time I try to approach Adam, something or someone gets in my way. I look like a stalker, and since people already think I stalk people, it's not the best look on me. I'm currently perched on the bar, waiting for him to get away from Lucas.

James is getting pretty drunk, too; I'm slightly worried about that.

Matt and Dani have disappeared. I went to the toilet and was gone for only two minutes, and bang, they were nowhere to be seen. I don't even have Alisha; she's sitting with Sarah, Steven and his girlfriend.

I can't stay at this bar much longer; people are looking.

That's it; I'm going inside.

I thought I might find the rest of my trio inside the house, but no such luck. Although no one is here, which means this is where I'm staying. If Adam wants to talk, he'll find me. It'll be hard to refrain myself, but I will.

It's weird how the home you grew up in can feel so foreign. I feel like a guest, a stranger walking through someone else's home. I'm still in some of the family photos, but I'm by far the least featured. Which is saying something, considering my mum hates photos of herself.

The lounge is still the same; it's smaller than the sitting room, but it's homely. It's also the only room downstairs with a TV, which is probably why I spent most of my time here. I had one in my room, but it wasn't the same; I wanted to watch my shows on a comfy couch. I don't have the same comfort feeling I used to have sitting here. It is nice to have a little peace and quiet.

'You hiding?'

God doesn't just hate me; he fucking despises me.

I look up to see Billy leaning against the doorframe. What a prick.

'Yes, now you're it. Go and hide.'

'James is being weird.'

'Is he?'

'Do you know why?'

That's a slightly menacing tone.

I don't know why he's sounding all aggressive, but he should cut it out.

'No, and I couldn't care less.'

'Well, did you say something?' he accuses.

321

'What I say to James is between him and me.'

'No, it isn't actually, and I suggest you stop making trouble.'

'You suggest? Who the fuck are you talking to?' I demand, standing up. I'm pissed off now.

'You're starting to sound like those two Glaswegians: rough and low class.'

'Get the fuck out.'

'This isn't your house. In fact, you're not even welcome here. Are you?'

'I won't say it again. Get out.' I warn.

He's standing there as if trying to intimidate me. People do have two sides to them, and he'll see my other side soon. I might take a lot of shit from people, but we all have our limits.

'Stay away from my brother,' he spits out before walking away

My hands are shaking. I'm that angry, my hands are shaking. What an absolute prick.

'What are you doing?' I know that judgemental tone.

Yeah, it's Mummy, replacing Billy at the door. I'm in a nightmare.

'Just having some quiet time.'

'I meant with Billy. Why can't you stay away from him? This is your sister's wedding.'

'Aw, you know what? You should really get that on a recording; save yourself some time.'

'This is why I didn't want you here. You start trouble wherever you go. I've never known anyone to make such poor life choices.'

Pot calling kettle.

'You didn't want me here? I would never have known. You hid it so well, Mother.'

I've never been this sarcastic towards my mother, but she's pushing me. Actually, it's a combination of everyone.

'Stop acting like a child, Dorothy; you're a grown woman.'

'Yeah, Mum, I am, which means I make my own decisions, the bad and the good. Just like you did.'

Oh shit.

'Don't you dare,' she rages at me, livid. 'And I don't see any good decisions from you. You live in squalor; you have no career prospects; you live with people who are...'

'Alright, Mum, you can think what you like about my life, and yes, there are aspects of it that I would change or that I hoped would be better by now, but Dani are Matt are two of the best people I know. Maybe a little rough around the edges, but they're decent and kind, and Dani has been by my side these last couple of years. She's wiped my tears, found me jobs, covered my bills when I couldn't, and made me laugh. She's someone I can depend on, who I know will always have my back. What the fuck have you done? I might be a mistake, but I'm still you're daughter.'

Oh my god, I think I might faint.

'I shouldn't have to do anything. I have taken care of you your whole life, and I gave you everything you could ever want. This was your mistake to fix. When are you going to grow up? You caused so much pain and dragged our family name through the mud.'

'Jesus, Mum, we're not in a Keira Knightly movie. These are modern times we are living in.'

'Yes, they are, and in these modern times, adult women take care of themselves. Do whatever you want. All I ask is that you stay away from Billy, at least until after the wedding. Then destroy your life however you wish,' she says, in complete disappointment.

With one last look of disapproval, she turns on her heel and leaves. Yeah, God really can't stand me. As I sit back down and put my hands over my face to block out the world, I sense someone walking in. Can't I have two minutes?

'Whoever you are, fuck off.'

'Charming.'

Adam. I look up and see him standing above me.

'Sorry, I thought you were...well, it's a long list.'

I stand up, making us two feet apart.

'You ok?' he asks.

His face is full of concern, which makes me feel instantly better.

'Yeah, it's just my mother being...my mother. How are you?'

A kiss or even a hug wouldn't go a miss.

'Yeah, I heard. What did she mean? When she said, "Stay away from Billy"?'

Fantastic.

'She thinks I'm going to ruin the wedding.' I smile, trying to break this weird, tense feeling. It doesn't work. 'She was being stupid; I have no intention of ruining anything.'

'But, why did she say stay away from Billy? Have you seen him?'

He's jealous. I know I shouldn't, but I actually like it.

'No, she saw him leave here and thought...I don't know.'

'Here? He was in here with you?'

'Yeah, he came in and told me to stay away from his brother.'

I'm doing my best, breezy tone, but he ain't giving it back.

'Why?'

'Oh my god, Adam, 'cause he's a moron. What is wrong with you?'

'Nothing, nothing. I was...Nothing.' He visibly relaxes. 'Hi.'

There's that stupid grin.

'Hi.' I smile back.

He pulls me close to him, wrapping his arms around me. 'Do you want to get out of here?'

He gives me a quick, soft kiss.

'I could be talked into it.'

This time I take the lead and kiss him.

'Ok, ok.' He pulls back from me. 'You win; let's go.'

We leave the lounge, and he takes my hand in his. We head outside, towards the gazebo.

'I just need to go tell Mum I'm leaving,' he says, letting go of my hand and walking ahead.

I shouldn't say it.

'If I ask you something, will you tell me the truth?'

He stops close to the entrance of the tent. 'Yeah, course.'

'You said the fight with Billy was about me. What happened?'

His face has gone from passionate and happy to mistrusting and annoyed. Instantly.

'Why do you care?'

'Because it was about me.'

'But, it's done with; it happened a long time ago.'

'Yes, but I only found out yesterday.'

'I don't think this is about you. I think it's about Billy.'

I don't get what he means.

'What?'

'You clearly still like him.'

'What?'

'I'm such an idiot. Of course, it's always about Billy, and I'm the consolation prize.'

'What?'

I don't love this insecurity of his, and now he's storming off like a child.

'Where are you going, Adam?' I shout after him.

Great, now I'm chasing after him, right into the gazebo.

'Stop following me; I'm going home.'

'Are you actually being serious right now?'

He stops and turns round to face me.

'Do you realise, in every conversation we have, we talk about Billy? For the last, I don't know, eight years or so.'

'I highly doubt that's true.' I know that ain't true 'cause we've barely spoken over the last eight years.

'There's my point. You doubt it, but you can't say it isn't true.'

'You know what, the jealous thing was cute at first, but I'm over it now.'

'Nice, but I'm not jealous. Just over being used.'

'Used? Used! I have never used you. What is even happening right now? I have a curiosity, a reasonable curiosity about something that happened in my life.'

'Four fucking years ago.'

'Four years, forty years; it's all the same.'

327

'Babe.' Dani appears on my right out of nowhere. 'I don't want to interrupt, but I thought you should know; it's a little loud, and people are looking.'

'Did you hear what he said? He's accusing me of using him.'

'Yeah, babe, I heard. Erm, again, people can hear you.'

'I'm not fighting about this,' Adam says. 'You know I'm right; it's always been the same. I don't get this obsession you have, but I'm having nothing to do with it; I'm out.'

'Obsession? I do not have an obsession. You seem to think you know everything, Adam, but you don't know shit.'

'Dorothy Peters, what are you shouting about?' my mum hisses, walking over.

'Not now, Mum, I'm in the middle of something.'

She's standing behind Adam, fuming.

'Sorry, Mrs Peters, we had a little disagreement.'

'Thanks, Adam, but I know you're not the issue here.'

'Thanks for the support, Mum, but I haven't done anything.'

'Oh, you never do, Dorothy.'

'What's happening over here then?'

Looks like it's time for James to join in on all the fun. He comes and stands next to Dani, and he attempts an arm around her shoulder, which she quickly smacks back down.

'Nothing. Go away!' I shout over to him.

'Doesn't look like nothing. Why are you two fighting?'

'We're not fighting. Me and Adam are having a conversation that I would rather not be a group discussion.'

'I think it's time for you and your friends to leave.'

Mum had a little extra disdain in her voice when she said 'friends.'

'You can't kick your daughter out of your home. Again.'

'Daniella, this doesn't concern you.'

Bit of extra disdain again on 'Daniella.'

'Who the fuck is Daniella?' Dani shouts.

'You know what? Mum's right; let's all leave. Adam, let's go.'

'Adam isn't causing the issue,' Mum spits.

'Erm, Adam raised his voice first.'

Dani jumps to my defence. 'Dotty hasn't done anything.'

'What's happening? Dani, have you started a fight?' Matt accuses.

This is getting out of hand; now Matt and David have arrived in our circle of hell. Matt has taken the spot on my left, with David beside him.

'This is ridiculous,' Adam says. 'I'm leaving.'

He turns round to leave, but I grab his arm back round.

'Absolutely not. I'm not finished with this conversation.'

'I am finished with this conversation. You stay here with the people you actually want.'

'Why are you being a complete arsehole? I asked one question, and you're acting like such a whiny little bitch.'

'Dorothy, there is no need for that kind of language!' Mum says. 'It is seriously time for you three to leave.'

'Let me guess. Adam, here, is upset about the whole Billy situation.'

'Shut the fuck up, James!' I shout.

'Adam, it's alright. We're in the same boat.'

'There is no situation; there is no boat. Adam is being a child and not listening to me. I'm getting annoyed that no one believes that there's nothing between me and Billy, and James; you're going to get a slap in a minute.'

'You're a lot more fiery these days, aren't you? You're also a fantastic liar. I believed you last night, but it was all bullshit, wasn't it?' James says.

'Actually, no, it wasn't. If you're about to tell more fantasy stories you were told from Billy, could you do me a favour and just not?'

'Fantasy stories!' James laughs.

'I'm not being a child; maybe I'm just tired of all this acting like teenagers bullshit,' Adam adds in.

'Dorothy!' my Mum warns, urging me to leave.

'Mum, I will leave in a minute, and I am not acting like a teenager. I literally haven't done anything wrong.'

'Really!' James declares.

James seriously needs to chill with the smarmy tone and attitude.

'Yeah, really.'

I let my stance down by talking like a teenager.

'So you don't count sleeping with Billy the other night as a mistake?'

Oh mother, fucking, Jesus, Mary, shitting bastard.

'For heaven's sake,' Mum gasps.

Why has no one carried my mother away yet? I need her in another room.

'You slept with Billy?' Adam asks in disbelief.

I was really hoping Adam hadn't heard that.

'Of course she fucking didn't.' Matt shouts.

'Billy's a fucking liar,' Dani interjects. 'We've been stuck with her this whole week, other than last night. Think we might have noticed Billy in our room. As if Billy doesn't talk utter shite.'

'Maybe they would believe that, but Billy didn't tell me. My mum did, and she definitely wouldn't lie about that.' James tells the whole fucking gazebo as he looks me dead in the eye.

I can tell his blood is boiling.

'Did you forget her room faces the garden?' he continues. 'She saw you two leave together, half undressed. Classy.'

This is bad. This is horrific, and I have no idea what I'm going to do. Dani and Matt can't lie me out of this.

331

'Are you fucking kidding me?' Adam says. 'You slept with him? What is wrong with you? What was last night? Was that you trying to make him jealous?'

I don't know what's worse, everyone watching this car crash or the look of hurt and disappointment in Adam's eyes.

'Course, it wasn't. Sleeping with him was a huge mistake,' I say quietly.

'Then why fucking sleep with him?' he screams.

'Don't shout at her.' Dani moves herself in between us. 'What she does is her business. If she wants to sleep with every guy in here, she fucking can.'

'I can't believe you are doing this,' Mum says. 'I knew you would ruin this wedding.'

'Oh fuck off, Anna, she didn't kill anyone!' Dani shouts at my mum.

'Thanks, babe, but let's have one argument at a time. Adam, I can explain.'

I totally can't.

'You don't have to,' Matt exclaims.

'Wait, you said, "What was last night?"'

Fantastic, James is using his brain.

'Did you two sleep together?' He starts laughing like a Bond villain. 'Well done, Dotty, you're really going for that slut title.'

'I'd rethink your next words there, James, before I beat you worse than I did your brother,' Adam warns.

'Adam, you didn't.'

Thanks for that, Mum. Loved the shaking of your head in disappointment. One for the core memory bank.

'Aw, he's still defending you. Look, Adam, I'm happy for you, but if I was you, I would definitely get tested.'

Jesus.

Adam just lunged at James. Thankfully, Jake and Matt pulled him back before he could do any real damage. Or unfortunately...I haven't decided yet. I don't even know where Jake came from.

'Alright, maybe we should take a little breather, talk later... or never,' Dani calmly suggests.

'Maybe Dotty should stop being a cheap WHORE!' James kindly screams.

'EXCUSE ME!' Dani screams before Adam gets a chance to attack him again. 'WHO ARE YOU SLUT SHAMING?'

'Volume babe, volume.' I plead. Suddenly aware of the many people looking at me.

'So what, she's a slut, but all you are blameless?'

She actually listened to me; her volume is considerably lower.

'Hypocritical bastards.'

'We heard "Slut" getting screamed; should have known Dotty was involved.' Chloe appears, grinning like those cats from Lady and the Tramp.

Chloe, Billy and Sarah have all arrived on my right; just what we need,

'I would recommend you leave, Chloe,' Dani warns.

'Is that right?'

'Yes. Trust me,' Dani advises.

'So what, because you sound like Vicky Pollard, I'm supposed to be scared?'

'It's time this ended,' my mum demands.

'Actually, no, Anna. I think it's just getting started.'

Dani moves towards Chloe.

'Dani,' I plead.

'No, babe, I've had it with these people thinking they can treat you like dirt.'

'Same,' Matt agrees.

'Why don't we start with James and Sarah?'

Sarah looks terrified as Dani starts her verbal assault. I should stop it, but I somehow can't.

'And how they were sleeping with each other, having an affair, the whole time you and James were together.'

'WHAT?'

I actually got a fright, hearing my brother there. I forgot he was here.

'Is that true?'

'It absolutely is. Tell me again, James, how you have the moral high ground?'

Adam turns again to leave.

'And where you going? You also have no higher moral ground, Adam,' Dani shouts after him.

'Why? 'cause he slept with Lindsey? Who the fuck cares about that?' James spits.

'Who is Lindsey?' Adam asks, confused.

'It doesn't matter. We know you didn't sleep with Lindsey,' Dani tells him.

'What? Yes, he did.'

James is the only one still behind on that one.

'Did you tell that rubbish about my sister to everyone?'

I think that's the first time I've heard Jake speak.

'Who do you think you are?' Jake shoots at Billy.

'I don't know what is even going on.' Billy defends himself.

'Wait! So you were cheating on Dotty the whole time?' David's catching up slowly.

'Not the *whole* time,' James reasons.

'Oh, I'm sorry, James, part of the time, and you let my sister take all that shit?'

All the men are getting heated now.

'Calm down, David; it's all in the past,' James tells him.

'Who is Lindsey?' Adam demands again.

'Billy's ex,' Dani tells him frustratedly.

'That you slept with while they were together,' James accuses.

'No, he didn't. I just told you that!' Dani shouts at him.

'What the hell is going on?' Adam shouts. 'Why is everyone assuming shit about me instead of asking me?'

'Or my sister. Who started this bullshit rumour?' Jake asks.

Billy tries to leave, but David pulls him back.

'I think Jake is directing that at you.' David scowls him.

'I didn't start a fucking rumour; it's what Lindsey told me,' Billy exclaims.

'What the fuck did you say? Don't be talking shite about my sister,' Jake threatens.

'Don't try and act tough, Jake,' James ridicules.

'Fuck off, James.'

'Don't talk to my brother like that,' Billy says.

'Aw, look who has found some loyalty at last.'

Dani apparently hasn't finished her rant.

'Don't start on my boyfriend, you little slut,' Chloe pipes up.

'Someone fill this moron in,' Dani says nonchalantly.

I would prefer that no one does fill her in.

'James, we should leave,' Sarah tells him.

'Really, Sarah? You just want to leave? You don't have anything to say to me? Like, sorry,' I suggest, suddenly finding my own rage. It sometimes takes a while when I'm caught off guard.

'Now isn't the time for this,' she tells me.

'Oh, isn't it? Because your boyfriend there had no trouble airing out my life.'

Is she actually crying?

'Aw, come on, Sarah. Isn't the whole innocent act wearing a little thin?'

'You tell her, babe,' Dani says. 'Acting like butter wouldn't melt after sleeping with all your men.'

Silence. That can't be good.

'What do you mean, "men"?' James questions.

Yeah, I never told him about Sarah and Adam.

'I mean her sleeping with Adam.'

Dani has no issue telling him, though.

'What?' James and Adam say in unison.

'She slept with Adam...' Dani repeats slowly.

'No, I didn't,' Sarah protests.

I can't blame her denial. I don't think everyone is loving their sexual history being put on display like this.

'Liar,' Dani spits.

'No, she isn't.'

Why is Adam backing her up?

'Why do you think that? Is this another bullshit rumour you've been told?'

Oh great, Adam's anger is directed back at me.

'And when was this meant to have happened then?'

'Why are you denying it?' I demand.

'Because it didn't happen. I've never slept with Sarah.'

'You two are quite the double act,' James starts, focusing his attention on me and Dani. 'Lying, scheming, whoring about town.'

'I'll give you one fucking warning to stop right now. I won't have bullshit said to them,' Matt demands, barging forward, to stand in front of James.

Dani pulls his arm back.

'I'm not lying. Sarah told me she slept with you,' I tell Adam.

Suddenly all eyes are on Sarah.

'She's lying; I did not say that.'

'Yes, you did,' Jane tells Sarah.

I have no idea when she got here.

'Jane, I don't know what Dotty told you.'

'She didn't tell me anything; I heard you tell her. I was only about four feet away, and I remember it very clearly.'

'Why would you say we slept together?' Adam demands to know from Sarah.

'Wait! So it didn't happen?' I direct to Adam.

'No!' He sounds angry.

'Sarah! Why did you tell me that?' I ask her. 'Did you do it to hurt me?'

Judging by the look on her face, she definitely did it to hurt me. She looks scared and spiteful. The innocent act is fading.

'You lied about Adam and slept with James behind her back. You bitch,' Dani states.

I turn to focus on Adam; he looks at me for a split second.

'This is fucking ridiculous,' he declares before walking away.

I don't try and stop him this time.

'We weren't seeing each other the whole time,' James announces.

'Yes, you were. Alisha told us, and Andy told her,' Dani says, dropping both siblings in it at the same time.

'Wait, let me get this straight. So, Sarah, you and James were seeing each other while he was with Dotty? And Andy fucking knew?' Jane demands to know.

'Yeah, alright, lay off her.' James leaps to his girlfriend's defence. 'Don't make Sarah out to be the bad one. Dotty's the one who cheated with my brother, then bedded both him and Adam this week.'

'One more word, James...say one more word,' Matt warns.

'Excuse me; she bedded Billy this week?' Chloe moves further into the hurdle.

There are many people who are angry right now. Emotions are flaring; feelings are hurt. Chloe, however, is the only one I would say looks murderous.

'Yeah, your precious boyfriend cheated on you – again. He didn't tell you?'

This is what you call Dani getting her revenge for Chloe's earlier comments.

'YOU FUCKING BITCH!'

Chloe basically flies towards me and slaps me hard across the face. Dani then pulls her, hair-first, to the floor and climbs on top of her. James just made the mistake of putting his hands on Dani, so now Matt has tackled him to the floor. Brilliant, now Billy is putting his hands on Matt.

Only one thing for it. Before I can even think, I'm on top of Billy.

Fuck, fuck, fuck. My hair, my hair. I'm being pulled off Billy. Thank god they've let go. I spin around and see that Jane has tackled Sarah to the ground. I've been flung into a table, probably by my mother, spilling wine and beer all over me before landing face-first on the floor.

'POLICE! Everyone stay where they are and let go of whoever they have.'

I stumble to my feet to see eight policemen charging in.

Perfect, this is perfect.

Chapter 28

Even though I once dated a policeman, I've never actually spent much time in a police station. Which I'm thankful for; they're disgusting. I have blood on my dress. I wasn't sure if it was blood or jam, but it's blood. At least it's not my blood. I feel like shit. Not only was that the worse rehearsal dinner in the history of rehearsal dinners, but now my best friend has been arrested.

The police couldn't not arrest her, to be fair. She was straddling Chloe, slapping her in the face and had a handful of her hair. On the plus side, Chloe also got arrested. She was biting Dani's arm when they walked in. Matt, James and Billy also got arrested since they were all on top of each other, punching. Thankfully, Jane didn't; she let go of Sarah in time to look like a bystander. I also avoided arrest since I looked like a victim, lying on the floor with blood on me. Chloe tried, though, by saying I started the whole thing, which isn't untrue.

'Dot, you should go home; they definitely won't get out until the morning.' Stan, one of James's colleagues, tells me.

'I know, but I won't leave without them.' I give a sorry, I'm taking up space smile.

He smiles back, clearly annoyed.

'To be clear, I mean Matt and Dani. I don't care about the others.'

'Noted.'

My mother is totally going to kill me this time.

'Oh my god, don't go to the toilet whatever you do!' Alisha warns as she takes her seat beside me.

Once the police had taken half the party away, Alisha drove us over here. I was unable to drive myself due to sheer devastation.

'He told me again that they won't get out until morning. You should go home.'

'I'm not leaving you here in this state.'

'Thanks, I really appreciate everything, but the wedding is tomorrow, and you're in it.'

'Do you actually think that wedding is happening tomorrow?'

'She'll calm down.'

After the police arrived, Andy finally appeared. It didn't take long for Jane to lose her shit with him, to the point where I thought the police would arrest her for Andy's safety.

'If you say so, but I'm still going to wait. Especially since I missed the show.'

It turns out that the bridesmaids were upstairs having their nails done for tomorrow. Alisha was not impressed that she wasn't there to witness the disaster for herself.

'You've been really nice to us.'

'I mean, I've been normal.'

'No, you spoke to us, told me the truth.'

'It wasn't because I'm a great person. I am, but that's not why I told you. Truth is, I can't stand Sarah.'

We both can't help but laugh.

'Yeah, I'm really off her too.'

'Why, were you friends with her before?'

'Do you know, thinking back, I don't think we really were. It's a small village, we were the same age, went to school together. It's like when you work with people, and they become your closest friends. Then when you finish working there, most of the time, you never see them again. Because you were never actually friends, you just spent most of your time with them. It's basically Stockholm syndrome.'

'So you're not broken up about her sleeping with James when you were with him?'

'Well, it would make me a pretty big hypocrite.'

'True.'

'To be completely honest, I never even missed her. When it first all happened, I was hurt and upset about losing her, but after a few weeks, I looked back and realised. She's dull and brought nothing to my life. That sounds horrible.'

'Yeah. True, though.' She grins.

'Anything you want to talk about?'

'My life isn't even a fourth as interesting as yours.'

'It wasn't interesting at all until this week.'

'As if! Dani told me all about what you two get up to. Random road trips, adventure days at rage rooms and bouncy castles. She told me, you bought flights to Paris, went in the morning and flew back that night.'

'Yeah, life with Dani is never dull. I meant drama-filled; my life had no drama until this week.'

'Can I ask you something?'

'I feel like you know absolutely everything there is to know about me, but sure.'

'Why did you sleep with Billy? No judgement, just why?'

'Which time?'

'I suppose. All the times.'

'It's a shit reason.'

'I've met him, so I thought it would be.' She grins, nudging my arm.

'The attention. He's very charming when he wants to be.'

'Again, I've met him. He's slimy at best.'

'Yeah, he is. Like I said, it's a small village. Is there a vending machine in here? I'm dying for a drink. All that talking and shouting has given me a dry mouth.'

'No, they have one in the staff room, I think, but they don't like you, so...'

Awesome end to my night.

My neck is killing me, which I guess makes sense since I woke up on Alisha's shoulder. I feel awful; I drooled all down her jacket. I don't know what I'll say when she wakes up.

It's only five in the morning; I must have only passed out for a few hours.

'Now then, what trouble has my little princess got herself into this time?'

I look up to see a six-foot man with a full head of salt and pepper hair, more salt than pepper these days. His brown eyes are looking down on me, filled with love and concern. Everything's going to be ok; my dad's here.

'Dad.' I sigh in relief.

I jump up and run as fast as I can over to him. He wraps me up in a bear hug, and I burst out crying. I don't know if it's 'cause it's been two years or because of the stress I've been under, but I am not in control of my emotions. I'm full-on sobbing.

'Shhh, it's ok, everything is going to be ok.'

'Mr Peters, you've missed everything.'

It must have been my sobbing that woke Alisha up.

'How about you two catch me up.'

I'm surprised they didn't call in backup before releasing everyone. I mean, here we all are, together again, after having a huge fight and being arrested. Dani and Chloe are standing side by side, waiting for their stuff. James and Billy are standing behind them, tension-filled. Matt didn't have anything on him, so he's standing next to me and Dad on the sidelines. Alisha went home since I had my dad with me.

'Tenner says Dani trips her up,' Matt whispers in my ear.

'Dani's smarter than that.'

I'm immediately proven right, although she does shove into her while walking over to us.

'I have never smelled worse in my entire life,' Dani tells us.

I can smell her and wholeheartedly agree.

'And I really need a pee, but was I fuck peeing in there. Hello, who's this?'

'My dad.'

'Aw, hello. I'm Dani, I would shake your hand, but I'm bogging. In fact, no one touch me until I'm clean.'

'Are you ok?' I feel so guilty.

'Course, not like it was my first time.'

'Shocker,' Chloe remarks, walking past us.

'Lovely to meet you, Dani. Why don't we all get out of here?'

'That is an excellent plan, Mr Peters.'

Matt takes the lead, and we all start heading towards the door.

'And no Mr Peters; call me Robert.'

I turn around to see James and Billy both looking in my direction. Being the mature adult I am, I give them the finger before walking out.

Chapter 29

I'm not surprised.
Matt is surprised.
Dani is raging.
Dad's confused.
But surprised, I am not.

We've arrived back at the bed-and-breakfast. Dad said we should get cleaned up, get our stuff and then he would take us back to the house. Once we pulled up and got out of the car, it didn't take long to notice all of our belongings spread across the front entrance in the dirt.

'Ok, I'm about to lose it,' Dani says calmly but coldly.

She walks over, and I swear I can hear her blood boiling.

'Why, Dani? I'm sure there's a perfectly reasonable excuse as to why all MY STUFF is outside with the worms!' Matt shakes with rage.

Dani charges towards the door and starts banging very aggressively on it. Me and Matt start picking up the innocent victims of this war. My poor, pink, fluffy jammies.

'GET THE FUCK OUT HERE!' Dani screams up at the window.

'Dani, would you mind if I handled this?'

Dani looks at my dad, torn. She clearly wants a physical fight.

'Fine.' She walks over to me and Matt.

'Don't tidy up yet, though,' Dad tells us.

We do as we're told, dropping what we are holding.

Kim opens the front door and looks at the three of us with, well, I don't think hatred is a strong enough word for it. She then notices my dad to her left.

'Robert!' Clearly, she's surprised to see him. 'I didn't know you were back.'

'Why are my daughter and her friends' belongings outside?'

Dad is always very calm and collected when he's angry, but you know when he's angry. You fear when he's angry.

'You haven't been here, Robert; your daughter has been up to her old tricks.'

'Is this bitch for real? Are you for real?' Dani shakes her finger at Kim. 'Dotty hasn't done anything, and me and Matt over there definitely haven't done anything to your precious sons. Who, by the way, are complete pricks. You did a grand old job there.'

'There were both happy and doing well – until she came back.'

'Course they were, darling,' Dani shoots back at her sarcastically. 'Matt! Robert said not to touch it.'

I turn round to see Matt stroking one of his shirts, looking pained.

'Sorry, Robert, but she's to blame, as usual.'

You know what? No. I ain't having that.

'I won't take the blame this time, Kim. James, Billy and Sarah have made just as many mistakes as I have.'

'Oh my god, look at my Emporio Armani,' Matt cries.

'Matt, suck those tears back in; there is such a thing as dry cleaning,' Dani says, as sympathetic as always.

'Those jeans are worth more than your car.'

'My car is a pile of shite.'

'Matt, why don't you go upstairs and check that there isn't anything left behind?' Dad tells him.

'Ok, be gentle with my shirts,' he warns Dani.

'They aren't welcome...'

'It isn't a suggestion, Kim.' Dad cuts her off.

Dani and Matt both stop and look over at me, shocked and impressed in equal measure at my dad's commanding and icy tone.

'Go, Matt,' Dani demands.

Matt does as he's told.

'Dani, could you take photos of this personal destruction of private property?'

'Absolutely, yes. Yes, I can.'

Dani whips out her phone and starts snapping like she's a paparazzi.

'I'm sure Trip Advisor will take you throwing your guests out in this manner interesting. I'll certainly be advising my customers and business associates to stay elsewhere in future.'

'There's no need for that.' Kim suddenly sounds professional. 'I shouldn't have let my personal feelings get in the way.'

Dad has sent quite a bit of business Kim's way; she's bricking it now.

'No, you shouldn't have. I'll expect them to have a full refund and a little extra for the damage to their belongings.'

Matt appears back from upstairs.

'No, the devil queen got everything.'

Matt walks back over to us. I'm having flashbacks to when Dad had to come down to my primary school because a teacher called me dumb during class the day before. I went home in tears, and he said he would sort it; he was fuming. The headmaster was terrified, and that teacher never even looked in my direction again.

'I'll expect that refund in the next three hours. I understand defending your children, Kim, but I won't have anyone treat my daughter this way. Especially since she's been nothing but dignified and gracious through all of this.'

Eh. Not sure about that.

'Which isn't something you can say about those pathetic sons of yours.'

Dad's definitely right about that.

'Let's go, sweetheart.'

This is why my dad is my favourite person.

I was hoping we'd just go home for the car, so I could make a clean getaway, but since we couldn't shower at the bed-and-breakfast, we now need to shower at the house. At least we have four bathrooms, so we can get finished quickly and then get the hell out of this village.

'Finally, we're here,' Dani says, exasperated.

We're pulling up outside the house, and Dani already has her seatbelt off and one hand on the door handle. Matt has fallen asleep next to her. I don't blame him; I'm knackered too.

'Ok, of course, you'll be in your old room; Dani can take Jane's old room, they're both already made up, and Matt will be in the guest room downstairs.'

'Dad! We ain't staying here; we'll grab a quick shower, then hit the road.'

'No, that's not happening.'

'I know you want us to be happy families, but it's not going to happen.'

'Your sister called off the wedding. The hotel staff aren't working, the cake can't be delivered, and the wrong drink order came. I need you; our family needs you.'

'I'm not being funny, Robert, but if Jane cancelled the wedding, then the other crap doesn't matter.'

Dani has a point.

My dad can't help but give a small grin at Dani's snarky comment. He turns to me with his big pleading eyes.

'She's upset; she needs her big sister.'

'Fine, I'll talk to Jane, but then we're leaving.'

I get out of the car before he can reply. I'm quickly followed by Matt and Dani. We make our way into the house to be greeted by David and my mum.

'Where is the shower?' Dani demands to know.

'Where's Jane?' I ask David.

'In a bit, babe, first – where is the shower?' she insists. 'We also need clothes. Ours are covered in all sorts.'

'Mainly dirt and insects,' Matt adds.

'I'll show you.' David leads them upstairs, giving me widened eyes as he passes.

'You should go with them; Jane finally fell asleep,' Mum tells me as Dad walks in.

'Ok.'

I head to my old room; hopefully, she didn't throw out my old clothes.

It turns out that Mum didn't throw out my clothes, which is actually unfortunate since I forgot how shit and old they were. I'm wearing ripped combats and a lime green tank top that says *Sunny Days* on it. The combats have a metal piece attached. I look like a middle-aged woman trying to hold on to her youth. What's making it worse is how tight it all feels; great for the old self-esteem. I haven't seen Dani or Matt since we split up, but I'm guessing they're probably still in the shower. I didn't want to leave mine.

I'm currently standing outside Jane's door. I don't want to wake her, but if she does want to get married, she better get moving. I gently knock, no reply. Fuck it; I'll just walk in. I didn't need to worry about waking her; she's wide awake, lying on her bed and staring at her engagement ring.

'Dotty!'

She looks like she's been crying for days. I close the door behind me, walk over and lie down next to her. Face to face.

'Did you have fun last night?' I ask her.

'So much.'

'My favourite part was the food. It was very nice.'

'Mum choose it all. I did pick the macaroons, though.'

'Dani was a fan of them...I hear we aren't having a wedding today.'

'You heard right.'

'How does Andy feel about that?'

'Upset.'

'How do you feel about it?'

'Upset.'

The only thing I've been certain of this week is that Andy loves my sister.

'Did you cancel because of me?'

'He let us all believe that...you were the only one in the wrong. He should have told me the truth.'

'I don't know. He wasn't in the best position...I would find it impossible to betray Dani's trust.'

'You're my sister.'

'I know! But what James and Sarah did doesn't matter. It doesn't change anything.'

'It changes everything. If I had known that, I wouldn't have...'

'You wouldn't have what? Disowned me? It shouldn't have mattered; you should have had my back anyway.'

I don't want to pile more on top of her, but it needs saying.

'I know. I'm sorry,' she whispers.

'I forgive you,' I whisper back, kissing her forehead.

'How? After everything.'

'Because life is short, and I love you...Do you want to get married?'

'Yes,' she pouts, her little bottom lip quivering. 'But it's too late. Everything's fallen apart. It's karma coming for me; it's over.'

'What did I always tell you growing up? That there was nothing I couldn't fix.'

She narrows her eyes at me.

'Other than my own life.' Didn't think that needed pointing out. 'If you want to get married today, we can make that happen.'

'You would do that for me?'

'How many times? You are my baby sister.' I can't stop the tears; they are flowing on both of us now. 'There's nothing I wouldn't do for you.'

'I really am sorry,' she cries.

'I know.' I pull her into a hug. 'And I really do forgive you…first things first though, you need to phone Andy. Make sure he still wants to marry you,' I tease.

'This is true. Can you do me a favour?'

'I'm about to save your wedding.'

'I know, but I really need you to change first. I don't want anyone to see you like that.'

'Agreed.'

Now that Jane and Andy are sorted, she phoned him; they cried, all is forgiven, blah blah blah. Now, I need to fix everything else. I'll need help, though, so I've enlisted the help of my A-Team. I have Dani, Matt, David and Jake. Maybe A-Team is being generous since they're tired, cranky and unwilling. We've gathered in the living room to plan our attack of action.

'So, Jake, you're good to get the cake, right? You know where you're going?'

'Yes. I think so.'

Good enough.

'Perfect, do your best. The rest of us need to head to the hotel and set up.'

'Who plans a wedding in a big, stupid, empty hotel with no staff?' Dani remarks, bewildered.

'That's why Mum hired staff, the same staff that have called in sick. I've already called about the booze. They can't deliver the correct order, so we need to set up the hotel, then take the booze from there to the warehouse and collect the right stuff.'

'How come Jake, over there, gets to pick up the cake?' Matt questions me.

'He has a car, and you can't even drive.'

He says it's a personal choice to protect the environment, but Dani told me he failed the test eleven times.

'How big is this hotel?' Dani asks.

'Big,' my darling brother replies.

I was trying to downplay the old hotel, which is now rentable event space.

It's stunning, though. It was built in the eighteen hundreds, has a huge grand ballroom, and an impressive entrance hallway with chandeliers. The rooms are filled with oak wood furniture, and then there are the gardens, which are incredible. A vast expanse of stunning greenery is surrounded by rose bushes, flower patches and enormous oak trees. Then surrounding that is a steam of water with pebbles and the cutest little bridge going over it, the perfect location for a wedding. Or at least it would be if it was already set up and it wasn't raining. Rain, which is getting heavier by the second, so the outdoor ceremony is out the window.

'Look, I know this is shit, and none of us want to fill a huge-ass ballroom, but the owners aren't thrilled that all the chairs, tables, and all the other crap is currently taking up their whole entrance space. We gotta move.'

'Don't we need more people? I would love more people.' Dani looks between the five of us, unimpressed.

'We don't have more people. All the other people who would help us are in the wedding,' I explain.

'I'm in the wedding,' David points out.

'Groomsman number four doesn't count. Plus, you're my brother; you need to help me. Now! We really need to go; the wedding has been pushed back to three, meaning we have just six hours. Time to hustle, people.'

Six hours to decorate, get the booze, get the cake, get ready and mentally prepare myself. Piece of piss.

I only wish the hotel wasn't an hour away.

Chapter 30

I can't do this.

It is not going well.

I mean, it isn't going terribly either, which I guess I should take as a win. David and Dani did great. Dani walked in and immediately went into boss bitch mode. She set out a plan of where to put the chairs and tables, where the altar should go, blah, blah, blah. David helped with the heavy stuff. He moved most of it into the ballroom, and then he packed up all the booze into the car for him and Dani to take back to the warehouse.

They left ten minutes ago, leaving me and Matt.

We don't know where to start.

We have our plan that Dani drew, but the tables are too heavy for our weak little arms. We are currently standing in the doorway of the ballroom.

'I ain't breaking my back setting up this room.'

'Yes, Matthew, you've said.'

The caterers are arriving any minute to start cooking; I think the kitchen is ready.

'Excuse me.'

Why do people keep sneaking up behind me? It's two women holding white ribboned boxes.

'Sorry, didn't mean to scare you. We're with Conner and Holly.'

Yep. No idea what that means.

'I'm sorry, I don't know who you are or who Conner is. Or who Holly is.'

'We're delivering the centrepieces and table decorations.'

'And who's setting them up?' I ask, panicked.

'Er. You.'

I didn't even think about that. I thought we would just set up tables and chairs. Crap. I don't know how to decorate tables all nicely. I'm not creative.

'Seriously, Dotty, I could kill you right now,' Matt angrily tells me with a thunderous stare.

He blames me for everything, although I did volunteer us for this.

'We'll leave the rest in the hallway,' one of the women nervously tells us.

'Thank you.'

Both women make their quick getaway.

Looking at this room isn't going to do anything.

'We should really get started,' I tell him.

'I'm not moving all that shit. Look at you, you weak ass bitch. How are we gonna do this alone?'

'How about some help?'

Turning around, we see a nervous Adam waiting in the hallway. He's surrounded by white boxes, tables and chairs. It's making me want to cry. We are never getting this done in time.

'I mean, as strong as you look, Adam, one more ain't gonna make much difference,' Matt snarls.

'Couldn't hurt, though,' I add.

I'm annoyed at him. I know he was upset and caught off guard, but he just left. Left me in the firing line. He also hasn't called or sent a text. To, you know, make sure I'm ok. I'm actually really annoyed.

'Great, it should only take 14 hours now,' Matt huffs.

How that boy has his own business baffles me.

'Well, then, we better get started,' Kate declares, striding in behind Adam, grinning. 'What, you think I'm too weak too?' Kate questions Matt.

'I think *I'm* too weak,' Matt reasons.

'The more, the merrier,' I tell them.

We've made progress. Not much, but something is better than nothing.

The tables are in place. The chairs are half in place. Jake arrived about ten minutes ago with the cake; he was soaked through. Apparently, we now have a thunderous rainstorm outside. Amazing.

Adam has kept his distance; obviously, he's been busy, but he's had enough time to apologise. I bet he's waiting for me to apologise; well, I ain't. He was a right whiny arrogant git last night.

But that's not the task at hand. The task at hand is me sitting out in this hallway, putting together the table centre-pieces.

'Looks like you're having some problems there.'

Kate isn't wrong. I'm looking through all the table decorations, and I have no clue how to make all this look impressive.

'I don't even know what half this stuff is.'

'I'll take care of the tables,' she kindly offers.

'Really? Thank god.'

'How are you, sweetheart?' She kneels down beside me.

'Good. I'm just trying to fix this wedding.' I offer a reassuring smile.

'It's very nice of you to do this.'

'Well, let's be honest. I'm not doing a great job.'

'Well, you did have a big night last night.' She shrugs, giving me the side eye.

Please tell me she is not wanting to talk about it, especially the parts involving her son.

'It was certainly a night to remember. Where should we start with all this?'

'I think it was for the best.'

'I don't know about that.'

'It was about time you stuck up for yourself. You bottle stuff up. You don't say what you want, and you let people walk all over you.'

Fuck's sake. Don't protect my feelings or anything.

'Well, I don't think...'

'You do.' She cuts me off. 'I think you need more family fights, especially with your mother.'

'I don't think that would be very nice for me.'

What is she on?

'You two need to talk. I know you've never spoken about... you know...But I think it would be good for you two.'

She is definitely on something.

'I don't think that.'

'It will be difficult. I'll admit.'

'Kate. It's not even an issue.'

She looks at me like I've said the sky is green and the earth is flat.

'It isn't. Mum has an issue. I don't.'

'There's nothing you want to ask her?'

'Nothing,' I snap.

'I know you think that she thinks you're some kind of...'

She pauses, probably trying to think of the best word for mistake.

'Mistake,' I say, helping her out.

'She doesn't think that. I know that's how it seems some-times.'

Sometimes! Sometimes?

'Kate. I'm not ten years old anymore. I'm the biggest mistake of Mum's life. If I wasn't already sure about that growing up, she actually said the words two years ago.'

'She says things all the time she doesn't mean.'

'Our relationship is what it is. I've made peace with that.'

This week really has been one hell of an emotional roll-ercoaster. What does she think is going to happen? Me and Mum have one heart-to-heart, and all our problems are solved. Our problems can't be fixed. I'm a constant reminder of her shame and embarrassment.

'This isn't my place, and I don't want to upset you, but you need to know. No one has ever thought you were a mistake.'

I'm sleep deprived. That's why my eyes are watering.

'We could put the candles in the middle of the tables.'

'Sweetheart,' she whispers.

'I don't need protecting, Kate; I know how it is. I mess up Mum's picture-perfect family, and when I'm not here, she can pretend it never even happened: that I don't exist. Unlike when I am here, then she can't pretend. It's best that we just get through this day, and then I go home,' I reason. 'Now, candles in the middle, yes or no?'

'No, we should use flowers,' she suggests, thankfully realising this conversation is over.

'They haven't been delivered yet.'

Thank god that's over.

We've managed, by some grace of god, to finish the layout. The flowers still aren't here yet, which make up most of the decorations, so that's annoying. There are around twenty round tables around the room, each set for ten. Then there's the long top table with eight seats; we also have a side table, which will be set up with the cake and extras. Kate has set up a prototype table, minus the flowers, which looks great. Jane has gone with a gold and blush pink colour scheme. The table has a gold vase in the centre, which will be filled with flowers. The table cover is natural Belgium linen with a blush pink runner, and the cloth napkins are also blush pink with a gold band. Then there's a tall blush pink candle in a gold holder on either side of the vase. The cutlery is gold, very grand looking.

Kate has also set up a table in the hallway in the same Belgium linen with a pink runner decorated with candles and the wooden guest book. There's a Welcome sign next to it, wooden with a pink centre and gold writing. That will also be decorated with the soon-to-be-delivered flowers. It's starting to come together; I'm starting to have faith that we can do this.

'DOTTY!' Dani screams frantically from the hall.

That doesn't sound good.

'What the fuck now?' Matt heads to the door, exasperated.

Me, Jake, Kate and Adam follow to see Dani drenched, covered in mud and raging.

'Have you seen outside?' she rages at me.

'We know it's raining,' I calmly tell her.

'RAINING?' she screams, infuriated. 'First of all, it's a fucking tsunami. Second of all, there is a great big, massive mudslide. Look at my shoes. LOOK at them!'

'Where's David?' Adam asks her.

'That coward, he's hiding in the car.'

'Ok, I know this isn't great.' Kate calmly takes control of the room. 'But Dani, could you please not walk in here any further?'

Kate gestures to the mud tracks Dani has trampled in.

'Fine, I'll not walk in further, but I ain't carrying all that booze myself. So I won't be the only one tracking in the dirt.'

'These shoes cost me two hundred pounds,' Matt states.

There isn't a chance in hell they were two hundred pounds. He's wearing crappy red trainers.

'No one is in their outfits yet, so we'll all go,' I say, volunteering everyone.

Dani wasn't exaggerating. It's like The Day After Tomorrow out here. The rain is thundering down, with a charming, powerful wind accompanying it. There are only ten steps to the entrance, which would be fine if the car was at the bottom of them. Unfortunately, the lovely mudslide Dani was talking about has taken over the dirt track/driveway from the car to the stairs. Basically, the hills surrounding the driveway have become waterfalls, crashing down onto the dirt-covered road, creating a mudslide. Both their cars are parked about five minutes away. I think David's car actually looks stuck. We're currently standing side by side at the entrance; Dani, Jake, me and then Adam. All we're doing is staring at the car. Matt and Kate passed on helping.

'He couldn't get closer?' Jake asks.

The look Dani gives him is hilarious. Brutal, so brutal, in fact, he moves away from her and stands next to Adam.

'Well, we can't stand here all day.' Adam points out the obvious.

'On you go then, Adam.' Dani gestures to the I'm a Celebrity style mud challenge. 'Honestly, babe, this might push our friendship to the limit.'

You would think I was asking her to walk through fire.

'You love a challenge,' I challenge her.

'You know I hate the wind.'

There is no other way for it. I take the first step and head down the stairs, instantly regretting it. The cover over the entrance was protecting me from the wind. A huge gust just whipped right into my face. At least I've been followed after my first step. Adam and Jake have already overtaken me down the stairs. Dani is behind me. I can't see her, but I can hear her.

'Fucking Highlands in the fucking winter,' she rages.

We make it down and start walking over the wet, sticky mud. It wouldn't be so bad if we were walking over a smooth road, not an unused road made out of stones and dirt. It's very hard to walk over now, so god knows how I'll carry heavy drinks over it.

'You two alright back there?'

'Fuck off, Adam.' Dani answers for both of us.

'It's not that bad,' he reasons.

'Not that bad! I'm definitely getting hypothermia from this bullshit. And it will be your fault, Dotty.'

Course it will be.

We've finally made it to the car.

David rolls down his window.

'I'm not feeling this.'

'Get out of the car,' I demand.

'Seriously, though, I'm in the wedding. I shouldn't do this.'

He might be the oldest, but with one look, he gets right out of the car.

He opens the boot of the car, and it's packed with booze, as is the entire back seat. Clearly, the wrong order they took back was also only half the actual order, as Dani's car is also completely packed.

With only the five of us, this could take a while.

The wedding starts in three hours.

Two hours and thirty-eight minutes until the wedding. We're fucked.

Physically and time-wise.

We have managed to empty Dani's car and half of David's, but my back is broken. I'm also soaked through. I mean, we all are, but I only have enough sympathy left for myself. We're all making our way back through the brown slush to the car.

'You know if you two carried more, we would be finished by now,' David groans.

'And if you don't shut it, I'll punch you in the face,' Dani warns my brave brother.

'Well, it's hard to be scared by you when you can only carry one box. Thought Glaswegians were meant to be tough.'

I don't know if it's what he said or if Dani's limit has been met. But with that comment, she leapt over and shoved my brother face-first into the slush.

'WHAT THE ACTUAL FUCK!' David screams.

He is completely covered. I thought my trainers being covered was bad enough. Adam and Jake are hilariously laughing at him. David has now found his feet and is chasing Dani over the slush.

'DON'T YOU DARE!' she screams at him.

While running from David, she attempts to hide behind Jake, but only manages to pull at him, causing him to fall onto his ass.

'Oh, man.'

'Shit, I didn't mean that.'

'Karma!' David tells him before picking up a makeshift mud ball and hurling it at Dani.

It misses and smacks Adam in the face. Although in her attempt to avoid the mud ball, Dani slipped and is now in the slush. I can't help but burst out laughing. They all don't seem to be impressed by my laughter, seeing how I'm not covered in dirt. Without even looking at each other, they all start chasing after me. I mean, come on. My little legs can't handle this. Great, that didn't take long. I think I took three steps before crashing down into this disgusting muck.

'Oh, babe, you looked like Bambi there.' Dani laughs at my misfortune.

It's horrible, wet, slimy, and it smells.

'Here, let me help.'

Adam is towering above me, his hand held out. Now isn't the time to be proud. He helps me to my feet but holds on to my hand longer than he needs to.

'WHAT THE FUCK IS HAPPENING HERE?'

We turn around to see Andy and two groomsmen standing at David's car.

'GIVING YOU A MAGICAL DAY!' Dani screams back, still laughing.

Thank god. This means I don't need to carry another box.

Chapter 31

As this hotel is now a rentable space, the old rooms are included, meaning the showers are in working order, thank the lord. I don't know if they accounted for me and my mini tribe taking a room, but it's too late now. We have truly set up shop. All our luggage is now inside and currently tossed all over the room. We have used every towel, and we're all currently in the provided robes. This room is ours, and what a room it is. Talk about a step up from the little room of horrors. There are two queen-sized beds, an actual bath and a shower. It's a tad old-fashioned in its décor, but classy and comfortable. There's a proper makeup table too, a couch by the window and the best part: there is a TV. We've all missed TV.

I'm showered and currently getting wedding-ready; Dani is still in the shower. I don't think she'll come out, to be honest. There's still loads to do, but I thought I might as well get semi-ready. Makeup and hair are done. I went with a half-up half-down look with soft, loose curls. Makeup is pretty basic, soft semi-glam. My look doesn't exactly go with my joggers and T-shirt get-up, but I ain't setting tables in my dress.

'DANI! I'm heading back down.'

She doesn't care.

This place is both beautiful and slightly creepy. With no other guests here yet, I'm walking down this hall in complete silence. I hope, since Matt and Kate weren't in need of a shower, they've got most of the work done. So that I can sit down, eat and get drunk. The way weddings should be.

Oh great, there's Adam. Right at the end of the hall.

'Is that what you're wearing?' he asks as I get within five feet of him.

'Yeah, thought I would give my mum something else to criticise,' I say, sounding as unbothered as I can.

He always looks like he wants to say something important but then doesn't.

'Well, I'd better get back down to the madness.'

I go to move past him, but he grabs my hand and pulls me over into a random cupboard.

'Sorry, I need a minute.'

'Oh, do you? Well, I need to go sort my sister's wedding, so move.'

'I only want two minutes.'

'Fine. Two minutes. Go.'

'I'm sorry about last night. I shouldn't have started that whole argument.'

'No, you shouldn't have.'

'And I shouldn't have left the way I did.'

'Right again, you shouldn't have.'

He signs, getting annoyed. Maybe I should apologise too, but I don't want to.

'You were right; what you do isn't my business,' he says, slightly irritated.

'It isn't.'

'Would you give me a break? I'm apologising.'

'So you should.'

'Seriously! There's nothing you would like to apologise for?'

'Absolutely nothing.'

'Really? How about all the shit about Sarah?'

'That wasn't my fault.'

It's weird. Like I know I'm not innocent, but I can't seem to admit it. I think this is a common problem for me.

'You are so goddam stubborn. If it wasn't for you not being honest and just talking to me, then all this could have been avoided.'

Well, since he's raising his voice, I will too.

'Me? What about you? Ok, I shouldn't have slapped you without telling you why I was slapping you, but why wouldn't I believe Sarah? And what about you?'

'What about me?'

Why can't I remember? Shit, what was my point? Oh yeah.

'You were flirting with everyone.'

'When?'

'Whenever you came to visit.'

'You mean when you were seeing James? Not to mention making eyes at Billy.'

'Eh? I didn't do that.'

'Bullshit, why do you think we fought?'

'Why did you batter him?'

'Because he was talking shit about you, but unlike you, I didn't believe it. Then he tried to punch me, so I knocked him out.'

We are both getting louder and louder by the second.

'What did he say?'

'That you were all over him and trying it on daily.'

'Was I fuck.'

'I KNOW, that's why I decked him.'

'Well, you should have told me.'

'You should have told me about the Lindsey and Sarah bullshit.'

'Well, I was upset and angry.'

'Why? I was single, and you were either with James or kind of with James.'

'Stop pretending to be thick. You know, you've always known how I feel about you, and you know that all it would have taken was one word, and James would have been history.

One word, and yes, ok, I might have flirted a bit with Billy to make you jealous. I admit it.'

I shouldn't have said that. Now I look desperate.

'What word?' he asks softly, moving closer.

I'm glad the shouting has stopped, although now my adrenaline is dying down, and I don't know what to do. He's looking right at me, my mouth is dry, and I feel faint.

'Anything. You could have said any word you like,' I whisper.

'I would never have touched Sarah...and I was jealous,' he says, completely serious.

He pulls me to him, lips straight onto mine, and we fall back against the wall. I should be helping downstairs, and we should probably talk more, but he's really good at all of it.

This looks amazing; the ballroom is stunning. The florist finally arrived. The tables are all done, and it looks like a professional setup. Andy says the booze is all set up, the chefs are sorted in the kitchen, and the humanist has arrived. The ceremony room is beautiful and ready. The wedding party have all arrived and are getting ready upstairs, leaving me and Dani to marvel at our handiwork. We didn't do all of it, but we did enough to feel proud. We've actually pulled this off.

'Who's serving the dinner?' Dani asks.

Fuck, I forgot we have no staff.

'I think it might have to be...'

'Us?' She cuts me off. 'It's us, right? Fantastic. I lift heavy objects, put out flowers everywhere, even though I have extreme hay fever, and now I get to serve two hundred people fish or chicken.'

'It's beef or salmon.'

'Like that fucking matters.'

'I'm sorry, Dani. I know this hasn't been the best adventure you've ever had.'

'It has not, but it's had its moments.'

'Like paintball.' I can't hide my smirk.

'That was fun,' she smirks back at me. 'The drive up was also kinda fun, and the morning at that bed-and-breakfast was hilarious.'

'Laser tag was fun.'

'Yeah, karaoke was a laugh. The hike too.... Actually, we have had a good week. Plus, we both got some,' she laughs.

'We sure did.' I smile at her. 'Thank you for coming with me and for making me come...I couldn't have done this week without you.'

'I got your back, babe.'

'And I've got yours. Even if you never actually need me.'

'I do.' She wraps her arm around me. 'Even if I don't tell you, I do.'

If the last two years have taught me anything, it's that having a good friend can change everything. They make the bad bearable and the good great.

'Once the food is served, we can join the party.'

'Babe! We *are* the party,' she states matter-of-factly. 'Now, are you going to tell Matt he's helping or make me do it?'

'Shall we both tell him? Take the wrath of Matt together.'

'Tell me what?'

We turn around to see a panicked Matt standing by the entrance. Aw, he's dressed in his suit; that's a waste.

Chapter 32

I never thought my sister would be a bridezilla, but she definitely is. I'm in the bridal suite with Jane, my mum, Alisha and Kate. Mum is completely ready and is wearing a lilac dress and jacket combo; she looks beautiful. Her hair is pinned, and she's wearing hardly any makeup. Alisha is wearing, I'm guessing, the bridesmaid dress. It's blush pink, silk, floor-length, one-shoulder and sleeveless. Alisha has her curls flowing loose and looks amazing. Kate looks immaculate as always; she's wearing a mid-length, surplice neck, off-the-shoulder red dress. Her makeup is glam, and her hair is down and straight. Jane isn't ready; her hair and makeup are, though. Her hair is pinned, and her makeup is glam, flawless.

'This is ridiculous, an absolute circus. We're cancelling, rearranging. I won't have this,' she shouts, pacing up and down in her bridal robe. 'What's the point? If it's already ruined, why go ahead? This is the worse wedding in the history of weddings.'

Even Mariah Carey would admit she's being slightly dramatic.

'Jane, we are not cancelling,' Mum tells her.

'We have no wait staff, no bartender. There's a thunderstorm outside.'

'It's fine. Me, Dani and Matt are going to serve,' I say, trying to calm the situation.

'Don't be stupid. My sister is not serving at my wedding.'

'Well, Dani thinks she caught hypothermia today, and Matt said he's definitely slipped a disc, so that can't all be for nothing,' I argue.

'I can serve,' Alisha offers.

She really is a sweetheart, that girl.

'None of the goddam bridesmaids are serving, Jesus Christ.'

Jane finally stops pacing and throws herself down on the bed.

'Your hair, Janey!' Mum shrieks.

'Doesn't matter, Mum, this is the most disastrous wedding in history.'

'Janey, would you please get a grip?' Mum sighs, exasperated. 'The wedding is happening. Let's get through the ceremony and worry about the dinner after.'

The door swings open, and a hyper Dani bounces in.

'Right, the wait staff are sorted. I've called in a few favours, and they'll be here in two hours. Can I start drinking now?'

'Staff are coming?' Mum asks her, perplexed.

'I used to work near Perth, in this hell hole hotel. Still got friends there and a few who moved further north. So help is coming.'

'Thank you,' Mum says sincerely.

'That's amazing; can't believe you did that,' I say, genuinely shocked.

'Come on, babe, did you really think I was going to serve? Grow up.'

'Well, it looks like we have a wedding today, then.'

'It's still a disaster, the weather, no best man,' Jane rattles off.

'What do you mean? Where's James?' I ask.

Everyone in the room turns to look at me. What?

'Obviously, he's disinvited,' Jane points out.

'But he's Andy's best friend.'

'Dot! Come on. After what he did.'

'Alisha, do you have his number?'

'Yeah,' she hesitantly replies.

'Can I use your phone?'

'Dot!'

'Jane! He's coming. I'm ok with it, so you're ok with it.'

Alisha hands over her phone. I know it's weird that I, of all people, will be the one to call him, but he should be here. Yes, I'm still angry, and yes, he was a dick, but I'm the bigger person. It's ringing.

'Hello?'

I hang up. I panicked.

'Babe, come on.' Dani berates me.

Ok, I'm ok now. Try again.

'Hello?'

'James-it's-me-get-your-suit-on-and-get-over-to-this-wedding.' I hang up straight away. That was plenty. Enough said. 'He's on his way.'

'I mean, did he even breathe? Let alone reply.' Dani asks.

'He'll come.'

He will. It would have been hard for him to miss it. He and Andy are close.

'Alright then, I guess we should get ready,' Jane says, with a hint of excitement.

'Someone pop some champagne and put the tunes on. This is a fucking wedding,' Dani demands.

That it is.

She looks incredible, absolutely stunning. My sister can wear a wedding dress. Floor-length, ivory, lace, thin straps, in at the waist, out at the bottom, with a low neckline. I got teary-eyed and emotional when I saw her. Mum was fine; her eyes didn't tear up, not even a drop.

'Right, Dani, we should go and get ready ourselves since it's almost go-time. Double check with Matt that everything is still in order.'

'Again?' Dani huffs at my request.

'Yes, again! Jane, stay calm, and we'll see you down there.'

'Wait! Er, I have a...' Jane stumbles. 'I have your dress.'

'My what? My dress is in the room.'

My horrible, disgusting dress.

'No, no, I have your bridesmaid's dress.' She blushes.

'Bridesmaid dress?'

'She won't fit into Chloe's dress,' Dani points out.

That felt unnecessary.

'It isn't Chloe's. It's Dotty's.'

'You got me a bridesmaid's dress?'

'You're my sister.'

I'm getting teary again. Dani will need to redo my makeup.

'How did you know I would come?'

'I didn't, but I hoped you would after getting the invite.'

'You sent the invite?'

'Again, you're my sister.'

Great, she's getting teary, and her makeup artist has already left.

'Aw. Kodak moment,' Alisha beams.

'Right, ok, come on, Dotty. Get ready; no time to waste.' Mum says, breaking the moment.

'I will.'

'Thank god, 'cause her dress was horrible,' Dani confesses.

I can't argue. It was. This also means Billy didn't send the invite; one more lie he told me. With every new piece of information about Billy, I feel stupider and stupider.

The ceremony was beautiful. I cried more than I did when I watched Dear John, and I cried for days after that movie. I was traumatised. Andy could hardly finish his vows, he was crying that much. It was sweet at first, then got kind of annoying. Matt was another one who wouldn't stop crying, although watching Dani roll her eyes at him every two minutes was really funny.

We then spent what felt like eight years outside taking photos. The downside to being in any wedding party: stand here, hold that, smile, laugh, look up, it was never-ending. I was finally released back into society and made a beeline for the bar, the free bar. Before anyone could ask me to do anything or talk to me, I hurried off to the back room of the hotel. I think it was the back office in the glory days. Now it's only a small room with a couch and a side table. Right now, though, it's perfection. I have a large gin, with peace and quiet.

Who is knocking on this door and ruining my alone time?

'I know you're in there, sweetheart.'

I hear my dad's soft and comforting voice.

'No, I'm not.'

He takes that as his opening and comes in.

'So this is where you've been hiding.'

'I'm not hiding.'

'No one has seen you in thirty minutes.'

'I haven't missed dinner, have I?'

He takes a seat next to me.

'Don't worry. It's not out for another twenty minutes.'

Thank god; I'm starving.

'Everything else ok?'

'Your sister has finally relaxed, and your brother seems happy enough. It's you I'm worried about.'

'I'm good, great even. Me and Jane are good; the wedding is going smoothly. Dani and Matt have stopped complaining. I'm good, Dad.'

'I spoke to Kate.'

Thank you very much, Kate. I won't have this conversation, especially with Dad looking so hurt right now.

'You know, Kate; she always wants to play peacemaker.'

'I don't want to upset you. I don't want to have this conversation, but I only plan on having it once.'

He's in total dad mode. Stern, protective and uncomfortable.

'Dad, we don't need to talk about anything,' I plead.

'You don't need to say anything. I only need you to know, without a shadow of a doubt, that you are not, nor have you ever been, a mistake.'

'Dad,' I whisper. 'I know you love me...'

'Dotty.' He cuts me off. 'I'm not going to sit here and explain in great detail my overwhelming love, pride and adoration of my three children. The thing I want to make painfully clear to you is that you were very much wanted.'

'I'm an adult, Dad. I know it broke your heart what happened.' My voice breaks. 'And the way that mum looks at me...'

I can't help the tears, now streaming down my face, from ruining my makeup. This isn't about my dad. I know he loves me; he's never treated me any differently from David and Jane. If anything, I'm the favourite, or maybe the one he just worries the most about. It's my mum who treats me differently, my mum who clearly doesn't think the same about me as she does my siblings. As if it's my fault, she left Dad for another man and then got pregnant.

'I had never felt worse in my life after your mum left. I understood, though; I was always at work or on work trips. David was only a baby; she was alone.'

I hate that he's putting himself through this, reliving his worst nightmare.

'After she got pregnant with you...'

'I know, Dad, you did the honourable thing. For David... and for me.'

'I didn't do the honourable thing. I love your mother, always have and always will, but after she left, I didn't think she would be back. I thought we would move forward, stay friends and co-parent David together...even after...he left.'

I can see his neck tensing at the very thought of my biological father.

'I wasn't thinking we would get back together...then I found out she was pregnant...You weren't something I had to accept or put up with. You're the reason we reunited. You put our family back together...without you...we wouldn't have Jane. Not wanted? You are my daughter; you have always been my daughter.'

'I know.' I nod.

'I hope you do, but just in case you don't. I'll be telling you every day until there isn't a doubt in your mind.'

This is the most we've ever spoken about it. My grandmother told me when I was fourteen, then me and mum had a very brief and emotionless conversation. Since then, it's been an unspoken truth that we all know and don't talk about. As far as I've always been concerned, my dad is my dad. The one who has raised me, loved me and supported me my whole life.

'I love you, Dad.'

He pulls me into a tight bear hug.

'I love you, my perfect beautiful girl.' He kisses my forehead and pulls away. 'Now, tell me about this you and Adam situation.'

Absolutely not.

Chapter 33

It turns out this wedding isn't the disaster I thought it would be. I'm actually having a good day. Which I didn't think would have been possible twelve hours ago. The only downside is my bloated stomach. The meal was great, but since Jane got my dress in a size ten, I'm feeling the pinch, even with the support of Dani's spanks.

Matt got sauce all down him, so our trio are back in our room, dealing with the disaster. Well, Matt is, me and Dani are sitting on the bed eating cupcakes. There's a whole dessert table downstairs, with cupcakes, macaroons, retro sweets and cookies; it's exquisite.

'Who fucking serves a meal swimming in gravy?' Matt shouts from the bathroom, frantically scrubbing his shirt over the sink.

'Who spills gravy down their shirt when they're a grown-ass man?' Dani shouts back through a mouthful of cake. 'Just put on another shirt.'

'Not before I salvage this one.'

'It's gone, Matt, let it go. Buy cheaper shirts.'

'Dani, shut up.'

'We should go dance and get drunk,' Dani suggests.

'I agree.'

'Then you can go find Adam and make up.'

'I think we already did.'

'You did?'

'Yeah. I think. Maybe.'

Did we? Or was it like a hate-sex thing for him? I haven't actually seen him since. That's the thing with weddings, everything happens so fast, and before you know it, the day is over. It's already eight.

'Well, then let us go find out.'

'No, he can find me.'

'Really?' she asks, shocked. ''cause you're looking absolutely gorgeous. Like, the best I've ever seen you look.'

Is that a compliment? Although she ain't wrong. I do usually look more scruffy and Vicky Pollard adjacent.

'But what's the point though? We're going home tomorrow.'

'Yeah, but I thought things might have changed,' she says, awkwardly avoiding eye contact.

She thinks I'm staying.

'Nothing has changed. We're going home tomorrow.'

'You've made up with your family; people aren't branding you with the letter A. You aren't slightly tempted to move home?'

'It's taken being back here to realise that I don't miss this village. I miss our flat; I want to go home, order in Chinese and binge Netflix with my best friend.'

'How about Chinese and Indian?' She grins.

'Perfect.'

'What about Adam?'

'What is it you always say? If it's meant to be...'

'It'll be,' she finishes.

I do believe that. Plus, I'm an independent woman who doesn't decide where she's going to live based on a man. Even an extremely decent and pretty one.

The wedding is in full swing, there are plenty of people on the dance floor, and most of us are pissed. Dani has dragged me onto the dance floor around a thousand times, so my feet are killing me. Every time I hear a 90s tune, I try to run, but she's faster than me. Luckily, they're playing Usher right now, which she hates, so I can rest my feet and watch Jane and Andy give it all they got on the dance floor.

'How's the wedding going for you?'

James has kept his distance the whole day until now.

'It's been good. How's it been for you?'

He takes my question as an invitation to sit down next to me. Ok then.

'It's been good... I wanted to thank you,' he tells me genuinely.

'You don't have to. You're Andy's best friend; you should be here.'

'You didn't have to insist, especially after last night.'

'Yeah, that was fun.'

He looks guilty and embarrassed.

'I'm sorry...for starting the fight...and for me and Sarah.'

'You don't need to apologise for Sarah. I have no moral high ground here. Although, I will accept the apology for the fight. That was bullshit.'

'Yeah, I didn't think that through, did I?' He smiles a small smile at me.

'I get it, though. You were angry, and you had every right to be.' Now it's my turn to look guilty and embarrassed. 'It's not like what you did suddenly makes me innocent.'

'Yeah, but let's face it, I knew you weren't "all in," shall we say?'

'I know this won't mean much, but I have always cared about you...I was stupid and selfish...and again, I'm sorry.'

'Call it even?'

He holds out his to solidify his truce. Might as well close this chapter, so we shake on it.

'What about Sarah?' I can't help myself.

'What about Billy?'

'Billy is a dick.'

'And Adam?' He grins.

'Private.' I grin back.

'Well, for it's worth, it's obvious to everyone he likes you.'

I should fucking hope so. The amount of time he's seen me naked these past few days.

'Well, who knows what the future holds?'

'Who knows...? But how about next time you come to visit, we are sociable with each other?'

'That could be nice. What about your mother? Do you think me and her could become best friends?'

'Now that,' he stands up and leans over me, 'really would be a miracle.' He chuckles before striding off.

Look at me, mending fences. I feel so grown up. Oh god, is that En Vogue playing?

'DOTTY!'

I hear Dani hysterically screaming my name.

Her song is playing. Which means my feet aren't resting. Which is a shame since they hurt so badly, but it is her favourite song.

Solitude. I love my friends and a couple of other people in there, but I'm tired, and I can't feel my feet. Thankfully, the rain has stopped, so sitting outside is actually possible.

Since the gazebo is covered, I've also managed to sit down on something that isn't soaked through. How the fairy lights are still working with that thunderstorm is anyone's guess. It is giving off seriously cute lighting, making the steam to my left glisten and sparkle. I feel like I am in Twilight at the prom.

'Who are you hiding from this time?'

Adam. Always appearing out of nowhere.

'You.'

'Really?' He sits himself down beside me. 'What did I do?'

'Nothing. I suppose I understand you keeping your distance after last night.'

'I haven't kept my distance.'

I can't help my look of disbelief and genuine 'what' face.

'I haven't seen you all day...well, not since the cupboard anyway.'

'My mum told me you needed to talk to some people.'

'Your mummy told you to stay away from me. Looks like you and James have something in common.'

'Hardly the same. Did you talk to some people?'

'I may have had a lovely chat with my father, but it didn't take five hours.'

'What about your mum?'

What is it with everyone wanting me to chat with my mother? It's clearly something I'm avoiding, with good reason.

'We'll chat next time I'm up.'

'When will that be?'

'Don't know, probably for another wedding or the prison reunion next year. Dani is already buzzing about it.'

'I'm sure Chloe would love that too.'

There's that smirk.

'Would you want to see me?' I ask.

He's taking his time answering, giving me only a tiny smile.

'There's nothing I would like more.'

'Is that right? So you kinda like me?'

'A little.'

'How long for?' I'm leaving tomorrow, so I might as well go all in.

'A while….a good while.'

'Same.'

'So, what if I came to Glasgow for a night away in the big city…? Would you show me the sights?' he says, inching ever so slightly closer.

'You know, Glasgow isn't that exciting. But my flat is, like, so cool.'

'Really?' His face breaks into a great big grin.

'Oh yeah. Total hotspot, and the best cooking in town.'

'Sold. How about a dance?'

'A dance?'

'I saw you on the dance floor; I know you can, kind of.'

'My feet hurt.'

'Pathetic excuse. You're just scared I'll show you up.'

'Terrified.'

'What would you like to do?'

This is difficult. It's my last night; I should take full advantage of being alone with Adam. Although, since I spent the night on a metal bench and then most of the day rushing around, I'm exhausted.

'What's on offer?' I might as well know my options.

'How about...' He casually puts his arm around me. 'A bath.'

Liking it.

'Cake.'

Loving it.

'And a foot rub.'

Heaven.

'You would rub my feet?' Forget roses and love letters; that is pure romance.

He places the softest and gentlest kiss on my lips.

'I would.'

'Then that is definitely what I want to do.'

Most people outgrow their childhood crushes. Move on from the first person they fell in love with. Then there's me. I have loved Adam for most of my life. I'm pretty sure I have never stopped, and I'm definitely certain I never will, especially if he gives foot rubs as well as he does other things. Something tells me he does.

Chapter 34

It's over. The week is done, and I survived. Not only did I survive, but I healed a little. My therapist of one session would be mighty proud, not that I plan on going back and telling him. Last night was the perfect way to end it, too. It turns out I was right; Adam gives fabulous foot rubs. I left him sleeping in his room to wake up the sleeping beauties and hit the road. I should say goodbye, but I want to leave last night as the lasting impression, what with me looking like a swamp creature this morning.

My hair is one great big, tuggy bird's nest; I washed off my makeup and now match the colour of the grey sky above me. My outfit of leggings and a grey hoodie isn't helping me look less shit. My companions weren't thrilled about the seven o'clock wake-up call and haven't stopped moaning about it. Luckily, the mud puddle has dried up enough for us to get the car to the front of the hotel. The car is packed and ready; time to go home.

'Eight fucking o'clock. This is inhumane,' Matt complains, squinting at the daylight.

'He has a point, babe; I'm pretty hungover. I don't even know if I should be driving.'

'We'll take turns,' I offer.

'You ain't driving, Dotty.'

'You three aren't trying to leave without saying goodbye, are you?'

I hear my dad calling from the entrance door. There goes my clean escape.

'You know I hate goodbyes, Dad.'

'I do.' He makes his way down the stairs towards us. 'But you're doing it. Your mum is awake upstairs. Go and see her, please.'

'We have a long drive,' I reason.

'It's not that long that you can't spare ten minutes.'

Ten? No chance, two tops.

'But, Dad.'

'No buts, move.'

'Ahhhh,' I whine, making my way up the stairs.

I know I sound like a child, but I don't care.

A quick goodbye won't take that long. In and out. Mum won't want to prolong this either. I swear my knock sounds nervous as I give three soft knocks. If I knock softly, she might not hear it.

'Come in.'

Damn it.

I reluctantly open the door and make my way inside. I must look like a child, going to see the headmistress. Mum and Dad's room is a carbon copy of ours, same layout and décor. There are even two double beds. Mum is standing by the window. If my sense of direction is correct, that means she's looking over the front entrance. Which is clearly how Dad knew I was making a run for it.

'Hi, Mum, I came to say goodbye.'

I feel like that's my job done, to be honest.

'Right.'

She's still looking out of the window. Rude.

'So...bye.' I turn to try and escape.

'When will you be back?'

I turn back around and see her looking over at me with sadness in her eyes.

'I don't know. I need to find a job, and Dani wants to go abroad for some summer sun.'

'Well, next time. Let me know...I'll get your room ready... and the guest room...in case your friends want to come too.'

What the fuck?

'Ok,' is all I can manage to say. Not only am I welcome, but Dani and Matt are welcome, too? Have I crossed into the multiverse?

'Maybe, if you all don't have plans. You could even come up for Christmas?'

Christmas is very soon.

'Maybe. It would be nice to give Dani and Matt a more thought-out trip. We had a few mishaps.'

'Hopefully, you can make it.'

'Hopefully,' I agree with a shy smile. Talking with your mum shouldn't be this awkward, surely. 'I'll be in touch then.' I turn to make my second attempt at escape.

'I also wanted to say...'

I turn back to face her, and she's fidgeting with her robe.

'What?' I press her.

'I wanted to say that I love you. Very much,' she tells me, seemingly feeling guilty. 'And I'm sorry.'

And I'm crying.

'You don't have to say sorry, Mum. I did something wrong, and you were disappointed in me.'

'That's not what I'm apologising for.'

Why isn't she apologising for that? I was being nice; she should apologise for it. My tears are drying up now.

'I'm apologising for making you feel...like a mistake.'

God damn Kate and her goddam mouth.

'Mum, I didn't mean it; I only meant that...'

'You did mean it.' She cuts me off. 'But you're wrong; you weren't a mistake. I know I've been hard on you; I didn't want you turning out like...'

'Him?'

I hate the thought of saying his name. My biological father. I know he might be a decent enough guy now, more grown up. He just isn't my dad. He's a stranger, a random guy that used to live in the village. He worked here for a season at the pub, then left when Mum got pregnant. He was some excitement for her, and she was a challenge for him. It wasn't love, at least; that's how Kate put it when she explained it.

'No...me. When I left your dad and got pregnant, the way people looked at me, spoke about me...it was awful, and my worse fear was that happening to you. My little girl.'

'James isn't Dad; it was a different situation.'

'It didn't feel different. I saw the way people were treating you, the way they were looking at me.'

'You could have stuck by me.'

'I should have, but I wanted things to not be like before.'

'And you thought if I wasn't around, it could be.'

'I don't know what I thought.'

What do I say? On the one hand, I'm still annoyed at how she reacted and how she's been this week. Then, on the other hand, I get that it must have been triggering for her, how she wouldn't have wanted people bringing up her past.

'I guess it's all over with now; what's done is done.'

'Yes, but no matter what was happening or how I felt, I have never thought of you as a mistake.'

'Ok.'

'Dorothy! I mean it. Do you know what your dad said? The day you were born.'

This will definitely make me cry again.

'That everything really does happen for a reason, because he now had the most perfect and beautiful daughter in the world.'

Yep. There are the tears. Oh my god, my mother, Anna Peters, is crying. I can't cope with Mum crying. I think it's time to move on from this emotional chat.

'If we do come for Christmas, Dani will need glass bottles of coke. She says if she doesn't have them, then it's not Christmas.'

'I can make sure of that.' She smiles an honest and real smile.

'Perfect.' I smile back. 'I better get moving; we have a long drive back to Glasgow.'

'Course, do you need anything?'

'No, no, I'm good.'

'Ok, then I'll see you soon and drive safe.'

'Yeah...I love you, Mum.'

'I love you too.'

We both move closer at the same time, and she pulls in tight for a hug. I can't remember the last time we hugged, but I really needed it.

Chapter 35

Three months later

This is typical of my life. When things are going well, when everything in my life is almost perfect, the shit hits the fan. Until today, I had it all in place.

A job I actually enjoy and that I'm good at.

I'm getting on well with my family, and we had a lovely Christmas together.

My friends are in good places, doing well in their lives.

I even kinda have a 'boyfriend' who is the whole package.

Then, after one conversation with Dani, everything changes. Well, maybe everything is going to change. We still have two minutes to find that out. How we both missed multiple periods and didn't notice is remarkable. Although when we did realise, Dani practically flew out of the door and down to the nearest shop. Now here we are, sitting at our makeshift dinner table, looking out for a blue line, while Matt watches on from the couch.

'We're overreacting. We are not pregnant,' Dani rambles nervously.

'Imagine if you both are! That would be hysterical, you must admit.'

'Matt, I told you to be quiet,' she warns.

Was that a knock on the door?

'Who's that at the door?' Matt asks, confused.

'Please tell me he isn't early.'

'Who?' Matt asks, confused, as I run over to the window.

'Shit, his car is outside,' I whisper.

I look over at Dani as she rushes to the door.

'Who is it?' she asks, knowing full well.

'It's me. I came early to surprise Dotty. Is she in?'

'Just a minute, Adam,' she shouts through the door at him.

Trust Adam to do something cute at the completely wrong time. I look at Dani. She doesn't know what to do; I don't know what to do. Matt won't know what to do. Where is Matt? Why is he by the tests?

'Well, one of you isn't pregnant,' he calmly says, like he's not delivering life-altering news. 'Whose test was on the right?'

Oh my god.

Printed in Great Britain
by Amazon